W9-CDL-880

A Fistful of Collars

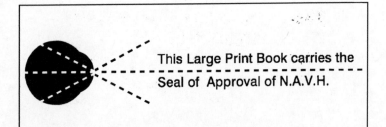
This Large Print Book carries the
Seal of Approval of N.A.V.H.

A CHET AND BERNIE MYSTERY

A FISTFUL OF COLLARS

SPENCER QUINN

THORNDIKE PRESS
A part of Gale, Cengage Learning

GALE
CENGAGE Learning·

Detroit • New York • San Francisco • New Haven, Conn • Waterville, Maine • London

GALE
CENGAGE Learning®

LIBRARY OF CONGRESS CATALOGING-IN-PUBLICATION DATA

Quinn, Spencer.
    A fistful of collars : a Chet and Bernie mystery / by Spencer Quinn.
       pages ; cm. — (Thorndike Press large print mystery) (A Chet and Bernie mystery)
      ISBN 978-1-4104-5520-8 (hardcover) — ISBN 1-4104-5520-3 (hardcover)
    1. Dogs—Fiction. 2. Private investigators—Fiction. 3. Large type books.
    I. Title.
    PS3617.U584F57 2013
    813'.6—dc23   2012039871

Published in 2013 by arrangement with Atria Books, a division of Simon & Schuster, Inc.

To Vivian

ONE

"Heard you drove another one off a cliff," said Nixon Panero. He spat a thin brown stream of chewing tobacco into an empty paint can, or maybe not that empty. Yellow paint, the yellow of egg yolks, now with a brown swirl in the middle: there's all kinds of beauty in life.

"You heard wrong," said Bernie.

Uh-oh. Bernie was looking at Nixon in an irritated sort of way. Wasn't Nixon our buddy? True, Nixon's eyes were too close together, even for a human, but he was one of the best mechanics in the Valley according to Bernie, and if Bernie said so, then that was that, and besides, Nixon was also one of our top sources on the street, even though we once put him away for a year or so. Or maybe because of it! Anything's possible with perps, believe me. We've taken down lots, me and my partner, Bernie. That's what we do at the Little Detective

Agency. He's Bernie Little. I'm Chet, pure and simple.

Sidling on over toward Nixon, just in case backsliding was on his mind? The right move at a moment like this, no question, so I sidled, keeping my eyes on his hands the whole time. That's where the trouble usually comes from with humans; their feet are too slow to bother worrying about. Nixon's big hands — fingers all oil-stained and as big as sausages — were hanging by his sides, doing nothing much. I hadn't had a good sausage in ages, or even a bad one, not that there's such a thing as a bad sausage, and was trying my hardest to actually remember the last time, when I became aware that Bernie was speaking. When Bernie talks, I listen and listen hard.

". . . three sticks of dynamite, maybe four — still waiting on forensics," he said.

"Somebody blew up the Porsche?" said Nixon.

"Kind of different from me driving it off a cliff," Bernie said, giving Nixon a hard stare. Loved seeing that hard stare of Bernie's: we've made hay with it, let me tell you, although why anyone would want to is a bit of a puzzler, hay being nothing but dried-up grass, of no interest to me at all.

Nixon nodded. "No comparison." He spat

another gob into the paint can; his aim was off the charts.

"Which is why," Bernie said, "we're in the market for a new one."

"A new old one?"

"Of course."

"As old as the last one?" said Nixon. "Or a bit younger, like the one before."

"Depends," Bernie said, and he went on with a whole long depends thing which I missed — on account of I'd been listening too hard! How weird was that?

The next thing I knew we were on our way to the yard at the back of Nixon's Championship Autobody. One of his guys was spray-painting a picture of a curvy woman on a black fender.

"More tit, Ruy," Nixon said as we went by. "What's wrong with you?"

Ruy raised his mask. "Sorry, boss."

We kept going. "Can't get good help," Nixon said. "What's going to happen to this country? We're competing in the global marketplace."

"Maybe the big breast thing isn't as important overseas," Bernie said.

"Talk sense, Bernie," Nixon said.

We came to the back of the yard, all fenced in with barbed wire. This was a bad part of town: across the street, some dudes lounged around doing nothing special, never a good sign. Parked by the fence stood two wrecks, one rusted out, the other torched. I'm not great with cars, but I know the shape of Porsches.

"Take your pick," said Nixon.

"You're paying me, right?" said Bernie.

"Love your sense of humor," Nixon said. "I was just mentioning it to the mayor, not two days ago."

"You're pals with the mayor?"

"Where do you think he gets the limo serviced?"

"Did you ask him how come he needs to ride around in that damn thing in the first place?"

"Huh?" said Nixon. "He's the mayor, that's how come. And anyways I wasn't talkin' to him directly. I was talkin' to his security guy."

"Cal Luxton?"

"Yeah. He was the one who actually mentioned your name. But then the mayor slid down the window and we got to talkin'."

"About what?"

Nixon shrugged. That's a human move I always watch for. It can mean lots of things. This time? Your call. "Wanted to know if I was named after Nixon. You know — the president."

10

"I know," Bernie said. "And are you?"

"Yup."

"Your parents hated you?"

Nixon gave Bernie a long look, a look I'd seen many times. It meant someone had just realized that Bernie was the smartest human in the room, no news to me. "How'd you know?" Nixon said. "I was the fifth boy. Long about then they were hankerin' for a girl. But — funny thing — turns out to be a big plus with the mayor."

"He's a Tricky Dick fan?" Bernie said.

"A secret fan," said Nixon. "Just between him and me, what with the election coming up. On account of the name being so — what would you say?"

"Toxic."

"Yeah, toxic with most people."

"You can always change it," Bernie said.

"Nope," said Nixon. "It's part of me." He took out his dip, bit off another chew. "Maybe someday I'll invade Cambodia."

Bernie laughed. "Let's take a look at these scrap heaps," he said, and then something else which I missed because of this growling I heard behind me. I turned and there was my old buddy Spike, the scariest junkyard dog I know, and I know plenty, amigo. Spike was part pit bull, part Rottweiler, part unknown, and we got along great: I have

11

lots of unknown in me, too. We'd had a nice tussle or two, me and Spike, including the night Bernie and I took Nixon down, something that maybe rubbed Spike the wrong way. What a barn burner! Although it was a gas station that ended up burning, but just as exciting, maybe more. And as for getting rubbed the wrong way? There's really no wrong way, in my opinion, only some that are better than others. I'm not fussy.

Spike lumbered up, gave me a bump. Just being friends: Spike was getting on now, that twisted warrior face almost completely white. I gave him a friendly bump back. He rose up and tried to . . . really? What a crazy idea! I shook him off, rose up myself, and tried to do the same crazy thing! What a time we were having! He shook me off and then we were racing around the yard — not really racing, since Spike was no speedster — nipping at each other and barking our heads off. Did we roll around some in an oily patch? Maybe, but I couldn't be sure, because all of a sudden Spike had one of those — what were they called? welding torches? — yes, welding torches in his mouth, and I had to have it, so —

FTWEEEEE!

Spike and I pulled up, coming to a dead stop.

FTWEEEEE!

And glancing back, saw Nixon with his hand at his mouth, finger and thumb between his lips, and looking real mad for some reason. Oh, no. He was one of those humans who knew how to make that earsplitting whistle sound. Please, not again.

FWTEEEEE!

"What the hell gets into you?" Bernie said.

We were rolling in the van, this beat-up van we use for surveillance but was our only ride at the moment. I lay curled up on the shotgun seat, waiting for the pain in my ears to go away. What gets into me? Was that the question? I thought about it. Sometimes I think better with my eyes closed, so I closed them.

When I awoke, I was back to feeling tip-top, so tip-top I knew I must have done some world-class thinking. I sat up straight, stuck my head out the window. Ah, the Valley. No place like it. The Valley goes on forever in all directions, and those smells! You haven't smelled till you've smelled the Valley. Hot rubber, hot pavement, hot sauce, hot charcoal ash, hot everything! Yes, even hot ice cream. Plus all kinds of grease — deep-fry grease, pizza grease, burrito grease, unwashed human skin grease, and human hair grease — not to mention the grease on my tail at this very moment. Where had that come from? I tried to remember, but not hard. Back to the lovely smells of the Valley, all of them with something in common, namely the dry dusty scent of the desert. I wouldn't live anywhere else.

Bernie glanced over at me. "Smell anything, big guy?"

He stuck his own head out the window and took a few sniffs.

"I don't," he said.

That Bernie! The best human sense of humor in the business, bar none. This had to be one of his little jokes, what with the whole river of smells flowing by and us smack in the middle of it. A nice refreshing breeze sprang up behind me so I turned to check it out — I can probably turn my head a bit farther around than you, no offense — and there was my greasy tail, wagging away. I just love Bernie.

We pulled into a strip mall. We've got strip malls out the yingyang in the Valley, just one more thing that makes it great. This particular strip mall was where Suzie Sanchez worked. Suzie's a reporter for the *Valley Tribune,* and also Bernie's girlfriend. If he had to have a girlfriend, then Suzie was a great choice. Compared to Leda, for example, Bernie's ex-wife and mother of his kid, Charlie, who we miss a lot, seeing as he's only around some weekends, plus every second Christmas and Thanksgiving, a complicated human arrangement that turned out to mean having even less of Charlie. Thanksgiving's my favorite holiday and Halloween's the worst, but no time to get into that now.

We entered the *Tribune* office, walking past the workstations, all empty, and there was Suzie at the back, fingers going tac-tac-tac on the keyboard, a sound I happened to like. If I had Suzie's job I'd make that sound twenty-four seven, faster and faster, and with all my paws in action that would be pretty damn rapid. Kind of a strange thought; probably better if it never happens again.

Some humans have the sort of brain where you can feel it at work, like a powerful, pulsing muscle. Suzie was one of those, but at the same time, she had a big warm smile and black eyes that shone like the countertops in our kitchen after Bernie polishes them, which doesn't happen often. Only when we got real close did she look up.

Then came a surprise. Suzie wasn't smiling, and her eyes, shining for a moment, lost that sparkle almost right away.

Bernie was smiling, though, that real big one, always so nice to see.

"Hey, Suzie," he said. "Lookin' good."

"Liar," she said, sweeping back a lock of her dark hair. Hey! What was that? A line on Suzie's forehead? And another? Those were new, unless my memory was playing tricks on me, something memories can do, Bernie says, although I don't remember ever experiencing that personally.

"How'd the car thing go?" Suzie said.

"Found a beauty," Bernie said.

We had? News to me, but I got most of my news from Bernie.

Suzie pressed a button and her screen went dark. "Bernie?" she said. "Got a moment?"

"More than a moment. How about we take you to lunch?"

Suzie bit her lip, another one of those human things I look for. In the nation within the nation, as Bernie sometimes calls me and my kind, we don't bite our lips, except by accident, when a bit of lip gets caught on a tooth, say. Human lip biting sends a message, a message I'd never gotten from Suzie before.

"I'm slammed today, Bernie," she said. "Let's just go out for a little walk."

"A walk? It's ninety-seven out there and just getting started."

"A short walk."

Bernie's smile faded and was gone. "Something on your mind?"

Suzie nodded, her eyes not meeting his. I got a sudden urge to chew on something; almost anything would do.

"We can talk here," Bernie said.

Suzie glanced around. Still just us in the office, but she said, "Outside's better."

"Okeydoke," said Bernie. Okeydoke is a way Bernie has of saying yes, but only when we're on the job, so what was up with that?

We went outside. There was some confusion at the door, but I ended up going out first. We walked toward a line of skinny, dusty trees that separated this strip mall from the next one. An old picnic table, weathered and lopsided, stood in the shade.

With picnic tables, it usually works like this: humans sit on the benches, facing the table, and I settle down underneath, waiting to get lucky, picnic food usually being pretty messy. But none of that happened now. No food, for one thing. Bernie sort of leaned against the table at a funny angle; Suzie sat at the end of one of the benches, but facing out, legs crossed and then uncrossed; I circled around. What was this? None of us

17

could get comfortable? I started panting a bit.

"Bernie?"

"Yeah?"

"I have some news."

"You're a newswoman."

Suzie's lips turned upward in maybe the quickest, smallest smile I'd ever seen. Then she nodded. "I've got a job offer."

"That's all?" said Bernie.

"What do you mean?"

"I thought maybe you'd met somebody."

"Met somebody?"

"Or Dylan was back in the picture."

"Dylan?" Suzie said. "Oh, Bernie." She held out her hand. Bernie took it in his.

Dylan McKnight back in the picture? He was Suzie's boyfriend long ago, a perp who'd done a stretch at Northern State Correctional, and was now where? LA? Hard to keep all the details straight, but the best one — that time I'd driven him up a tree — was still so clear in my mind!

"Let me guess," said Bernie. "The *Trib*'s making you managing editor."

She laughed, one of those tiny laughs that's just a little jet of air from the nose. "That would never happen," Suzie says. "It's another reporting job, but somewhere else."

"Not the *Clarion*?" Bernie said.

Suzie shook her head.

"Whew," said Bernie. "Not sure how I'd handle that. They won't stop until every square inch of the whole state's totally developed."

"It's the *Post,* Bernie."

Bernie has very expressive eyebrows, one of his best features, although they're all so good, it's hard to choose. Right now, his eyebrows were sort of trying to meet in the middle, a puzzled look you didn't often see on Bernie's face. "The *Post*?" he said.

"The *Washington Post,*" said Suzie.

Bernie let go of Suzie's hand. "Oh," he said.

Something was up — I could just tell. But what?

"I'm so torn," Suzie said. "And the irony is it's all due to that series I wrote about the Big Bear case."

Whoa. Big Bear Wilderness Camp? The sheriff? Those deputies? That judge? The mama bear? All of them breaking rocks in the hot sun by now, or very soon. Except for that mama bear, of course. Let's not get started on her.

"Don't be torn," Bernie said. "You deserve it."

"There's no deserving, Bernie. Not in this

business."

"I wouldn't know about that," Bernie said. "But —" He went silent.

"But what?" said Suzie.

Bernie took a deep breath. "Could you turn it down, walk away, and then never think about it again? The what-ifs, what-might-have-beens, all that?"

Suzie went quiet. Then she took a deep breath, too. "I love you," she said.

Bernie's lips moved, just the slightest, like he was about to say something, but he did not.

"I've been checking flights," Suzie said. "They're cheap if you book far enough in advance. Weekends would be way more do-able than you'd think."

"So," said Bernie, his voice getting kind of thick in a strange way, like there was something in his throat, "it's all good."

What was this? I'd been gnawing away at one of the legs of the picnic table? And it didn't even feel that great? Not bad, exactly, just more like . . . nothing. I stopped.

Two

The bourbon's in the cupboard over the kitchen sink. Cigarettes are harder to find because Bernie quit smoking and one of his tricks when he quits smoking is to stop buying cigarettes cold turkey and scrounge around for them instead. Bernie's got tricks for just about everything — he's always the smartest human in the room, might as well get that out of the way right now, if I haven't already. As for cold turkey: a puzzler there's no time to go into, not now and maybe not ever. Except does it mean cigarettes are in the fridge? I didn't smell any, but sometimes I can't detect every single little thing that's in the fridge. As for cigarettes — one of those unmissable smells, lit or not — there was one under the end pillow on the living room couch, and another behind Bernie's desk in the office, both places he'd already searched unsuccessfully, a little bourbon sloshing out of his glass each time

21

he bent down.

We went out to the patio. We have a nice patio in back — this is at our place on Mesquite Road — with a stone fountain in the shape of a swan that Leda had installed before the divorce, but then wanted no part of when Bernie said she should take it with her. We had trouble understanding Leda, me and Bernie.

Bernie sat in his favorite patio chair, the one with the drink holder, and I sat beside him. The sun was going down, changing the colors of the canyon that runs behind Mesquite Road, a canyon inhabited by lots of creatures, including some fat javelinas. Until you've chased a javelina you haven't lived, and I wouldn't dream of living anywhere else, although once I did dream I was living in a Dumpster, sort of a nightmare until it turned out the Dumpster stood behind a fast-food place. Dreams: don't ask me to explain them.

Bernie swirled his bourbon around, stared into it, took a sip. "Suppose I said let's get married. What would happen then?"

I waited to hear.

Bernie drank some more. "Why shouldn't she be ambitious?" He gazed at me, his face reddening in the evening light. "She's got every right. So that leaves the option of picking up stakes and going with her. Which, you may have noticed, she didn't mention." Bernie drained his glass, went inside. I went with him, right on his heels. He took the bottle down from the shelf, refilled his glass. "Heading east," he said. "How would that work? My ancestors headed west. Going back would be like —"

The phone rang before Bernie could finish, but not a problem since I'd lost the thread long before. Bernie picked up.

A man's voice came over the speaker. "Bernie?"

"Yup."

"Cal Luxton here."

"Uh-huh."

"From the mayor's office."

"I know."

"How're you doin'? It's been a while."

"No complaints," Bernie said.

"Suppose I should congratulate you on that wilderness camp case."

"Not necessary."

"Heard you drove another one over a cliff."

"You heard wrong."

Silence on the other end. In that silence, Bernie knocked back a big slug.

"Got much goin' on these days?" Luxton said.

"How do you mean?" said Bernie.

"Work-wise."

"We're pretty busy."

We were? First I'd heard of it. Hadn't done a stitch of work since the Big Bear Wilderness Camp Case, for which we'd been paid, yes, and plus there'd been the bonus of that gold nugget, now at Mr. Singh's on account of some tax bill coming due, not something I'm clear on and neither was Bernie although he finally gave up on getting an explanation and just cut the check; which bounced, so he cut another one. In short, our finances were a mess. There hadn't even been any divorce work, which we hated, me and Bernie, but took when nothing else — mostly meaning missing persons cases, our specialty — came along. The Teitelbaum divorce! Mrs. Teitelbaum at the wheel of that forklift, crushing Mr. Teitelbaum's classic car collection! And what he did to her boyfriend right after that! Only it wasn't her boyfriend! I gave myself a good shake. Meanwhile that Luxton dude was talking again.

"I'm sure you are," he said. "But maybe you could squeeze in a little job for us."

"Who's us?" said Bernie.

"The mayor, who else? Did I wake you or something, Bernie?"

24

Bernie put down his drink. "Wide awake, Cal. So wide awake that I'm thinking, Why me?"

"Why not you?"

"We have a little history, the mayor and I, maybe from before your time."

"Back before you got — back when you were still with the force? I know all about it. Water under the bridge, as far as the mayor's concerned. And what with the election coming up, he wants to reach out, to be more inclusive."

"Has he heard of the aquifer yet?" Bernie said.

The aquifer? Bernie talks about the aquifer a lot, but he hasn't shown it to me yet. Something about water, of which we've got a lot in the Valley — check out our golf courses every morning and evening, sprinklers spraying rainbows out the yingyang — although, come to think of it, none under any of the bridges. Whew! I'd taken that one pretty far! Right up to the point where Bernie always says "so therefore." Bernie handles the so therefores. I bring other things to the table. That's how come the Little Detective Agency's what it is.

"You can ask him tomorrow at ten," Luxton said.

"Huh?"

"That's the only time he can see you this week."

"See me about what?"

"This job, Bernie. Are you listening?"

"What's the job?"

"He'll tell you in person."

Bernie reached for his glass, downed some more. "I'm not interested."

"No? What's your normal fee?"

"Eight hundred a day. Plus expenses."

"Yeah? You can make that stick in an economy like this?"

"Not always."

"What I thought," Luxton said. Another phone rang at his end, and he spoke a little faster, so maybe I didn't hear right. "The fee for this job is three grand a day, plus expenses, guaranteed, plus a bonus at the end if they like you."

"Who's they?"

"See you at ten." *Click.*

Humans tend to go to sleep in their beds and stay there all night. It's different with me and my kind. For example, I often start in Bernie's bedroom, on the floor at the foot of the bed, and later move across the hall to Charlie's old room, even though he's hardly ever there, the bed stripped, and after that I like to lie with my back to the front door.

The sounds and smells of the night leak in through the crack under the door. Security is part of my job.

On this particular night, my pal Iggy who lives next door got a little restless and did his yip-yip-yipping once or twice, and Mr. Parsons tried to shush him, and later a toilet flushed in their house. Our neighbor on the other side, old man Heydrich, went outside not long after that, and what was this? *Whisk-whisk, whisk-whisk.* He was sweeping the dirt from his part of the sidewalk onto ours? I barked, the low muffled kind of bark, not wanting to disturb Bernie. The *whisk-whisk*ing stopped, and old man Heydrich muttered something about curs, a new one on me. Then came the *pad-pad-pad* of his slippers, his door opening and closing, and quiet. I dropped down into dreamland. Did a car come down the street sometime later, moving slowly, pausing in front of our place, driving on? Maybe. Dreams can be so strong, and then you wake up and poof! It doesn't work the other way. You always remember real life. Sort of. But forget all that.

Except if a car did go by, its engine was making a little ticking sound. *Tick-tick-tick.* That tick-tick-tick happened once with the Porsche, not the blown-up Porsche but the

27

one that actually did go off a cliff. Bernie'd taken out the tools. You never wanted to see that.

"Knits up the raveled sleeve of care?" Bernie said the next morning. "I wish."

Uh-oh. We were in the van, headed downtown, possibly on something work-related, and now was when the linen shirt episode comes up? Linen: a complete unknown to me at the time, specifically on a visit I paid to the laundry basket not long after Suzie gave Bernie a long-sleeved linen shirt for his birthday. I prefer Bernie's Hawaiian shirts, of which he's got lots, including the one with palm trees and martini glasses that he was wearing at the moment, but that had nothing to do with what happened. It was just the strange feel of linen, and when it comes to feeling things, well, you always do better with your tongue, no news there. And what's close to the tongue? Teeth. So there you go.

But still, I felt bad. I moved across the bench seat, a little closer to Bernie. The van made one of those quick swerves across the lane that sometimes happens, not sure why. It's not the smoothest ride in the world, but no complaints.

"Hey, you're crowding me, buddy," Bernie said.

I was? How had that happened? I shifted away, but not before giving Bernie's face a quick lick, just showing him that everything was cool between us. Bernie's great-looking, even if he wasn't at his best today, dark patches under his eyes, and possibly a patch or two where he'd missed with the razor blade, although he'd clearly made a good try; there was still a dab of shaving cream on the side of his neck.

The downtown towers rose in the distance, their tops kind of merging with the copper-colored sky, a sight that always made me uneasy, hard to say why. We got off the freeway, drove past the college — a Frisbee soared by, went right into the window of a passing bus! I love college kids! — and parked at a meter in front of city hall, which I recognized from the two huge stone birds, very nasty looking, on either side of the tall arched doorway. Don't get me started on birds. Bernie dug in his pocket for change, found none, but did come up with a cigarette, or part of one. He straightened it out, lit up, and said, "My lucky day."

"This must be Chet," said Mayor Trimble. "What a handsome dog!" The mayor turned out to be a round little guy with more than one chin, very big ears, and a string tie. In short, what wasn't to like? "Happen to be in possession of some nice rawhide chews," he said. "Can he have one?"

Bernie sighed, for no reason that I could come up with.

What a mayor did, exactly, was anybody's guess, but one thing for sure: we had the best mayor around. Soon I was lying on the floor at Mayor Trimble's side, working on a rawhide chew, tough and tasty, just the way I liked. The mayor introduced everybody — " 'Course you already know Cal Luxton, head of security, and this is Vera Cobb, chief of staff." Then came handshaking, hello hellos, and nobody took a single sniff of nobody, all very human, and everyone sat down.

Mayor Trimble rocked back in his chair. "Pleasure to have this opportunity to renew our friendship, Bernie."

"Is that what we had?" Bernie said.

"Any mistakes were mine," the mayor said. "Real or imagined. I should have patched things up long ago. Everything goes by so goddamn fast. Agreed?"

"That everything goes by fast?" Bernie said. "I won't argue."

"Bernie's known for his sense of humor," said Luxton, sitting in a shadowy corner of

30

the room. Luxton was a thin dude with swept-back hair and the kind of long sideburns you sometimes see out here in the Valley, but not many other places, Bernie says. It's a look, he also says, that goes with cowboy boots, which Luxton was wearing, and cowboy hats. Luxton had a big white one resting on his knee. A smell goes with hat wearing. I detected it now; not unpleasant.

"One of the most important senses going," said the mayor. Then came a silence. The mayor looked around, maybe waiting for someone to chip in. No one did. He cleared his throat — I can do that, too, especially if a bone was caught in it — and checked a note on his desk. "Vera here tells me your great-great grandfather once owned all of Mesquite Canyon."

Vera, sitting at the end of the same couch as Bernie — he was at the other end, but it wasn't a big couch — said, "From where the airport is now all the way up to the Rio Seco railroad bridge." She glanced at Bernie. Vera was blond, wore a dark suit, had her hair in a bun, always interesting to me. Human hair, big subject, maybe later.

Bernie glanced at Vera, eyes going to that bun almost immediately — Bernie and I are alike in lots of ways, don't forget — and

31

said, "Um."

"Just think if your family had held on to that spread," Luxton said.

"Kind of pointless," Bernie said.

Which I didn't quite get, because more than once, walking the canyon, Bernie has said almost that exact same thing to me: *What if we still owned all of this, Chet? Rio Seco would have water in it — that's for damn sure.*

"No living in the past for you, huh, Bernie?" said the mayor. "We're on the same page, us two."

"Uh," said Bernie, "I wouldn't —"

The mayor smacked his hand on his desk, not hard. He had fat little hands, wore a nice big pinkie ring. One thing I've noticed about pinkie rings — they're never pink. But Bernie says I can't be trusted when it comes to colors, so don't bet the ranch. "The future, Bernie. I'm all about the future of this beautiful city, and my guess is you are, too."

"It won't be so beautiful when the aquifer's dry," Bernie said.

The mayor smiled. He had one of those real big smiles you see sometimes, a smile too big for the face, if that makes any sense. "Truth to power," he said. "Not afraid of that, are we, Vera? In fact, we encourage it.

32

Fill Bernie in on the water commission."

"I'm not sure we have time for that, mayor," she said. "Shouldn't we be getting on with the business at hand?"

The mayor's smile faded, down to normal size and then nothing. "What would I do without you, Vera?"

Vera gazed at the mayor, her face showing nothing that I could see.

"Vera here's a Stanford graduate," the mayor said. "My opponent's chief of staff went to North Valley CC. What does that tell you?"

"The Unabomber went to Harvard," Bernie said.

The mayor's smile started going upside down. Vera laughed. Maybe not the nicest-sounding laugh I'd ever heard, kind of loud and harsh, but human laughter? One of the best things there is. The meeting was going great. I gnawed on my chew strip and soon my mind was wandering pleasantly. That's part of the fun of chew strips, maybe news to you.

". . . water commission some other time," the mayor was saying, or something like that. "What do you know about our Millennial Cultural Initiative, Bernie?"

"Zip."

"Vera? Bring him up to speed."

Vera turned toward Bernie. Their gazes met, unmet, then met again. "Cutting to the chase," Vera said, "the may—"

"Cutting to the chase," the mayor said. "That's a good one, considering what we're about to discuss. So — what's the expression I'm searching for, Vera? Foreign, maybe?"

"A propos," said Vera. "The mayor believes that with proper planning and incentives, the Valley could be a mecca for movie production."

"Isn't half the nation's porn already shot in South Pedroia?" Bernie said.

"Thirty-seven percent," said Vera. "But the mayor is targeting mainstream Hollywood movies."

"Like *Wild Horseman,*" said the mayor.

"Don't know that one," Bernie said.

"Because it's not out yet," the mayor said. "Not even in production. But the whole world's going to know about it in a year or two. Guess who plays the horseman."

"John Waters," Bernie said.

Vera laughed her harsh laugh again. The mayor blinked. I watch for that. When Bernie gets them blinking, it's usually a good sign.

"Tell him who's starring," the mayor said.

"Thad Perry," said Vera.

The mayor chuckled. Suddenly all sorts of different laughs were in the air. Did it mean anything? I waited to find out. "Heard of him?" the mayor said.

Bernie nodded.

The mayor leaned forward, rubbing his hands together. "Now we're getting somewhere," he said. His pinkie ring caught a ray of brassy light coming through the window and glittered in a dull sort of way.

THREE

Thad Perry? Didn't ring a bell. There was Mad Thad Thatcherton, who'd hijacked a beer truck that turned out to be full of empties and was now wearing an orange jumpsuit at Central State Correctional — Bernie made him recycle them all before we took him in — but other than that no Thads came to mind.

"Hottest action hero in Hollywood," the mayor said, "and that's *Variety* talking, Bernie, not me. Familiar with *Variety*?"

"No," Bernie said.

"Don't worry about it. Neither was I. We're on a learning curve here, lots of hard work ahead of us. But think of the payoff!"

"What's the payoff?" Bernie said.

The mayor gave Bernie a long look. Then, over his shoulder, he said, "You were right, Cal."

"About what?" Luxton said.

"Didn't you tell me I'd love how his mind

worked?"

"Something like that."

The mayor pointed a pudgy finger at Bernie. "I love how your mind works," he said. "Loop him in, Vera."

"I'm sorry?" said Vera.

"The payoff, for Christ sake. Tell him about the payoff."

Humans can sometimes squeeze their mouths into very small puckered shapes, which Vera did now. "You already did," she said.

"Huh?" said the mayor.

Vera turned to Bernie. "If the studio has a successful experience producing *Wild Horseman* here in the Valley, then —"

"The mecca thing?" Bernie said.

The mayor smacked his desk again. "Exactly! Hollywood West!"

Then came a long silence. Vera gazed down at the floor. Bernie's mouth fell open a bit, not a good look on most humans, but just fine on him.

"Think of the revenue," the mayor said. "And all those jobs — carpenters, electricians, drivers, cooks, waiters — what are the latte people, again?"

"Baristas," Vera said.

"Baristas, et cetera, et cetera," the mayor said. "Too many to list. But you catch my drift, Bernie?"

"Voters," Bernie said.

The mayor laughed. He laughed and laughed, his face kind of jiggling. "I'm getting a real good feeling about this," he said. "Welcome aboard, Bernie. I have complete confidence in you."

"What am I doing?" Bernie said.

"Finger on the button," the mayor said. "Just what we need around here. Walk him back, Vera."

"Starting where?" said Vera.

"The money," the mayor said. "Where else?"

"The budget for *Wild Horseman* is one hundred million dollars," Vera said, "excluding advertising and promotion. The studio — Paragon — and the producers — Rapscallion Entertainment — need to protect that investment. The success of the movie depends to a great extent on the performance of Thad Perry. He's in every scene."

"Give Bernie the script," said the mayor.

"I'm not sure we can do that," Vera said.

"Then just slip it to him on the side."

Vera opened her briefcase, handed Bernie a thick sheaf of papers. Bernie set it down on the couch without a glance.

"Ever read a screenplay, Bernie?" the mayor said.

"No."

"It's easy. And way quicker than a book, although I didn't get through the whole thing. Want the elevator pitch?"

"Why not?" said Bernie.

"Vera?" the mayor said.

"A man in a present-day big desert city —" Vera began.

"Like let's all guess which one," said the mayor.

"Wakes up in the night," Vera continued, "and finds a beautiful white horse in his yard. He gets on and rides back to 1839, where he ends up a prisoner of the Apaches and, guided by a beautiful female shaman, decides to change the whole future of the West."

Another long silence. Then the mayor said, "That shaman is hot. Check out page thirty-five, I think it was. At your convenience. But what Vera's trying to say is that there's no way we can let Thad Perry screw this up. Which is where you come in."

"I don't get it," Bernie said. "You want me to teach him how to ride?"

Hey! Bernie could ride? Just when you think he's done amazing you, he amazes you again. That's Bernie. I thumped my tail on the mayor's nice soft rug.

"Hell," said the mayor, "never thought of

that. What if he can't ride?"

"They'll have stuntmen for that," Vera said. "Thad Perry's problems are behavioral. We have to keep him out of trouble for the duration of the shoot."

"You want us to babysit him?" Bernie said.

"We've got way more respect for you than that," the mayor said. "And who's us?"

"Chet and I," Bernie said.

The mayor glanced down at me. "Where'd that chew go?"

Where did it go? Was that the question? I had no answer.

"Crazy," said the mayor, "but from the way he looks at you, you'd almost think he knows what's going on."

"Crazy," said Bernie.

"Where was I?" the mayor said.

"Too much respect," said Vera.

"Right," said the mayor. "And besides, he's already got a babysitter in the form of that bejeezus bodyguard of his. Fine and dandy, but what we want you to do is keep watch on things from our lookout."

"Keep watch on things?" Bernie said.

"Act as our eyes and —" Vera began.

"Vera?" said the mayor. "Did I ask for your help?"

Vera's mouth got very small again. For no particular reason I tried to do the same with

40

mine, got nowhere. Instead I opened it up nice and wide, stuck my tongue way out, actually touching the tip of the mayor's tassel loafer, and then curled it back in. I tasted shoe polish, not bad at all, if on the tangy side for my taste.

"We want you to be our eyes and ears on this project," the mayor said. "There's some history of Thad Perry and illegal substances. That right, Cal?"

"Of every kind known to man," said Luxton, from the shadows in the corner, everything about him indistinct except for his eyes. They were the probing kind.

The mayor rubbed his hands together again. "So," he said. "Any questions?"

"Why me?" said Bernie. "And who's paying?"

"Why you?" said the mayor. "Because I'm a bridge builder."

The mayor was getting more and more interesting. We'd worked a bridge building case, me and Bernie, all about pilfering rebar, whatever rebar was, never clear in my mind, but the point was that the bridge building dudes had big hard hands and the mayor's were small and soft. Did he wear gloves on the job? That was as far as I could take it.

"So you picked me because of you?" Bernie said.

The mayor sat back and his face, soft like his hands, hardened a bit. "Cal?"

"Sir?"

"He's a hard-ass."

"Pointed that out in preliminaries."

"Maybe not with enough emphasis."

Luxton dusted off his cowboy hat and put it on. "He's a goddamn hard-ass and pisses a lot of people off, big-time," he said. "Is that better?"

"Much," said the mayor. He looked at Bernie. "As for who's paying, my campaign fund's running a convenient little surplus at the moment."

"Meaning we're working for you," Bernie said.

"Not me personally," said the mayor. "My office. Which really means you're working for the men and women of the Valley."

Bernie gets a look in his eyes when he's having fun. It's just the tiniest gleam, there and gone, so you have to be on your toes. But I'm pretty much on my toes all the time — it's the way we're built in the nation within, according to Bernie — so I didn't miss it now.

"And the children?" Bernie said.

The mayor squinted at Bernie. Squinting, never attractive, in my opinion, is something

42

humans do when they're trying to see more clearly. Finally, he nodded and said, "Yes, and the children. Goes without saying. Children are our most important resource, Bernie."

"Next to water," Bernie said.

Silence. Then the mayor laughed and said, "I love this guy." No surprise there: who wouldn't love Bernie? "Don't you just love this guy, Vera?"

Everyone turned to Vera. "He hasn't said yes yet," she said.

"Three grand a day plus expenses?" Bernie said.

"Also a five-thousand-dollar bonus if Thad Perry is incident-free when location shooting wraps," Vera said.

"How long does that take?" said Bernie.

"They've scheduled twenty-one days," Vera said.

"Yes," said Bernie.

"You left out the two tickets to the premiere, Vera," the mayor said.

"Black tie," Luxton said. He came out of the shadows and handed Bernie a check. "This do for a retainer?"

Bernie glanced at the check, nodded, and tucked it away in his shirt pocket. *Not that pocket, Bernie.* We'd had problems with the shirt pocket in the past. Front pants pocket, always.

After another round of handshaking, we split. There were more chews in the mayor's desk drawer — I didn't lose the smell until we were in the elevator — but he didn't open it again. I'm not greedy, although more is always better, stands to reason. As for the case, if it depended in some way on black ties then we were all right, on account of the single tie Bernie owned being black. But was it even actually a case? A puzzler to deal with some other time.

"What's with you?" Bernie said.

Uh-oh. Had I been kind of clawing at Bernie's shirt — specifically in the pocket area — and not just thinking about it? I put a stop to that pronto, sat up straight in the shotgun seat, alert and professional. But Bernie wasn't mad, not at all — in fact, even though we were bumper to bumper on the freeway, he seemed to be in a great mood, tapping his fingers on the steering wheel like maybe to some music happening in his head, possibly one of our favorites like "Death Don't Have No Mercy in This Land" or "Cry Me a River."

"See what this means?" he said. "Banner year, big guy. In three weeks we're going to rake in more than we made in the last . . . Christ knows how long. Have to check the spreadsheets."

Please not the spreadsheets. Spreadsheets, whatever they are, get Bernie upset. Last time he ended up giving the laptop a smack, which is what led to the duct taping. Bernie's very good with duct tape — if you ever visit us at our place on Mesquite Road, you'll see lots of it.

We got off the freeway, crossed the railroad tracks — a cat was walking on one of the rails! like he owned the — "easy, Chet" — and pulled into Donut Heaven. A black-and-white sat in the lot. We parked beside it, cop-style, driver's-side door to driver's-side door. The window of the black-and-white slid down and our buddy Sergeant Rick Torres from the Valley PD Missing Persons Department handed over a coffee.

"Shaving cream on your neck," he said.

Oh, that. Was it a problem? I was much more interested in the cruller crumbs in Rick's mustache.

Bernie dabbed at his neck, checked his hand. "Damn. Was it there the whole time?"

"The whole time you were with the mayor?" Rick said.

"How do you know about that?" Bernie said.

"Word gets around."

"But it just happened."

"I've got spies everywhere," Rick said. He looked past Bernie, over at me. "How you doin', Chet? Got half a cruller left if Bernie gives the okay."

Bernie's eyes shifted, as though he was thinking it over. What was there to think over? Whatever half was, it had to be better than none. I have this low rumbly bark I can do that sends a message of much louder barking coming soon. The next thing I knew I was curled up on the seat, getting busy with the cruller. There are lots of great human inventions — the car being the best, of course — but the cruller's got to be right up there.

"How'd the meeting go?" Rick said.

"You tell me," said Bernie.

"Why they chose you for this I'll never know," Rick said. He sipped his coffee. "Although actually I do know."

"Yeah?" said Bernie.

"Insurance."

"Huh?"

"The insurance company asked for you specifically."

"Me specifically?"

Rick nodded.

"And what's insurance got to do with

anything?"

"Insurance is when you pay a premium to protect yourself from loss," Rick said.

"For Christ sake, I know what insurance is." Wow! But of course he would: that was Bernie. "I'm asking what insurance has to do with this movie thing."

"What do you care? It's a paying gig."

Yes! So nice to hear that again.

". . . name of the insurance company?" Bernie was saying.

Rick shrugged. "I assume it's whoever Valley government uses for everything." He took out a little screen device, tapped at it. "The Stephan K. Gronkovich Insurance Group," Rick said.

Bernie went still for a moment, then nodded.

"What's up?" Rick said, ripping open a little packet and sprinkling sugar in his coffee; then he opened another packet and did it again.

"Nothing," Bernie said. "And that's refined sugar."

"Want me to mash my own cane?" said Rick. He stuck his finger in the cup and swirled it around. "You're taking the job?"

"Yeah."

"You could do me a favor."

"What?"

"Marcie's a big fan," Rick said. "She'd love an autograph."

"From the mayor?" said Bernie.

We were turning onto Mesquite Road when Bernie's phone rang. He picked up and a voice came through the speakers.

"Hi, Bernie. Stine here."

That would be Lieutenant Stine, another cop pal of ours, although maybe you couldn't call him a pal like Rick. With pals like Rick, you don't feel Bernie watching everything like a hawk; with pals like Lieutenant Stine, you do.

"Congratulations on landing this new job." Lieutenant Stine had a harsh, hoarse sort of voice, like he partied every night, but when you saw his face, you knew he wasn't the type.

"What new job?" Bernie said.

A pause, and then Stine said, "For the mayor's office."

"No such thing as secrets anymore?" Bernie said.

Stine laughed. "There are plenty. The Valley's like an iceberg, nine-tenths hidden, which I'm sure you know by now." He paused. "If there's anything you need, don't hesitate to ask. Call me on my direct line anytime."

"Sure."

"Do you have the number?"

"Must have misplaced it."

Another pause. "Got a pencil?"

"Yup," said Bernie, although he did not.

Maybe he was thinking about icebergs. I sure was. Had Lieutenant Stine forgotten how hot we had it in the Valley? Ice melts here just like that. Supposing an ice cube falls on the patio: by the time you get there to lick it up, it's turned to water. And the water isn't even cold.

I don't like elevators, not one little bit, but Bernie promised me a treat. We rode an elevator up to the very top of one of the tallest of the downtown towers, just the two of us, which made it better. There were a lot of rapid panting sounds in the elevator. Then at last the doors opened and I burst —

"Ch — et?"

And we stepped outside.

"Here you go," he said, and then came treats, small ones but a whole handful. I made quick work of them. We were on the job.

We went down a long hall, the floor covered with a soft, thick rug, offices on both sides, people hard at work, the kind of human work that involves sitting in front of a screen for a long time. I thought we were headed for a raised, glassed-in office at the end of the hall, but as we passed a conference room with a bunch of people around a long table, a big guy at one end saw us, and jumped up, saying, "Son of a bitch!" Then he ran toward us, grabbed Bernie and hugged him tight. They pounded each other's backs real hard while everyone around the table watched with their mouths wide open.

"Bernie!"

"Gronk!"

Gronk — maybe not as tall as Bernie but a lot broader — turned to the people in the room. "Here's your chance to fix the shit you've been feeding me," he said. "Five minutes, everybody."

Then he took Bernie by the arm and marched him down the hall, up the stairs, and into the glassed-in office. Whatever had been going on in the conference room — it sounded pretty bad — remained a mystery to me. Sounded pretty bad, yes, but hadn't I once seen Iggy —

"And this is Chet," Bernie said, as they settled on a huge leather couch.

"Know all about him," Gronk said. He held out his hand, a real big one. I went over, just to the edge of his reach. He scratched behind my ears. This Gronk dude, whoever he happened to be? A gem, in my book.

"In fact," Gronk said, "I've followed your career closely — especially since you went private."

"Not exactly my choice," Bernie said.

"So what? You're doing great."

"What makes you say that?"

"Read all about that Big Bear case," Gronk said. "And the elephant thing, down in Mexico? Who else could have pulled that off?"

"It was mostly Chet," Bernie said. "But thanks. That's what I'm here for, actually — to thank you for recommending me to the mayor's office."

"Recommend, hell," said Gronk. "I made it a stipulation for underwriting the goddamn policy."

"I don't get it," Bernie said.

"See, that's you — your mind's always on the bigger things."

"Huh?"

"Point is, down here in the money-grubbing world, the mayor's sinking taxpayer dollars into this movie scheme of his, and the law requires him to insure Valley government against loss. That actor asshole, what's his name?"

"Thad Perry."

"Looked into his history. Keeping an eye on someone like him requires someone like you, and the only person I know like you is you."

So complicated, impossible to follow, but it was clear that Gronk was one of the good guys, so why worry about the details?

"You haven't seen me in a long time," Bernie said. "Maybe I've changed."

"Feel bad about that," Gronk said. "Thought about calling you many times when I first came out here. But building something like this, it gets kind of consuming."

"That's not what I meant," Bernie said.

"I know what you meant," Gronk said. "I witnessed you get tested like hardly anybody ever gets tested, and I know what I need to know."

"I got lucky that night."

"The hell you did," Gronk said. "How's the leg?"

"No complaints," Bernie said. "What do you think of the mayor's idea?"

"Cockamamie," said Gronk. "Which is good for our balance sheet — we charge extra for cockamamie."

Bernie glanced around the office. "I never knew you even wanted to get rich."

Gronk laughed. "I never did. That's the best part."

FOUR

Nixon Panero delivered our new wheels in person. Bernie and I had been watching out the window, so we were already outside when he pulled in the driveway.

"Whaddya think?" said Nixon, getting out and handing the keys to Bernie. Nixon eyed the back of the outside mirror, blew on it, buffed whatever was bothering him with his sleeve. "Turn heads or what?"

Bernie gazed at our new Porsche. "This, uh, pattern on the front fenders?"

"The martini glasses?" said Nixon. "Coulda upped the scale — I went back and forth on that. But guess what."

"I give up."

"I copied them right offa the shirt you were wearing the other day!" Nixon spat out one of those thin brown streams of tobacco juice. I toyed with the idea of licking the damp spot on the pavement and rejected it. "Moment of pure inspiration,"

Nixon continued. "Didn't see the point of running it by you. Knew you'd go for it — woulda bet the ranch."

"Where's the ranch?" Bernie said.

Nixon's eyes and mouth opened wide at the same time, one of those human expressions I watch for. What does it mean? Not sure, but I've seen all sorts of unexpected things right after, including shouting, tears, and an airborne machete. "Whoa," said Nixon. "I did bad?"

Bernie smiled. He has the nicest set of human teeth going, and the implant matches perfectly, in my opinion, no matter what anyone says. "Nah," he said. "I love it. The constantly getting pulled over part will take getting used to, that's all."

"Didn't think of that," said Nixon. "But patrol guys know you, Bernie. Once a cop, always a cop."

"Where'd you get that idea?" Bernie said.

"When I was in the pen," said Nixon. "We talked a lot about cops, kind of the way dogs think about cats."

"Dogs think a lot about cats?" Bernie said.

"Makes sense, don't it?" said Nixon.

Then suddenly they were both looking at me. The subject was cats? At the moment, I had no interest in that at all. What I wanted was to take this new baby for a spin, see what it could do, and pronto. I gave myself a good shake, the kind that starts at my head, travels all the way to the tip of my tail and ripples back up again.

"Bet that feels good," Nixon said.

"He wouldn't be doing it otherwise," said Bernie.

Well, of course not. Went without saying. But that hardly ever stops humans, no offense.

"Come on inside," Bernie said. "I'll cut you a check."

"Twisted my arm," said Nixon, which had happened once before, the night we took Nixon down, but why now? And in fact, no arm twisting took place. I pushed all of this out of my mind — *whoosh,* just like that, a nice feeling — and we moved toward the house.

"Notice those two different shades of red?" Nixon said.

"I did," said Bernie.

"Too subtle?"

"No."

"Cheers," said Bernie.

"To the open road," said Nixon.

They clinked glasses. We were at the kitchen table, Bernie on the bench seat, back to the wall, which was how he liked to sit, Nixon in Leda's old chair, and me over by the floor vent, catching the AC. Yes to the open road, and what was wrong with right now?

"Goes down real nice," said Nixon. "Bourbon?"

"Yup."

"That your drink?"

"Guess you could say so."

"Classy."

"This isn't the classy kind."

Nixon took a sip, glanced at some pages on the table. "Don't tell me you're working on a screenplay?" he said.

Bernie shook his head. "Don't even know how to read the goddamn thing." He picked up a page. "What's INT?"

"Interior," Nixon said. "INT or EXT, lead item in every slug line in a script."

"Slug line?" said Bernie.

Nixon leaned over, pointed to the top of the page Bernie was holding. "Right here, after Fade In. Fade in is how you start a movie. Then comes the first scene — interior, bedroom, night. After that, they put in what's going on, like here — a man tosses in his sleep. Then see here? Cut to. That's how they get to the next scene."

"That's a whole scene?" Bernie said. "A guy tosses in his sleep?"

"All depends on how it's handled," Nixon said. "Film's a director's medium — gotta keep that in mind. Take the cigarette lighting scene in *Now, Voyager* — what would that look like on the page? Zip. But on the screen . . . well, there are some things you never forget."

"*Now, Voyager,*" said Bernie. "That's Bette Davis?"

"Shit, yeah," said Nixon. "And Paul Henreid — he did the cigarette thing."

"Forgot you were a fan."

"A fan of a particular period, Bernie. Ain't been acting like hers outta Hollywood before or since."

Bernie poured more bourbon in both their glasses. "What do you think of Thad Perry?"

"Zip."

"I'm talking about his acting ability."

"He don't have no acting ability," Nixon said. "Checked out any of his movies?"

"No."

"He's hype, Bernie, hype that walks and talks. Hype don't get it done. Bette Davis had what gets it done."

"Which was?"

"Hell of a question, Bernie," Nixon said. "Hell of a question."

He closed his eyes real tight, the way humans do when they're about to take a swing at some very hard thinking. I always feel sorry for them at moments like that.

"Had much experience with mushrooms, Bernie?" he said.

"Nope," said Bernie.

Whoa. Nope? Had he forgotten that huge and tasty mushroom we'd found in the woods on the Big Bear Case? And didn't Bernie love to throw little white mushrooms on the barbecue when we grilled burgers? Which I hoped would be happening again real soon. I could just about smell them! In fact, with a little more effort, I actually . . . yes! I smelled burgers. I'd made myself smell burgers when there were none around — wow! What a life! Had something just been bothering me? Whatever it was: poof!

"Once on 'shrooms," Nixon was saying, "— this was down in Mexico, bad idea as it turned out, but that came later — I was sitting by this campfire and all of a sudden I rose up out of the flames." Nixon opened his eyes. "Not me, but this vision, you see what I mean."

"Gotcha," said Bernie.

"Only I was in black-and-white," Nixon said. "Shimmering. Is that a word?"

"Think so."

"I was shimmering," Nixon said. "There was me, this real person, and then me, this

59

unreal person — but cool, you know? — at the same time." Nixon shrugged and went silent.

"That's what Bette Davis had?" Bernie said. "Real and unreal at the same time?"

"You left out cool," said Nixon.

They drank some more, in a no-hurry kind of way. Burgers, anybody? But there was no sign of burgers in the works, no sign of any kind of food at all in the near future, which is the only future that interests me.

"Do me a favor," Bernie said. "Read this script and tell me what you think of it."

"Who's the writer?" said Nixon.

"Says on it."

Nixon studied the top page. "*Wild Horseman,*" he said. "Screenplay by Arn Linsky. Never heard of him. What's this all about?"

"They're shooting it here in the Valley," Bernie said. "The mayor's making a play for the movie business."

"Who's the mayor, again?" said Nixon.

"Doesn't matter," Bernie said. "What matters is that he hired me to keep an eye on Thad Perry."

"Good luck with that," said Nixon.

"How about we swing by Suzie's and take her for a test drive?" Bernie said.

Next thing I knew I was hopping into our

60

new ride for the very first time. Up, up, and in there, a nice soft landing in the shotgun seat, a very comfortable shotgun seat covered in red leather, although red's not supposed to be something I can spot, according to Bernie, so maybe it wasn't. But the best shotgun seat I'd ever sat on: no doubt about it, even though a member of the nation within — namely Spike — had already done some sitting on it, too. But his smell would soon get overwhelmed by mine, the best smell in the world, if I haven't mentioned that already — a heady mixture of salt, pepper, leather, with a soupçon — not of soup, that was a tricky one — but of a scent a lot like Leda's mink coat; plus, to be honest, a topping of something male and funky.

Bernie turned the key, tapped the pedal, cocked his head to one side. "Maybe a little too noisy?"

No way!

And then we were off, out of our neighborhood, up onto the freeway, into the passing lane. Vroom! I sank against the backrest.

"This baby can fly!" Bernie said.

Or something like that, his voice drowned out by a siren. Then a motorcycle came whizzing up beside us, blue lights flashing, and we pulled over. But no problem: it was

61

Fritzie Bortz, an old pal. He got off the bike, not without some trouble — Fritzie was a terrible motorcycle driver with lots of crashes on his record — and came up to Bernie's side.

"Hey!" he said. "Bernie!"

"Hi, Fritzie."

"And Chet — lookin' good, Chet."

So nice to see Fritzie. My tail started wagging.

"How're things?" Fritzie said.

"No complaints," said Bernie.

"New wheels?"

"Uh-huh."

"Cool. Love those martini glasses — wouldn't have bothered pulling you over otherwise. I was actually on my way home — haven't had a day off since last Tuesday."

"No one's ever said you're not a hard worker."

"Thanks, Bernie. I do what I can." Then he took out his ticket book, flipped a page, reached behind his ear for a pen.

"Fritzie? What are you doing?"

"Writing you up," Fritzie said. "Might even make my quota on this — I had you at one-oh-three."

Suzie lived in a garden apartment not far from Max's Memphis Ribs, the best restaurant in the whole Valley, in my opinion, and not just because the owner, Cleon Maxwell, was a friend of ours and gave us two-for-one coupons, but mostly on account of those ribs: the juicy meat and then when you're done with that — the bone! Was Max's Memphis Ribs in our near future?

"Chet! What the hell are you barking about?"

Oops.

We drove down Suzie's street. There are lots of garden apartments in the Valley, but Bernie doesn't like any of them, those little lawns and plants always being the wrong kind, bad for the aquifer. Suzie's yellow Beetle was parked out front and . . . what was this? Hooked to a small trailer? Bernie's face changed. For a moment it looked sad, not something you often see from Bernie. Then he sat up straight and took a breath. That was Bernie making himself do what had to be done. His face went back to normal. We pulled up behind the trailer and hopped out, me hopping, and Bernie stepping out after a bit of a struggle with the door handle.

At that moment, Suzie came out of her house holding a lamp. She saw us and her face went through some changes, kind of like Bernie's but different in a sort of female way, hard to describe. She lowered the lamp.

"Hi," she said.

"Hi," said Bernie. "Didn't think you were leaving till tomorrow."

Had I known that? Did tomorrow count as near future? I wasn't sure.

"Yeah," Suzie said. "I'm just trying to get . . ." She made a little gesture with the lamp and it slipped from her hand and fell on the stone path, the shade — the multicolored glass kind, like they have in the lobby at Rancho Grande, Bernie's favorite hotel in the Valley, and mine, too, no surprise — shattering into tiny pieces. They caught the light in a beautiful way and then Suzie was crying.

Bernie took her in his arms.

"I can't do this," she said.

Bernie patted her back. I kind of nudged at both of them, helping out in my own way. "Sure you can," he said. "You've got the goods."

"It's not that." Suzie drew back, wiping her face on her sleeve. "It's you," she said. "Us."

"Um," said Bernie. "I . . . uh, everything'll turn out."

"What do you mean?"

"For us."

"How can you know that?"

64

Bernie shrugged. "I just do."

They gazed at each other. Suzie's eyes were dampening up again.

"Got a new ride," Bernie said.

Suzie turned toward it. Eyes dampening, yes, but now a smile was trying to break out at the same time, one of those real complicated human looks.

"How about an inaugural spin?" Bernie said.

Normally, meaning pretty much always, the shotgun seat is mine, but on this particular occasion I hopped right up on that tiny shelflike thing in back. How come? No clue. Sometimes I just do things. One of Bernie's rules is not to overthink. I'm totally with him on that. Perps fell into that overthinking trap all time. Take Fishhead Hobbs, for example, and that jewel heist he'd tried to pull at the Ritz. "Fishy," Bernie said to him. "Don't overthink." But Fishhead had swallowed the emeralds anyway, so we'd had to spend the whole afternoon waiting in the hospital before collecting our reward from Mort Gluck, house dick at the Ritz.

Did an inaugural spin mean one that ended up at Max's Memphis Ribs, and pretty damn quick? Must have, because just about the next thing I knew, there we were at our favorite table, the one in front of the painting of the pink pig. I've only had one experience with an actual pig, and don't want to go into it at the moment, or ever.

Cleon Maxwell's the owner. We'd helped him out on a case once, the details escaping me, and he was also a friend of me and my kind — whether or not that's the case is something I've known from the get-go with every human I've ever met.

"We didn't order this," Bernie said when a bottle of champagne arrived.

Cleon appeared at the round window in the swinging door that led to the kitchen, smiled, and waved at us, then disappeared. Things were always humming at Max's. I lay under the table and worked on a rib, then another, and possibly one more. Up above, Bernie and Suzie were doing the same thing, plus drinking champagne. Water's my drink.

"Who's going to win the election?" Bernie said.

"Until a few weeks ago, probably the reformers," Suzie said. "Now it's too close to call — the mayor's smart."

"He is?"

"More like shrewd," Suzie said. "The smart one's his chief of staff. Wherever it's coming from, he's made some good moves lately."

"Like the Hollywood thing?" Bernie said.

"You know about that?"

"I'm a player." And then Bernie explained all about this new job we were on, or if we weren't already on it, soon would be. One or two details seemed familiar.

"Thad Perry?" Suzie said. "Isn't he from here originally?"

"Didn't know that," Bernie said.

"Did you meet the chief of staff?"

"Vera something?"

"Yes," said Suzie. She seemed to be about to say something else but did not, just giving Bernie a quick sideways glance instead.

Soon after that came a struggle between Bernie and Cleon, Cleon saying dinner was on him and Bernie refusing. They arm wrestled over it — Cleon's got these popping forearms, way bigger than Bernie's — and Bernie won, as usual. But it took a long time and I missed the very end — arm wrestling gets me too excited and I ended up waiting with Suzie in the parking lot.

We spent the night at Suzie's place. A nice crib, but I never sleep my best at Suzie's. One thing about apartments: you're not alone. There were people up above, a woman and a man. The man said, "What did you do with my pills?" and the woman said, "I didn't touch them." Clear as a bell

— although I've seen humans miss ringing bells, too — but Bernie and Suzie didn't seem to hear. And on the other side of Suzie's wall there was a cat. He knew I knew, by the way, and also knew I knew he knew I knew, which is the maddening way it goes with cats, so no surprise that I had a restless night.

And was just settling down by the front door — Bernie and Suzie slept in her bedroom, door closed, fine with me this particular night, kind of a surprise — when I heard a car go by. Did it make a little ticking sound? *Tick-tick-tick?* I thought so. I rose and went to the window. Yes, a tick-ticking car, driving real slow, a dark car with darkened windows, all closed except one at the back. And poking out of that back window? The head of an enormous member of the nation within, an open-mouth dude with the angriest eyes and the longest teeth I'd ever seen; a real bad combo. The car sped up and vanished in the night.

FIVE

"You know what was on my mind the whole time?" Bernie said. We were on the street outside Suzie's place and the Beetle, towing the trailer, had just turned the corner and disappeared from view. Its sound shrank and shrank, and then the entire Valley went quiet, which hardly ever happened.

I waited to hear what was on Bernie's mind. At that moment a car towing a trailer a lot like Suzie's drove up. A woman got out, glanced at us, then walked to Suzie's door and fished some keys from her purse. She tried one or two, opened the door, and went inside.

"I was thinking of popping the question," Bernie said.

A new one on me. Popping? I knew popcorn — not my favorite, on account of how it can stick between your teeth — and that was it.

"There's a tide which taken at the flow,"

69

Bernie said, not losing me at all, on account of the trip we'd taken to San Diego a while back — we'd surfed, me and Bernie! — so I knew tides were some trick of the ocean. Were we headed there again? Like now? A fine idea, but that was Bernie.

"On the other hand," he went on, something he hardly ever says, because of this belief of his that if humans had more or less than two hands they'd think differently, or something like that, "a wedding means a happy ending only in the movies. In real life, real life goes on."

Okay. Now I was lost, and completely. San Diego: yes? no? I didn't have a clue.

"Come here, big guy."

I moved closer to Bernie. He gave me a nice pat. His gaze was still on the empty intersection down the street. I let that slip from my mind and just concentrated on the pat. You can feel things in the hand of humans, things that are happening deep inside them. I felt what was happening inside Bernie.

We pulled into Vin's Discount Liquors, which was in the West Valley, next to a strip club. Strippers: they crop up in our line of work, each and every one a fan of me and my kind. From time to time you run across

70

a person who actually seems to prefer us, from the nation within, to their own, in the nation without, if that makes any sense. Probably not, but the strippers I'd met were all like that.

"You goddamn son of a bitch," said Vin as we walked inside. "Not you, Chet, but the asshole you're dragging along."

He came around from behind the cash register and rolled toward us in his wheelchair real fast, long hair lifting off his shoulders in the breeze. Vin was another old army pal of Bernie's, he had a massive upper body and below that a lower body easily covered by a small blanket. They shook hands, Bernie's hand, which normally looked so big, lost in Vin's.

"What's doin'?" Vin said, reaching into his pocket and tossing a biscuit my way. I was ready, caught it in midair.

"Not much," Bernie said. "You?"

"No complaints," said Vin. "Lookin' for something special, or your usual cheapo rotgut?"

"Maybe not rotgut tonight."

"Yeah? Celebration?"

"More like the opposite."

Vin laughed. "I know that one." He waited, like maybe for Bernie to say more, but Bernie did not. Vin wheeled around, sped down the aisle, grabbed a bottle off the shelf, and returned.

"Maybe not bourbon strictly speaking, bein' from Texas," he said, "but nice toffee overlay, long, soft finish, big in the mouth."

A woman stuck her head around the corner from the next aisle just as Bernie took the bottle from Vin. She gazed, blinked, and backed out of sight.

No idea what went down there, and no time to figure it out, because a moment later Vin had decided on a little tasting, and they'd opened the bottle.

"Remember that five-hour leave in Amsterdam?" Vin said.

"I try not to," said Bernie.

"How tall was the blonde, do you think?" said Vin. "The one with the speargun."

"Six three?"

"Nah," said Vin. "Six six at the very least. Never ran so fast in my goddamn life."

Bernie was silent for a moment. He sipped from the little plastic sampling glass. "It is nice," he said.

We bought three bottles.

"Ship come in?" said Vin.

We were driving away from Vin's when the phone rang. Bernie has it rigged so the voice of the caller comes through the speakers.

72

"Bernie? Cal Luxton here. You all set?"

"All set for what?" Bernie said.

"Meet and greet," Luxton said.

"Who am I meeting?"

"Thad Perry, of course. You feeling all right?"

"Where and when?" Bernie said.

"Forty-one hundred High Line Road in an hour," Luxton said.

"The old Comstock place?"

"I'll leave your name at the gate." *Click.*

Bernie checked his face in the rearview mirror. "No time to swing by the house." He rubbed his chin, which made a little rasping sound. "Do I look all right?"

What a question! He looked great! We're talking about Bernie here.

We drove toward the sun. It was sinking now, just over the mountains across the Valley, reddening everything, including Bernie's face. That bothered me for some reason.

"What are you barking about?"

Was that me? Oops. But then I barked some more, this time just to bark when I was back at the controls of my own barking, if that makes sense.

"Another chewy? Forget it?"

Up and up we went — yes, this baby could move, and what a loud rumbly voice it had!

— first on freeways with heavy traffic, then on a mountain road with hardly any.

"Like how it corners?" Bernie said, the wind whipping at his hair.

I loved how it cornered! I felt like cornering forever. Corner, Bernie, corner!

"Whee-ooo!" said Bernie. At that point, with us in the middle of a corner, and sliding over the yellow line, a big pickup came barreling down from the other direction, also sliding over the yellow line.

"Still alive," Bernie said, after all the honking and burning rubber was done with.

Yes! Totally. But that turned out to be it for the fast cornering part of the drive.

The mountain got steeper and houses started to appear, real big ones, some of them sticking right into the sky. We went past a huge red rock, taller than any of the houses, and came to a gate.

"Bernie Little," said Bernie to the guy with the clipboard.

The guy gave Bernie a close look. "Thought it might be you," he said.

Bernie gave him a close look back. "Boo Ferris?"

"At your service. Hey, Chet, lookin' good."

Boo Ferris! And no longer sporting an orange jumpsuit. What a nice perp! He'd hijacked an eighteen-wheeler loaded with tequila that actually turned out to be prom dresses and he'd tried to make his escape by wearing one. The fun we'd had!

"What the hell are you doing here?" Bernie said.

"It's a job," said Boo Ferris.

"A security-type job," Bernie said, giving Boo Ferris a long look, the meaning of which escaped me.

Boo Ferris leaned closer, lowered his voice. "The company thinks I'm my brother Bo," he said. "Our Socials are just one number different, so I can rattle his off like nobody's business."

Bernie smiled. "It'll be our little secret."

"Much obliged, Bernie. I always tell the boys I'd rather be busted by you than anybody else."

"Let's not test that again," Bernie said.

A car came up behind us. Boo Ferris raised the gate and tapped on our hood. We drove through. Beyond the gate, the houses were more spread out and even bigger. We drove along a high ridge, nothing but blue skies on both sides, and turned up a long winding driveway lined with flowers. At the end stood a huge adobe house with a black SUV out front. We parked behind it. Cal Luxton got out of the SUV and walked over.

"He's not here yet," Luxton said. "But this is where he's staying during the shoot, a little fact we'll keep under our hats."

I was on board for that, although Luxton was the only one of us wearing a hat, that big white cowboy hat of his. All I ever wear is my collar, the brown one for everyday and the black one for dress-up. Everyday means on the job, so brown's what I wear when we're collaring perps — and then they end up sporting orange! Not collars actually, but jumpsuits, even though they're collared: kind of confusing. Let's drop it.

"Doesn't that hedge fund guy still own this place?" Bernie said.

"He's renting it out to the studio," Luxton said. "Ten grand a day."

"When's the revolution?" Bernie said.

"Seventeen seventy-six," said Luxton. He gave Bernie a quick sideways look from under the cowboy hat shadow, missed by Bernie but caught by me. At that moment, I heard a buzzing in the sky. A distant chopper appeared, like a black insect against the red ball of the sun. Then came a surprise.

"Think I hear it now," Luxton said, and he turned his probing eyes in the right direction.

Wow. A human who could hear, no offense. We watched the chopper come closer and closer, then circle over the other side of the ridge, changing from black to white. *WHAP-WHAP-WHAP.* The chopper, a real big one, tilted a bit to one side, flew over the house, stopped in midair, and then settled slowly down and down, coming to rest on a flat part of the driveway, not far away. The engine went silent, the blades spun for another moment or two, and then everything was quiet and still.

A cabin door opened and stairs swung out from the inside. People appeared and started climbing down: first a woman with short dark hair, wearing glasses, then a very big guy in a suit, after that another woman, this one with long blond hair, and finally a scruffy-looking dude in jeans and a torn T-shirt, a cigarette hanging out the side of his mouth. After that, nobody.

"Where's Thad Perry?" Bernie said.

"That's him, the last one," said Luxton. "You don't know what he looks like?"

"I know what he looks like on screen," Bernie said.

The scruffy dude was Thad Perry? Not Thad Perry? This was hard to follow, and we were just getting started. He and the others moved toward us, the huge guy first, then the women, scruffy dude last, scratching under his arm. That made me like him from the get-go.

"Hi, Jiggs," said Cal Luxton to the huge guy. "Nice trip?"

"Uh-huh," said Jiggs, shaking hands. "This here's Nan Klein, Mr. Perry's assistant."

"Luxton," said Luxton to the glasses-wearing woman, "head of security for Mayor Trimble's office."

"Mr. Perry's friend Felicity," Jiggs went on.

"Hi," said Luxton.

The blond woman gave him a tiny wave, barely any movement at all.

"And," said Jiggs, "Thad Perry."

Thad Perry spun his cigarette butt toward a low bush.

"Love your movies," Luxton said.

Thad Perry took out another cigarette and the next moment Nan was right there with a lit match.

"Want you to meet Bernie Little," Luxton said. "Bernie's going to —"

"Hey!" said Thad Perry. "Where the fuck's Brando?"

"Oh my God!" said Felicity. "Did we leave him in LA?"

Nan was already running toward the chopper, wobbly but surprisingly quick in her high heels. She raced up the stairs and disappeared inside.

"Oh my God!" said Felicity. "I don't remember seeing him on the plane."

"It's not a goddamn plane," Thad Perry said. "It's a chopper. How many times do I have to tell you?"

"Sorry, baby," said Felicity. She gave his arm a little rub. He moved away.

I glanced at Bernie. That's something we in the nation within can often do without turning our heads, on account of not being locked into a straight-on view, something we learned on the Discovery Channel, me and Bernie. But forget all that. The point is that when things get confusing, I like to touch base with Bernie — that time at Charlie's T-ball game when I stole the base! What a memory! It wasn't nailed down! I got as far as the concession stand before Bernie . . .

Bernie. I glanced at Bernie. He had on one of his unreadable faces, but he was thinking, and plenty. I could feel his thoughts in my own mind, although I couldn't break through to see what was inside them. He walked over to the bush and stamped out Thad Perry's cigarette butt.

Nan appeared in the doorway of the chopper and called out, "The little scamp was curled up in the copilot chair!"

Or something like that. I couldn't really concentrate on account of what she was holding in her arms. Of course, he saw me right away and gave me one of those superior looks. Yes, a cat. Not particularly little, by the way, in fact, kind of monstrous. And ugly, besides. If a deep golden coat except for snowy-white feet and a snowy-white nose wasn't ugly then what was?

"Brando!" said Thad Perry. "Come to Poppa!"

Brando was the cat? And Thad Perry thought he himself was the . . . I couldn't take it past that. Meanwhile, Brando stayed right where he was, in Nan's arms. She came down the ladder.

"Brando!" said Thad Perry, raising his voice. His voice had a strange harshness, and the louder he talked the harsher it got. "Come to Poppa!"

"He's a cat person?" Bernie said.

"Guess so," said Luxton.

Cat person? I tried to make sense of that idea and failed completely.

"Nan, let him go, for Christ sake," Thad Perry said.

"I'm not holding him, Thad," Nan said. "He's holding me. I think he's scared of that big dog."

"What big dog?" Thad Perry said. And then he was looking at me; so were they all.

Bernie moved my way. "This is Chet," he said. "He works with me."

Thad Perry turned to Bernie. "What do you do?"

"Right," said Luxton. "I was just getting to that. Bernie here's going to be the mayor's special liaison for security during the shoot. Any problems, take them to him, and they'll get fixed pronto."

"I don't understand any of this," Thad Perry said. "Nan? Do you understand any of this?"

"I saw some emails about it," Nan said, "but I wasn't aware —"

"You saw some emails!" Thad Perry said. Hey! His voice could get really huge, booming right off the ridge. Except for all the added harshness, I kind of liked that. Also I liked how he'd scratched himself. But of course the whole cat-person thing now ruled him out. So was it time to hop in the car, get the hell on the road?

"You weren't aware!" Thad Perry went on. "Am I all alone out here? In this godforsaken hole? Like Jesus on the mountaintop? Has everybody forgotten what's riding on this?"

Nan gazed at the ground, said nothing.

"Baby?" said Felicity. "I think this man — Bernie is it? — is just here to help."

Thad gave her a hard look. "Yeah? Why do you think that?"

Felicity rubbed his arm. "I get an aura."

"Yeah?" said Thad. "You're sure? It's not one of those fake auras?"

Felicity shook her head.

"Remember what happened in wherever the hell that was," Thad Perry said.

"St. Barts?" said Felicity. "Oh, no, this is different."

"And everyone here wants nothing more than for this movie to be ginormous," Nan said.

"Yeah?" Thad Perry said, quieting down. He turned to Bernie. "Okay," he said. "You're in. But the dog's got to go."

"It's Moses on the mountaintop," Bernie said. "And the dog stays in the picture."

It got real quiet up on this ridge. I thought of a biker bar we'd been in once, me and Bernie, the moment before things cut loose. But this wasn't a biker bar, and nobody looked dangerous, except that Jiggs guy, maybe a bit. Bernie can be very dangerous, of course, as dangerous as they come, but he doesn't look it, at least most of the time.

And then Thad Perry started laughing. He had a big, loud laugh, actually kind of jolly.

He wasn't the kind of laugher who shook with it, not being at all fat, in fact pretty much ripped, now that I saw him up close, but the sound was just like one of those Santa Clauses in the movies. At that moment, I made a connection, which didn't happen every day — just nailing it. Thad Perry was in the movies, too! So I knew everything was cool before he even said it.

Six

Had I ever been in a house this big? Not close. It spread across the whole top of the ridge and also had levels going down the mountain, kind of like the decks of this cruise ship we saw on our San Diego trip. There was even a gym with a boxing ring. Thad Perry, dressed in shorts, stood near the ring, working the speed bag. I'd seen lots of dudes working the speed bag — comes with the territory — and Thad looked pretty good to me, his hands *bap-bap-bapping* real fast, the bag itself a blur. Bernie watched from a stool in the corner. Jiggs sat at a desk near the door, paging through a magazine.

"How'm I doing, Jiggsy?" Thad said.

"Better and better," said Jiggs, although he didn't take his eyes off the magazine.

Thad stepped away from the bag, turned to Bernie. "I've been training with Carlos Longoria," he said. "Carlos thinks I could've gone pro if I'd started young enough."

"Who's Carlos Longoria?" Bernie said.

"Who's Carlos Longoria?" Thad said. "You hear that, Jiggsy?"

"Uh-huh."

"Where have you been, Bennie?" Thad said. "Mars? Carlos Longoria's the middleweight champion of the goddamn world."

Bennie? Mars? This was confusing.

"I don't keep up with boxing anymore," Bernie said. "And it's Bernie."

Thad went to work on the bag again. "Bennie, Bernie," he said, and then lots of *bap-bap-bap,* faster and harder than before. "Don't like boxing? Too violent for you?"

"Boxing's okay," Bernie said. "It's prizefighting I don't like."

"Huh? I don't get it."

"Doesn't matter — just my opinion."

"Whoa," said Thad, winding up and giving the bag a tremendous blow. He wheeled around and stared at Bernie. Thad had great big blue eyes, maybe slightly farther apart than usual. "I said I didn't get it. I like to get things."

Jiggs looked up.

"Yeah?" Bernie said.

"Yeah," said Thad. "So help me get it."

"Two guys trying to beat each other senseless in front of a paying crowd bothers me,"

Bernie said. "I've got no problem with them doing it for fun."

"Still don't get it," Thad said.

Bernie shrugged. "Like I said, doesn't matter. Just one man's take."

Thad seemed to think that over. Sweat ran down his big, muscular chest. "What makes you an expert?" he said at last.

"Didn't say I was."

"Like, for example, have you ever actually boxed?"

"A little," Bernie said.

Hey! That was a surprise. We'd been partners, me and Bernie, practically as long as I remember, and here I was, still finding out things about him. I'll never get tired of Bernie.

"What does that mean?" Thad said.

"Just fooled with it when I was in high school," Bernie said.

"Jiggs?" Thad said.

"Boss?" said Jiggs.

"Remember that line from *The Last Warrior*?"

"Which one?"

"For Christ sake — the best line in the goddamn picture, where I say 'Make me believe it, bro.' "

"Oh, yeah," said Jiggs. "Brilliant line — who was the writer?"

"Writer? No goddamn writer. Improv, Jiggsy. I improvised that line right on the set."

"Brilliant line," Jiggs said.

Thad nodded, took a few steps toward Bernie, and smiled — a little smile, but there was something real cool about it that made you want to keep looking. "Right now, Bernie, I've got a strong urge to say that line again, only this time in real life."

"Yeah?" said Bernie.

"Yeah," said Thad. "You say you boxed in high school. I say make me believe it, bro."

Bernie gazed at Thad for a moment, then rose off the stool. They were close together now, so it was easy to see that Thad was taller and bigger, and way more ripped. Bernie wasn't soft — oh, no, not at all — but you couldn't call him ripped. And, kind of a strange thought for me, Thad looked younger, too, a thought I didn't like and hoped would go away soon. That's something I've been lucky with in my life.

"Jiggs?" Thad said. "Go find the sixteen-ounce gloves. Nothing to worry about, Bernie. It'll be like a pillow fight."

Jiggs checked his watch. "The manicurist is due in fifteen minutes," he said.

"Jesus Christ, she can goddamn well wait," Thad said. "When am I gonna start getting some cooperation around here?"

Jiggs got up, opened a wall cabinet, took out boxing gloves.

Not long after that, they were in the ring, both wearing head protectors. Bernie still wore his jeans, but he'd taken off his shirt. Not ripped, but no flab on Bernie, excepting the tiniest bit around the middle. You had to look real hard to see it. In fact, it might have been my imagination. I'm almost sure of it.

"How do two three-minute rounds sound?" Thad said. Or something like that. The mouth guard made him hard to understand.

Bernie shrugged.

"Count it down, Jiggs," Thad said.

"Sure thing," said Jiggs. He was looking at Bernie in a careful sort of way. Was it because of the scar on Bernie's shoulder from his baseball days? Or the one from when he got slashed by Spiny Price, who was now sporting an orange jumpsuit up at Northern State Correctional? Or was it something else? No time to figure it out, because the next moment Jiggs said, "All set?"

"Whee-ooo," said Thad, his chest swelling way up. "Raging fucking bull."

Bernie turned to me. "Sit, boy," he said. "Sit and stay." Like Thad, he was hard to understand with the mouth guard, so I just stayed how I was, standing by the ring. "Ch—et?" Bernie said, in this special way of saying my name. I sat. I sat and promised myself to stay until further notice.

"On three," said Jiggs. "One, two —"

Was three coming next? Not for me to say: I stop at two, which is a real good number, in my opinion. But if three was coming next, Jiggs never got to say it, because right at two, Thad lunged forward and launched a heavy roundhouse punch right at the middle of Bernie's face, the part not protected by the head guard.

Bernie and I never watched boxing anymore, but we'd gone through a stage of running old fight videos on TV, back around when he and Leda were going through the divorce. "Our own little rumble in the jungle," Bernie said to me at the time. Not sure what he meant by that, but the rumble in the jungle, Ali and Foreman? Forget it! And the Thrilla in Manila, Ali and Frazier? Shut up!

But that's not the point. The point is I've watched a lot of fights and I know the lingo. Slipping the punch, for example, is the way Bernie handled that first blow Thad threw

89

at him. He shifted his head to one side, just enough so that Thad's punch hit nothing but air. Funny thing about the look in Bernie's eyes: he'd been expecting that punch. Hard to explain how I knew, I just did. I was on my feet now; very hard to stay sitting at a fight.

Boxing has its own time, Bernie says, speeding up and slowing down in a way that proved Einstein was right. He'd lost me there — the only Einstein I knew being Wilbur Einstein, a forger from down Arroyo Rojo way who'd been totally wrong when he'd said no jury would ever convict him, and was now breaking rocks in the hot sun — but I got the idea about speeding up and slowing down. Now, for example, after the speed of Thad's roundhouse and Bernie's head shift, things were slowing down. Bernie hadn't even raised his arms. Bernie! And Thad was just sort of gaping at him, like this fish Charlie used to keep, before the unfortunate accident.

Then came another slow thing. This reddish color appeared on Thad's face, spread all the way down his neck. And just like that: boom! We were back to full speed. Thad stepped in, threw a whole flurry of punches at Bernie's midsection. Somehow Bernie's arms were up in time. Thad's blows landed,

thud-thud thud-thud, the sound echoing off
the bare walls of the gym and coming back,
thud-thud thud-thud, real hard, but Bernie
said in boxing you had to watch where the
punches land, and Thad's punches were
landing on Bernie's arms and shoulders.
Lots and lots of hard punches and they had
to hurt — red welts were already showing
on Bernie's skin — but I knew that was better than getting hit in the head or the guts
or the kidneys, wherever the kidneys happened to be.

And then Bernie kind of got Thad in a
clinch and they danced around together,
their heads very close, both of them already
sweating.

"You want to waltz or fight?" Thad said.

Bernie pushed him away, and then got up
on the balls of his feet and started moving
sideways, circling Thad. Bernie on the balls
of his feet! Wow! Have I mentioned the way
one of Bernie's legs gets tired sometimes,
on account of his war wound? It didn't look
tired now.

Thad lowered his head, moved into the
circle Bernie was making, tried a jab to
Bernie's chin, caught by Bernie with his
gloves, and then a hook that landed on the
side of Bernie's head, and landed good.
Bernie's eyes went a bit blurry, then came

back to normal, just as Thad moved in with another one of those roundhouse swings. Bernie slipped that one, too. Uh-oh. Maybe not completely.

And now he was against the ropes, ropes, by the way, that I could jump through, no problem, and take Thad down before you could say Jackie Robinson, Bernie's favorite baseball player of all time, Teddy Ballgame being second. Not all of that: only the Jackie Robinson part.

Thad started in on another one of those punch bombardments, some landing, some not. Bernie sagged against the ropes, leaned one way, then another, couldn't get free of Thad. Thad had a hot glow in his eyes, wild and mean. He lined Bernie up, let loose with another big hook. Hey! Bernie ducked it! No time to go into the whole duck thing now. Bernie ducked that big hook and came up with a hook of his own that whapped Thad on the side of the face. A snapping hook, yes! You could hear it snap! And then Bernie jabbed off the hook, so quick it almost happened at the same time. That jab was a stinger, popping Thad right on the button, the button meaning the nose in boxing lingo. *Snap, pop,* and then *crack:* loved the sounds of boxing!

Crack? Turned out that was Thad's nose,

now lined up kind of sideways and dripping blood. Why did I glance over at Jiggs at that moment? Not sure. He'd slid his hand inside a suit jacket pocket and was pulling out a gun.

Thad was staring at Bernie in an out-of-his-mind-with-rage sort of way. "You fucking cheeseball son of a bitch, I'm gonna kill you."

Then we were back up to full speed again. Thad charged at Bernie, hurling punches, wild and ferocious, giving me no time at all to go back over the cheeseball thing, get my mind around the concept. Bernie stepped inside and threw a short uppercut to the chin, landing it square, bang on. Thad's eyes rolled up. His face went all white. Then he toppled over on the canvas and lay flat on his back, sort of like Sonny Liston at the end of the second Ali fight, except that Sonny Liston was one scary dude and I now knew for sure that Thad Perry was not.

Jiggs? Maybe a different matter. I looked at him again. He was moving toward the ring now, mouth hanging open a bit, no sign of the gun. I trotted over behind him, following close. He climbed through the ropes and hurried to Thad. Bernie was already there, leaning over him.

"Why the hell did you have to go and do

93

that?" Jiggs said. "Is he dead?"

Uh-oh. Hadn't thought of that. But no worries. Thad's chest was rising and falling, rising and falling, and they're never dead when that's happening.

Bernie spat out his mouthpiece. "He was beating the crap out of me," he said. "It was just a fluky punch."

Jiggs glared down at him. Jiggs was really a big, big dude. "The fuck it was. You played him like a goddamn fish."

Bernie glanced down at Jiggs's suit jacket pocket, the one he'd taken the gun from, then looked back up at Jiggs, meeting his gaze and saying nothing.

"Not saying I don't blame you," Jiggs said. "But I know what I saw."

"It was still pretty fluky," Bernie said. "And I didn't know he had a glass jaw."

"Of course he has a glass jaw," Jiggs said. "And look at his goddamn nose. They roll film day after tomorrow." He shook his head. "Christ. Starting with the bar scene."

"What happens in that?" Bernie said.

"He beats the shit out of a whole mess of renegades," said Jiggs.

They gazed down at Thad.

"I'm gonna lose my goddamn job," Jiggs said. "And what happens when the media gets hold of this?" He gave Bernie an angry look.

"They won't get it from me," Bernie said. "And why does the news have to travel beyond these four walls?"

"What's the matter with you?" Jiggs said. "You're not seeing that hooter of his?"

"I know a good doc," Bernie said. "Completely trustworthy."

"Yeah?" said Jiggs. "You really think —"

Thad groaned. His eyes, such an amazing shade of blue, like the early morning sky out in the desert, fluttered open.

Jiggs got down on his knees. "You okay, Thad?"

"Do I look okay?"

"Uh," said Jiggs, "yeah, pretty good."

Thad's eyes shifted toward Bernie, then away, real quick. "Must have passed out," he said.

"Hardly at all," said Jiggs. "Not worth mentioning."

"Fuckin' dehydrated," Thad said. "This goddamn altitude."

Jiggs blinked. "You fainted on account of the altitude?"

"Not fainted," Thad said, strength returning to his voice, and with it some of that harshness. "Passed out."

"Passed out," Jiggs said.

"Scratch that," Thad said. "Blacked out."

"Blacked out," said Jiggs.

"Happens when people first get here," Bernie said.

"Yeah?" said Thad, looking at Bernie and then quickly away one more time.

"More often than not," Bernie said. "Practically the rule. Drink some water, get a full night's sleep, you'll be good as new."

"Feel like sitting up?" Jiggs said.

"Huh? Don't talk to me like I'm some kinda candyass," Thad said. "If I want to sit up, I'll sit up."

Back up. Candyass? A new one on me, and very, very interesting. Not that I'm a big candy lover, but the whole thing together — candy, ass — for some reason reminded me of a night when we were working a case down in Mexico, and a brief interlude with a member of the nation within named Lola. Funny how the mind works.

Meanwhile, Bernie and Jiggs were pulling Thad up into a sitting position. For a moment, Thad's eyes went all glazy. Then he shook his head and went, "Whew. Thought I was gonna puke there for a second."

Jiggs and Bernie let go of him, stepped back.

"I hate puking," Thad said.

Me, too, although it's nice how you feel

right after, so nice — and this is kind of crazy — that sometimes the next thing you knew you were licking up all the stuff that just got puked, putting it back inside you. What a life!

"Think about something else," Bernie said.

"Like what?" said Thad.

"A cool breeze," Bernie said.

Thad went very still. His face began to change in a way that was hard to explain. He became a different sort of Thad, one that wasn't pukey. Then, mostly on his own, he rose to his feet.

"Jiggs?" Thad held out his hands. Jiggs unlaced the gloves and pulled them off. Thad stood there for a moment, then reached up and touched his nose, or rather, where his nose used to be.

SEVEN

"What would you call it this time?" Jiggs said. "Fainting? Blacking out? Passing out?"

Bernie took a look at Thad Perry. He was lying on the canvas again, but this time he'd gone down gently, sagging into Bernie's and Jiggs's arms a moment after he'd located his poor nose, angled over to one side of his face.

"Tough call," Bernie said. Thad made a little moaning sound. His big chest rose and fell. "Looks like he's in great physical shape."

"He can bench three oh five," Jiggs said.

"I'm impressed," Bernie said. He pulled his cell phone out of his pocket, started fiddling with the buttons. "I know I've got Doctor Booker's private number here somewhere."

"Booker?" said Jiggs. "He black, by any chance?"

Bernie nodded. "Is that a problem?"

"Nope. Any relation to the DA?"

"Cedric? Yeah — the doc's his brother." Bernie gave Jiggs a quick glance. "I assumed you were from LA."

"I am," Jiggs said.

"But you know our DA out here in the Valley?"

"Know of him," Jiggs said. "I do my homework."

"So — no objection?"

"As long as he stays away from the goddamn media."

Bernie nodded. "Here we go," he said, hitting one more button. At that moment, there was a knock at the door. Jiggs whipped out some tiny device and clicked it. I heard bolts sliding in the walls.

"Thad?" Nan called. "The manicurist is here, if you're ready."

Bernie and Jiggs looked at each other.

"Thad?" Nan called through the door.

"Uh," said Jiggs, "he's, um . . ."

"In the whirlpool," Bernie said. "His shoulder's a little sore." Jiggs nodded vigorously.

"Oh my God!" Nan said.

"Nothing to worry about," Bernie said. "Jiggs is just checking to see if he's ready."

Jiggs did some more vigorous nodding. Then he bent down, picked up Thad like

99

nothing, threw him over his shoulder. He stepped through the ropes, took Thad into a room on the other side of the gym. Before the door closed, I glimpsed a whirlpool bath and a pile of fluffy white towels. I made — what's that expression of Bernie's? A mental note? Yes. I made a mental note about those towels. A fluffy white towel can be fun to drag around, maybe something you already know.

"Jiggs?" Nan called. "Mr. Little?"

"Call me Bernie," Bernie said.

"What's going on?" Nan said. "The door seems to be locked."

"It is?" Bernie said. "I'll just step into the whirlpool room and . . ."

Bernie didn't go anywhere, just stood in the ring. He gave me a smile. So nice. Now I knew that everything was going smoothly. I liked to be in the picture. And hadn't Bernie said something about that very recently? I tried to remember. But not my hardest, on account of what was the point, with everything going smoothly and all?

"Nan?" Bernie said after a while. "Thad says for the manicurist to come back tomorrow. He wants to sit in the whirlpool and, quote, that's that, end quote."

"Oh," said Nan. "Sure. Of course."

"And the door's locked because Thad

didn't want any distraction during his workout," Bernie said. "He seems to take it very seriously, maybe with filming coming up so soon."

"Yes, he does," Nan said. "For sure. Okay, then — I'll take care of it."

"Thanks," said Bernie.

He cocked his head, as though listening for Nan's departing footsteps. Did he hear them? No idea, but I did. There was a pause of a few moments before she actually started walking away.

I'd never met Doc Booker before, but his brother Cedric, the DA, was a pal of ours. Cedric had been a basketball star down at the college and could have gone pro, Bernie says, but he couldn't play with his back to the basket. A puzzler, but basketball was full of puzzlers, starting with the ball, pretty much impossible for me, despite my best efforts.

Doc Booker, not as tall as his brother, was still the tallest human in the whirlpool room. Then came Jiggs, after him Thad, now on his feet and wearing a robe, and Bernie last, the very shortest! Had that ever happened before?

"Love your movies," said Doc Booker.

"Thanks," said Thad, only it came out

more like "Danks," what with his nose the way it was.

"My wife would be thrilled to have your autograph," Doc Booker said. "How about signing my prescription pad?"

"Always the wife," Thad said, taking the pad and pen Doc Booker handed him and writing on it. "Maybe I'll prescribe myself a whole mess of Oxycontin."

Doc Booker laughed. "That's a good one." Bernie didn't laugh, although the corners of his mouth turned up a bit. As for Jiggs, the corners of his mouth — not a very nicely shaped mouth, especially compared to Bernie's — were way down.

Doc Booker tucked the prescription pad away. "Thanks a bunch," he said. "Let's take a look at this situation." He peered at Thad's nose, extended his finger as though to touch it, but didn't, Thad wincing anyway, said, "Totally fixable. You can either come to the hospital where I'll get you into the OR and reset you under anesthetic —"

"Hospital?" said Thad. "What about the goddamn media?"

"Or," Doc Booker continued, "if you're up for it, I can do it right here, quick and dirty."

"Quick and dirty?" Thad said.

"Sting a little," said Doc Booker. "But it'll

be over in two seconds."

"And I'll be back to normal?"

Doc Booker nodded. "Or even more rugged than before."

"What the hell?" said Thad. "I don't want to be more rugged than before. I need to be the exact same amount of rugged, for Christ sake."

"Got it," said Doc Booker.

"And no one ever hears about it," Thad said.

"Bernie has already filled me in," Doc Booker said. He shook his head. "You're a brave man, mixing it up with ol' Bernie."

Bernie shot Doc Booker a quick look.

"Or not," said Doc Booker. "Bernie's bark is worse than his bite."

Whoa. What a stunner. Bernie's bark? Bernie's bite? Neither one had ever happened, not in all the time we'd been together. Maybe Doc Booker was getting the two of us confused. Did that mean that my own bark was worse than . . . ? I lost the thread, and none too soon.

Thad took a deep breath. "Okay," he said. "Do what you gotta do. Should I sit down?"

"Nah," said Doc Booker, and he reached out and in one smooth motion took hold of Thad's nose and gave it a hard twist.

■ ■ ■ ■

"In hindsight," Doc Booker said, "sitting down would have been preferable."

"Not your fault," said Bernie.

"I didn't take him for a fainter," Doc Booker said.

"I was trying to figure out how to put it," Bernie said.

"Good luck with that," said Jiggs.

They gazed at Thad, now lying on a training table, eyes closed and a peaceful look on his face.

"You did a great job, Doc," Jiggs said.

"Thanks."

"Just send in a bill."

"No bill," said Doc Booker. "Bernie and I go way back. How's the leg, by the way?"

"No problems," Bernie said.

Even though there were. But that was Bernie.

Jiggs glanced at Bernie's leg, maybe about to say something, but before he could, Doc Booker turned to me and said, "Chet's looking great. Happen to have a biscuit on me."

Old news: I'd known the instant he stepped into the room, had almost stopped wondering if the biscuit was going to make an appearance. Now I was wondering again, wondering my hardest.

"Down, Chet," Bernie said.

"Should I make him sit?"

"Way past that," said Bernie. "Just give him the damn thing."

Doc Booker reached into his pocket and gave me a biscuit. Maybe I took it, would be more accurate.

"My God, he's quick," Doc Booker said. Then came a discussion of how much I weighed — I'm a hundred-plus-pounder — but I wasn't paying attention, on account of the quality of the biscuit, very high.

We drove past the gate — a different guy on duty now — along the ridge, and started down the mountain. After not too long, we came to a construction site with a partly built house and a Dumpster out front. All of a sudden, Bernie pulled off the road and parked behind the Dumpster. He shut off the engine.

"If you know someone does his homework," he said, "then you've got to do your homework, too."

At that moment, he noticed the fluffy white towel — just washcloth size, really — in my mouth, and took it away. No problem. My mind was on other things, namely homework. Once Charlie had to do some homework. This was on one of his every-second weekend visits, and did we look forward to them or what? Every-second weekends couldn't come fast enough! But the point was, I knew about homework. You opened a book or two, did some writing, yawned, gazed around, got up and had a snack, turned on the TV. So I waited for Bernie to take out a book. The sooner the book part, the sooner we'd get to the snack.

No book appeared. Bernie rubbed his shoulder. "How does he know he's the exact right state of rugged?" he said, losing me completely. I didn't sense a snack coming anytime soon. Kind of frustrating because there was a ham sandwich, or at least part of one, somewhere in that Dumpster: pretty much impossible to miss the smell of ham.

Bernie glanced over at me.

"You're slobbering," he said.

Uh-oh. I wasn't sure how to stop that. I tried panting. It worked a bit.

Bernie smiled at me and gave me pat. "Let's just keep in mind the three grand a day," he said, rubbing his shoulder again.

Bernie's always been a great thinker, one of our strengths at the Little Detective Agency. I bring my own things to the table. We're a real good team. Ask some of the dudes sporting orange jumpsuits up at Northern State Correctional.

"Thad Perry," Bernie said. "I've already changed my mind about him three times. Maybe that's why he's an actor. What's that word? Sort of means changeable."

I waited to hear.

"It's on the tip of my tongue," Bernie said.

I gazed at him closely. At first his mouth was closed, then it opened slightly, and I saw the tip of his tongue. A beautifully shaped tongue tip, nice and pink, but there was absolutely nothing on it.

"Suzie'll know," he said.

Whoa. Suzie would know what was on the tip of Bernie's tongue when she wasn't even here?

Bernie took out his phone, raised a thumb to start pushing buttons, then paused. "But maybe this isn't the kind of thing I should be doing, now that . . ." He put the phone away. Why? I'll leave that to you. All I knew was that he'd been happy when we started down the mountain — you can always tell by his eyes, the clearer the happier, the murkier the sadder — and now he wasn't.

We sat. "Starts with P," he said after a while. My eyelids began to get heavy — what a strange thing, how eyelids could put on weight like that — and were just about to close when I heard a car coming down the road, and a few moments later a black SUV with tinted windows rounded a bend and whizzed past us. Tinted windows, but rolled down on the driver's-side door, and I could see him: Jiggs. He now wore a T-shirt and his huge bare arm rested on the door frame. Bernie turned the key, let Jiggs get by the next turn, and pulled onto the road.

We've tailed a lot of dudes, me and Bernie, and once I did some tailing with Suzie at the wheel. She did a fine job for a rookie, but Bernie was an expert. He could follow from far behind, from closer in, from different lanes, even from in front! Two tricks, when it comes to tailing, Bernie always says. Don't let them lose you. That's one. The other may come to me later.

The road curved back and forth all the way down the mountain. We followed Jiggs from two curves behind, so he was always below us, making it hard for him to — yes! That was it. The other trick: Don't let them spot you. I'd known it would come to me, just didn't expect it so soon.

Jiggs got on a freeway, headed back across the Valley, traffic pretty heavy. We followed from two lanes over, only a few cars behind, but on the passenger side of Jiggs's car. Shadows got longer and longer, and soon

Jiggs and lots of other drivers were switching on their headlights, but not Bernie. After a while, we reached Spaghetti Junction, this huge tangle of freeways that had once made Leda so mad she'd done something too upsetting to go into — in the end, Bernie persuading the tow truck guy not to sue — and Jiggs took one ramp, then another, with all these changes of direction and us now following real close. When we came out on the far side we were crossing the bridge over the Vista City arroyo and it was night.

We hadn't done much work in Vista City — just one case I could think of, and I never wanted to think of it — but I'd been down in that arroyo. It was dry, like all the arroyos in the Valley, although Bernie said that back in Indian times water had flowed in them all year long, and I had smelled water that one time, under the pebbly ground. That was just before I'd found the kid's backpack, but too late. We've solved every missing kid case we ever took, except that one. I'll never forget when we opened the broom closet. And later that night, we'd taken care of justice on our own, me and Bernie. That was part of what I never wanted to think about.

EIGHT

We have some tough neighborhoods in the Valley, South Pedroia being one, and Vista City another. They're both in flat parts of town, where the heat gets hottest and the air dustiest. Also they've both got lots of boarded-up buildings, dive bars, and too many people just sitting around, watching. That's never good when it comes to humans. We had the headlights on now, and they shone on the eyes of one of those watchers, an old guy sitting on a wooden box by the pumps of a closed-down gas station. His eyes followed us down the street.

The black SUV turned at the next corner and went down a block of small, low houses, their yards all dirt, or grass burned brown by the sun. At first only a few of the streetlights were working; and then none. The night sky went dark and sort of pink, the way it got in the Valley, not a star showing.

"This is getting interesting," Bernie said.

I waited to find out how. Meanwhile, we tailed the black SUV down a long street where there'd been a fire sometime back — I could still smell the ashes, very faint — and most of the lots stood empty. Some guys sat on lawn chairs on one of those empty lots, drinking beer from the real big cans. A block or two after that, the brake lights glowed brighter on the SUV. Bernie pulled over right away. That was him every time. He senses things.

The SUV stopped in front of an unlit house that looked a bit bigger than any of the others in the neighborhood; had two stories, for one thing. Jiggs got out. He didn't glance around — that's something Bernie always watches for at a time like this, can't go into it now — but just walked right up to the house. The door opened without him knocking and he went inside. Was he carrying something? I thought so. A moment or two passed, and then a light shone at the back of the house.

"Curiosity killed the cat?" Bernie said. "Never bought into that, myself."

Then we had something in common; a lot, in fact, and finding more all the time. Once we even howled at the moon together. What a night that was! Too bad about those bikers, of course. Back to the curiosity killing

111

the cat thing. I'd never really understood it, curiosity being a bit of a puzzler. But it's always nice to have a takeaway — that's one of Bernie's beliefs — and my takeaway was that curiosity must be a good thing.

We hopped out of the car — the only actual hopping done by me, although I'd seen Bernie try it once, back when he and Suzie were first getting to know each other and we'd gone to pick her up — and started down the street, side by side and real quiet. That was just one of our techniques. We had a bunch, including me grabbing the perp by the pant leg, which was how we knew the case was closed. Was it going to happen tonight? You never knew, not in our business.

Another technique we had was to get off the road and walk through vacant lots. We were doing it now. These lots were vacant when it came to houses, but there was plenty of other stuff — broken bottles, broken furniture, rusted-out parts of this and that, plus the smell of drugs, all kinds of different drugs. Two of my guys had passed this way recently, laying their marks at exactly the places where I wanted to lay mine. What an annoying coincidence! No time now for me to do anything about it, what with us on the job. Well, except maybe for one quick squirt on the side of this slashed-up couch, taking no time at all. Who could resist?

We swung around a strange greenish puddle that smelled like metal when the welder gets his torch on it — Bernie always told me not to look, but I did anyway, then could never see right for the rest of the day — and squeezed through a hole in a chain-link fence; me first, although there was a little confusion about that. We stepped into the yard behind the house Jiggs had entered. The house had a small deck at the back. Bernie put his finger over his lips: our signal for quiet.

We crept onto the deck. Right away, one of the boards made a cracking sound under Bernie's foot. It sounded like a gunshot to me, but you never knew how humans would hear something. We went still, waited. There were two windows on the back wall, one above, one below. The top one had an air conditioner in it, making a high-pitched rattle that bothered my ears. A light shone in the lower window. No one came to peer out, meaning we were good to go; not good to go is something I have trouble with, I admit it. We went closer, Bernie bending down to my level, right at the sill, and looked in.

We saw a small, bare room, with peeling paint and holes in the walls, plus a card table and two chairs. Jiggs sat on one, and a dude in a wifebeater with slicked-back hair and lots of tattoos sat on the other. They weren't doing friendly things like playing cards or drinking or smoking or eating; they were just talking in an unsmiling sort of way, but with the window closed and the AC so loud I caught hardly any of it. Jiggs said something about someone named Ramon. The tattooed dude said he wasn't here to talk about Ramon. Jiggs said he didn't want this goddamn messed-up situation to get anymore messed up. The tattooed dude told him to stop acting like a girl. Whoa! Imagine a girl who looked like Jiggs. I couldn't. Meanwhile, Jiggs had a real pissed-off expression on his face. The tattooed dude said it was just an expression, take it easy. Then he held out his hand. Jiggs reached down, raised a brown paper bag, set it on the table. The tattooed dude glanced into the bag and nodded. Jiggs got up and left the room. The tattooed dude just sat there. A moment or two later, I heard the front door close. Then the SUV started up. Bernie heard that part: I could tell from the slight turning of his head.

What next? Go back to tailing Jiggs? Stay

where we were? The what-nexts I pretty much left up to Bernie. He reached toward me, like he was about to tap my shoulder, meaning, Let's go, big guy. But at that moment, the tattooed dude picked up the paper bag. Bernie's hand went still. The SUV drove away, the engine sound fading. Was the tattooed dude, too, listening for that? He tipped the bag over and money spilled onto the table, lots of it. Then he started counting — when humans count money their lips move, like maybe there's some connection between money and their mouths, about as far as I can take it, maybe farther — and then arranged the bills in stacks, snapping rubber bands around each one. After that, he dropped all the stacks back in the bag except for one, which he pocketed.

The tattooed dude grabbed the bag, rose, and left the room, shutting off the light on his way out. I heard his footsteps; then running water; and the tiny squeak of mattress springs. After that, nothing but the AC.

Bernie spoke, his voice very soft. "Wonder what's going on?"

What was going on? Did he mean besides the tattooed dude zonking out? If he did, I had no answers. I stood where I was, outside the back door. Soon the AC began dripping.

I shifted out of range of the falling drops and sat down. Bernie went on gazing through the window at the dark room. Somewhere in the neighborhood a woman shouted, "Get out of my goddamn house!" A man laughed at her in a way that made my teeth feel like biting.

Bernie tapped me on the shoulder. We went back to the car and drove home. On the way, Bernie said, "I'd sure like to know what Jiggs and that guy were talking about."

I wondered why. Nothing I'd heard had seemed particularly interesting, not even the parts I remembered.

Nixon Panero came over for breakfast. Had that ever happened before? Not that I could think of, but I sure hoped he'd do it again. For one thing, he brought the food: coffee and egg sandwiches for him and Bernie, a nice fat sausage for me. Did we mind that his fingers were grease-stained? Not us. Some days you just hit the ground running; I knew this was going to be one of them.

We sat out on the patio, water gurgling from the swan fountain, steam rising from the coffee cups, not a care in the world, at least not on my part.

"What's with the ice pack on your shoulder?" Nixon said.

"You don't want to know," Bernie said.

"Hope it was one of those you-should-see-the-other-guy dustups."

"Wasn't any kind of dustup."

"Whatever you say," said Nixon. He took a big bite from his sandwich, talked with his mouth full, saying something like "I read the script." He tossed it on the table. "Guy who wrote it, Arn Linsky? They paid him a cool million."

"How do you know that?"

"*Hollywood Reporter,*" Nixon said. "He's A-list. That's what they get. Minimum."

"So it's good?"

Nixon shrugged. "Not claiming there aren't good lines in it," he said. He bit into his sandwich again, pawing — yes, just another nice thing about Nixon — pawing through the pages. "Like here, where Lolotea — she's the shaman — says to Croomer — that's Thad Perry's character — 'I am unready to embrace the white man,' and he says, 'You could try closing your eyes.' "

"That's good?"

"Guaranteed to get laughs. Plus it's when he starts to appeal to her. And now you know there'll be a hot scene with her and Thad Perry coming up. Heard who's playing Lolotea?"

"Nope."

"Kina Molenta," Nixon said. "The brunette from *Hothouse Flowers.*"

"Didn't catch that one," Bernie said.

"It's a TV show, not a movie," Nixon said. "About strippers in a place called the Hothouse."

"She's playing an Apache shaman?"

"There are some — what's the word?"

"Authenticity?" Bernie said.

"Yeah," said Nixon, "authenticity issues you're not going to like."

"For instance?"

Nixon turned a page. "This part, where Croomer gets shot right through with an arrow, back to front, and then kills this other guy by falling on him so the same arrow goes —"

"For Christ sake."

"It's only a movie, like they say."

Bernie gazed at the script. "Do the rivers flow?"

"Rivers?"

"The arroyos, the washes, the gulches — do they flow in the movie?"

"No," Nixon said. "It's dry as dust. They talk about that a lot. There's even a scene where Lolotea takes one of those forked sticks and tries to —"

"Water flowed," Bernie said. He put down

his coffee — actually sort of banged it down, a tiny black wave slopping over the rim — and pointed to the canyon beyond our back gate. "Flowed right past where we're sitting now."

"Maybe you gotta pay two mil for that kind of detail," Nixon said.

The phone rang while Bernie was shaving. Bernie hated shaving, didn't do it every day, not even close — causing some problems, back in the Leda days — and he looked great shaved or not, in my opinion, except for that one camping trip where he'd ended up with an actual beard. Too much for me, and we'd had to drive into the nearest town, hardly even a day's ride, for a disposable razor.

He hit the speaker button.

"How's it goin' so far?" said Rick Torres.

"Don't like the script," Bernie said.

"Yeah?" said Rick. "What's wrong with it?"

"It's not accurate."

Silence. Then Rick said, "Don't forget it's a director's medium. The script doesn't mean squat. It's what happens on the set and in the editing room."

"They pay a million bucks for something that doesn't mean squat?" Bernie said.

"That's Hollywood."

"How do you know all this?"

"It's common knowledge," said Rick. "Met Thad Perry yet?"

"Yup."

"What's he like?"

"You know," Bernie said. "Just a guy."

"Puts on his pants one leg at a time?" said Rick. "C'mon, Bernie. Help my marriage."

"What are you talking about?"

"I told you — Marcie's a big fan. She needs details. And don't forget about that autograph."

"Always the wife," Bernie said. And then: "Ow." Uh-oh. A fat drop of blood welled up on Bernie's chin, trickled down. I wanted to lick it up, but sort of remembered Bernie not liking that when I'd tried it before, and all the other befores. Bernie cut himself shaving just about every time.

"Shaving?" said Rick.

"No," Bernie said. "Can you check out twenty-four hundred sixty-three North Coursin Street, Vista City? Ownership, residents, the usual."

"Bad neighborhood — I can tell you that right off the top of my head," Rick said. "What's the story?"

"Just following up on something," Bernie said.

"I'll see what I can do," Rick said. "But nothing's free in this world."

"You'll get the goddamn autograph," Bernie said. He clicked off. "Chet! Down!"

Oops.

Soon after that, we were on the open road, headed up, up, and out of the Valley, passing the last development, then one more golf course, and into the desert. *Rumble rumble* went the engine, sending shudders through the whole car. Bernie slowed down a bit.

"Is that a new sound?" he said.

He tapped the gas pedal a couple of times. *Va-vroom! Va-vroom!*

"Wonder if it's something to worry about."

Of course not, Bernie. Couldn't be better, our new ride. But on his face I could see that a bout of worrying was on the way, those tiny forehead lines growing deeper. The phone rang just in time.

"Bernie? Cal Luxton here, mayor's office. How you doing?"

"Headed out to the set," Bernie said.

"Seen it yet?"

"No."

"You're gonna be impressed," Luxton said. "How're things going with Thad Perry?"

"Good."

"That's what I hear," Luxton said.

"From who?"

Luxton laughed. "Word gets around."

There was a silence. The sky went from the dusty blue of the Valley to lovely pure blue. Hey! The moon! I'd forgotten all about that, seeing the moon in the daytime. What a treat! Nothing like a treat you eat, but pretty nice.

"Anything I can help you with," Luxton was saying, "don't hesitate."

"Thanks."

Another silence. "Any questions so far?" There was something . . . probing, yes, probing about his voice; kind of like his eyes, if that made any sense.

"When are you going to ask me for his autograph?" Bernie said.

Luxton laughed again. "Already got it," he said.

NINE

I'd been in a lot of bars — comes with the territory in our business — but never one quite like this. Yes, it was Old West–style, our favorite, mine and Bernie's: rough wooden floor, long bar with a few tough-looking dudes hunched over their shot glasses, rows of dusty bottles, a wagon wheel leaning in a corner. But this bar had no ceiling; the shot glasses were filled with tea — no putting a switcheroo like that past me; and there were bright lights all over the place, plus microphones dangling down here and there, and a big camera in the middle of things. A dandruffy guy — a real easy smell to pick up — dressed in torn jeans and smoking a big cigar was peering into the camera eyepiece. Everything about him said perp to me, but I was sitting quietly, on my best behavior or even better: Bernie had been very clear about that.

He was right beside me now, in one of

those movie-set chairs. Hey! A connection! Beside Bernie were Nan and Jiggs. On my other side sat Felicity. And on her lap was Brando, which is maybe where I should have started all this, but it's hard to keep so many details organized, kind of like — what's that expression? herding cats? Whoa. Another connection, and so soon. Was I cooking or what? Brando was sleeping, or possibly dozing, in a very annoying way, hard to explain.

Nan leaned toward Bernie and spoke in a low voice. "He's brilliant," she said. "IQ of one seventy-two."

"Thad?" Bernie said, his eyebrows rising. Bernie has great eyebrows, if I haven't mentioned that already — and eyebrows like his, beautifully thick and heavy, are worth mentioning again — with a language all their own. Right now they were saying he was real surprised. About what? No idea.

"Thad's brilliant, too, of course," Nan said. "Goes without saying. But I'm talking about Lars Karlsbaad, the director."

"With the cigar?" said Bernie.

Nan nodded.

Bernie watched Lars Karlsbaad. So did I. He turned from the camera and nodded to a man standing beside him, who now took Lars's place at the eyepiece. A woman with a clipboard said, "Places, everybody. Quiet on the set."

At that moment, Brando opened his eyes and stared right at me. His eyes were gold and narrow, like edgewise gold coins, very unpleasant. I stared back — what choice did I have? — and missed a bit of what followed. When the staring came to an end — Brando turning away first — I noticed that the swinging doors of the bar were opening and a man with a gun on his belt and a rifle over his shoulder was walking in. His spurs — I'd had a run-in with spurs once, the only perp whose pant leg I'd ever had trouble with, a story for another time — went *jingle-jangle,* a sharp, clear sound that sends a pleasant little shiver down my back. He wore a black cowboy hat pulled down low, kind of hiding his face, but I knew it was Thad Perry from his smell, although it was almost completely hidden by the scent of makeup; he had to be wearing more than Leda on her most dressed-up day.

Thad took a few slow steps, turning toward the dudes at the bar. He stopped near one of those dangling microphones and raised his face a little. He was mad about something but had it under control. Bernie had that same look, exactly! For a moment he seemed something like Bernie — strong and tough and nice — even though I knew he didn't come close to Bernie in any of those things. Wow.

The dudes at the bar turned to him, real slow. All the movements going on were like that, real slow. It made me want to do something real fast, and soon, not sure why. The dudes at the bar were nasty-looking — with sweaty, hairy faces — and reeked of makeup. The one with the eye patch said, "Lookin' for somethin', cowboy?"

Thad gave him a long stony look. It went on and on. Then he said, "Lars? That line kind of sucks."

Someone yelled, "Cut."

The cowpokes at the bar got up and stretched, and there was some milling around in general. Lars went over to Thad and said, "Sucks in what way, Thad?"

Thad shrugged. "I just don't like it."

"But you don't say it. Sam says it."

"What the hell?" Thad said. "I have to work off it, don't I? If I don't know what I can work off and what I can't, who does?"

Lars puffed on his cigar as though thinking things over and nodded. He was standing in a way humans stand sometimes, hands behind the back. I only mention that because I noticed that at the same time Lars was puffing on his cigar and nodding, his hands had balled themselves into fists.

"Get Arn," he said, speaking around his cigar. The clipboard woman went running out of the bar, returned with a guy who reminded me of this hopeless junkie we'd saved from getting beaten up by some gangbangers in South Pedroia. Just like the junkie, this guy was skinny and pale, with messy hair and bad breath: I could smell it from across the room.

"Shot forty-three, Sam's dialogue, top of the page," Lars said. "Thad has some concerns. Met Thad yet, by the way?"

"No," said the skinny guy.

"Thad, this is Arn Linsky, wrote the script."

Arn Linsky's arm moved, like maybe he thought handshaking was about to happen, but it did not.

"Hear it's great," Thad said. "Only read my lines so far, but I plan to go over the whole thing when I get some time."

"Thanks," said Arn. "Can't tell you how happy I am to be working with you. Loved what you did in *There and Back,* and also —"

"Arn?" Lars said. "We're hoping to clear this up on the fly and get back to the scene ASAP." He handed the script to Arn, more shoved it at him, really.

Arn glanced at it, spoke to Thad. "These, um, concerns. They're yours? Or Sam's?"

"Interesting point, but we've moved beyond it," Lars said. "This is more a question of Thad's internal response to the line."

"Can't work off it," Thad said.

"What, uh, part, if you don't mind my . . . ?" Arn said. "The 'lookin' for someone' part? The word 'cowboy'?"

Thad shrugged, turned to Lars. "Back in a jiff," he said. "Gotta take a piss."

Thad walked out.

"Actually serendipitous," Lars said, or something like that. The movie business — if that's what this was — turned out to be confusing. "Get makeup."

The clipboard woman went running off. Bernie spoke in this small voice he sometimes uses for talking to himself; himself and me, of course. "Jiff?" he said. Where was he going with that? Before I'd gotten to square one, the clipboard woman came back, now trailing an older woman who wore a white smock.

"Lars?" said the older woman. "You wanted to see me?"

Lars put his hand on her shoulder, kind of maneuvered her to the side. Very quietly — but not so quietly I didn't hear — he said, "What's with his nose today?"

"I did what I could," the older woman said.

"But what's the problem?"

"Allergies. He says he forgot to take his medication."

"Christ," said Lars.

Arn stepped forward. "How's this?" He handed Lars a scrap of paper. Lars eyed it, nodded his head.

"Quiet on the set," the clipboard woman said again. "Take two."

The saloon doors swung open again. *Jingle-jangle.* Thad came in, his movements real slow, maybe even slower than before. He stopped below the hanging microphone, mad again but under control, the expression on his face exactly the same as one Bernie had. Was he even standing like Bernie, too, and looking like Bernie in general? I started getting upset, not sure why, the kind of upset where I need to pant. But panting would be bad now, so I hardly did it at all.

Thad turned to the tough guys at the bar. The tough guys at the bar turned to him. The one with the eye patch, maybe named Sam, spat a thin stream of brown liquid on the floor — just the way Nixon Panero would have done it, except this particular stream didn't smell of tobacco, smelled more like licorice — and said, "You look lost, friend."

Thad gave him a long, long look. He was still giving him the long, long look when a mouse crept out from under the bar. A pointy-nosed mouse with big ears and long whiskers: I had time to notice those details, and then things started happening fast. First, Brando sprang off Felicity's lap and flew across the floor. Second, the mouse whipped around and zoomed straight up the leg of the dude with the eye patch. Brando leaped up after the mouse, grabbed the little bugger in his front paws, maybe scratching the eye patch dude at the same time, because he screamed; a surprisingly high-pitched scream for a tough guy. And then — what was this? I was airborne, too? Was it possible? More than possible, amigo. There I was crashing into Brando, not to hurt him, or protect the mouse, or . . . or anything else I could think of — only to be part of things, really. Did the eye patch dude get knocked right off his stool? And did he knock off the next tough dude on his way down, the whole sequence that followed reminding me of a fun time Charlie and I had once with dominoes? I couldn't be sure.

"Cut!"

The only sure part was that somewhere in all of that, Brando had got me a real good one with his claws, right on the button, meaning nose in boxing lingo, maybe a detail I've included already. What the hell was wrong with him? How come he didn't realize it was all in fun? Cats. I don't know what to tell you.

After, out on the dirt street of the little town — a strange town, most of the buildings having fronts and nothing else — Bernie dabbed some kind of medicine on my nose. I licked it off.

"Stop licking it off." Bernie looked displeased about something or someone. I wondered what or who, came up with no answers. He dabbed on more medicine. "I mean it." I tried and tried not to lick it off. Then I licked it off. "Christ."

Uh-oh. He sounded kind of displeased, too. I nudged up against him, a surefire way to take his mind off whatever was bothering him. At that moment, the clipboard woman came walking up.

"You're from the mayor's office?" she said. Bernie nodded.

"The producers appreciate the mayor's

131

support," she said. "But Lars has asked me to inform you that the set is now off-limits."

Bernie nodded again.

"And he requests, with all due respect, that the mayor's office send a new representative."

Bernie stopped nodding. His face hardened, although he didn't turn that hard look on her. Instead, he said, "Chet," and we started walking to the car. Off-limits meant what, again? And new representative? Was it possible we'd lost the gig? On account of . . . ? My mind didn't want to go there. I tried to make it think of snacks, or Frisbees, or riding shotgun, but it skimmed over all those things and landed on . . . oh, no — another bad thought. Bernie nailed Thad right on the button and then Brando did the same thing to me! So I'd let down the whole team, the whole team being me and Bernie.

My tail dragged in the dust. I didn't do anything about it.

We got in the car. I didn't hop in. Bernie opened the door for me. He turned the key, glancing my way at the same time. "Hey," he said. "Cheer up. It's only money."

Only money! What a thing to say: our finances were a mess. But I started to cheer up, partly because Bernie told me to and partly because, well, how long can you stay down in the dumps?

He backed out of our spot between two huge trailers.

"Wait! Wait!"

What was this? Felicity running up? The girlfriend, right? Tall, thin, blond, dressed in tight jeans and a little T-shirt, plus red high-heeled shoes that made running look dangerous. Bernie stopped the car.

"Bernie?" she said. Felicity had big golden-brown eyes, kind of damp. Hey! She'd been crying. The sun shone on a tiny tear track on her cheek.

"Yeah?" Bernie said, cutting the engine.

"I'm very sorry," Felicity said. "It was all my fault."

"Huh?" said Bernie.

"I let him off my lap," she said. "But he's so sneaky. I just hate the way he —" She stopped herself. "And Thad's so pissed at me now." Her eyes got damper. "I don't blame him — there's so much pressure, that's what no one understands."

"What kind of pressure?" Bernie said.

Felicity blinked. "You know," she said. "The industry."

"Anything else?" Bernie said.

"Anything else?" said Felicity. "I don't

understand."

"Forget it," Bernie said. "And no need for you to apologize."

"Oh, yes, there is," Felicity said, her hand now clinging to the door frame. "And please, please say you accept it."

Bernie gave her a look, one of his long looks, but not hard. "Okay," he said. "Apology accepted."

She touched his shoulder. "Thank you. And Thad says to tell you" — She checked her palm; I saw some blue writing, right on the skin; Charlie did that sometimes, but no other humans I'd ever seen — "forget whatever the studio people told you." She looked up. "You're still welcome on the set."

There was a silence. Out in the desert the wind was stirring. It fluttered a tuft of her hair, so soft and light. "How old are you, Felicity?" Bernie said.

"Almost twenty-two."

Bernie didn't say anything.

"You're thinking he's too old for me?" Felicity said.

"No," Bernie said.

"And you're wondering how old he is."

"I'm not," Bernie said. "But what's the number?"

"Forty-three."

"Wow," said Bernie. "I would have guessed

134

at least ten years younger."

"A lot of work goes into that," Felicity said. "It's part of the pressure." She wiped her eyes on the back of her hand.

We drove out of the desert, down into the Valley. Bernie was real quiet. Me, too. My nose felt almost back to normal, totally normal if I didn't think about it. When you really need not to think about something, sleep comes in very handy. I closed my eyes.

When I awoke we were turning onto Mesquite Road, almost home, and Bernie was on the phone. Rick's voice came over the speaker.

"That address in Vista City, twenty-four hundred sixty-three North Coursin Street?" he said. "Owned by the Territorial Bank."

"Foreclosure?"

"Yup. And according to them it's boarded up, hasn't been occupied for a year and a half."

Bernie slowed down, made a U-turn. My nose felt perfect.

TEN

Back in Vista City, only now it was day.

"Looked better at night," Bernie said.

Exactly the thought I might have been moving toward. We didn't use any of our sneaking-around techniques, just rolled right up to the house on North Coursin Street and parked. First time we'd seen it from the front: a stucco house, all peeling, with a crooked little porch and a kid's bicycle lying on its side.

"Try to look like we're from Territorial Bank," Bernie said.

I wasn't sure what he meant by that. Was it something I could do? My ears didn't match and I was a hundred-plus-pounder, info I'd picked up from humans discussing me in my presence, maybe not nice of them. Other than that, I had no facts, not about my looks or Territorial Bank. We hopped out of the car, crossed the hard-packed dirt yard, stepped onto the porch.

"We'll ask why they're not boarded up," Bernie said, "and improvise from there." He knocked on the door. "Just like Thad Perry."

No answer from inside, no movement, no sound. Didn't mean no one was in there. In fact, someone was, kind of.

Bernie knocked again. Nada. He peered at the lock, then checked up and down the street. Not a human in sight — although a curtain twitched in a window down the block — the sun shining straight down, that shadeless baking we get in the Valley happening big-time. Bernie reached into his pocket and took out this tiny jimmy we'd taken off a perp name of Fast Freddie Walsh, expert burglar, who'd designed and made it himself; Fast Freddie had lots of talent, Bernie said, could have made it big as an inventor. "Really think so, Bernie?" he'd said as Bernie snapped on the cuffs.

Scratch, scratch, click. "Quiet as a mouse, now," Bernie said, one of those human expressions that made no sense, mice being very noisy, especially considering their small size. He pushed the door open and we went inside. We moved — Bernie as quietly as he could, me silent — through a bare room, nothing in it but empty bottles and cans, past stairs leading up, and into the room

137

with the card table that we'd seen through the window. Bernie picked a rubber band off the table and gazed at it for a moment. Then he pulled back on it, sort of like a bow and arrow — don't get me started on those bow hunters we chased down out in Agua Roja — and snapped it across the room. It made a *thwap* against the window, a brand-new sound for me — I'd heard plenty of *thwaps,* but never so tiny — and was hoping Bernie would do the rubber band thing again. He did not. We turned and climbed the stairs.

There were two small rooms upstairs, plus a bathroom in between. Nothing in the first room, except for more empties. The bathroom had a towel on the floor and a medicine cabinet hanging open, a toothbrush and a razor inside. A bar of soap lay on the floor, white soap but with a little red blot at one end. Bernie bent down, gave it a close look, didn't touch it. When he rose he had the .38 Special in his hand.

What a surprise! Loved the .38 Special! Hadn't seen it in way too long, and Bernie's a crack shot. Was gunplay coming up? Just what we needed, me and Bernie; no idea why I thought that, but I did.

The door to the last room was open a crack. Bernie gave it a hard kick and we went in fast. And then slowed right down.

The last room had a mattress on the floor. The tattooed guy lay on it, tucked in under a white sheet, all except for his head, his slicked-back hair still slicked-back, neat and tidy. Eyes closed: he might have been sleeping, except for the red stain where the sheet covered his chest. This was a little confusing because dead humans start to smell different right away, and I wasn't quite picking up —

His eyes opened. He looked right at me. "Outlaw?" he said. I looked right back at him. Was the red stain getting bigger? I thought so.

"Who's an outlaw?" Bernie said.

The tattooed dude's eyes shifted, real slow, over to Bernie. "You a cop?" he said.

"No," said Bernie, lowering the .38 Special.

"Look like a cop," the tattooed dude said. "And you're dumb like a —" He coughed a little cough. A red bubble appeared on his lips, got bigger, and popped like a balloon. I'm no fan of popping balloons. "— like a cop," the tattooed dude went on.

Bernie took out his cell phone, pressed some buttons.

"What the hell you think you're doin'?" the tattooed dude said.

"Getting help," Bernie told him. He spoke quickly into the phone, then put it away. "Who did this to you?"

The tattooed dude gave Bernie a cold look, then closed his eyes.

"Was it Jiggs?" Bernie said.

The tattooed dude's eyelids twitched, like they might be about to open back up, but remained closed. "Dumb like a cop," he said. "No question."

"Then give me some help," Bernie said. "Who's the outlaw?"

The tattooed dude's eyes opened. "There's no outlaw, you stupid fuck." His gaze shifted back over to me. The expression in his eyes changed. I got the feeling he was about to smile, kind of crazy in a situation like this. "Outlaw's a dog," he said. No smile came.

"Whose dog is he?" Bernie said.

"Think you're gonna open me up like a tin can?" said the tattooed dude.

"Too late for that," said Bernie. "Someone already opened you up, but good." The tattooed guy winced, like Bernie had just hit him, something Bernie would never ever do when a dude was down. "I can make them pay," Bernie said. "Just need the name."

The tattooed dude's eyes closed. "Not how we do things, bud," he said.

140

"How do you do things?" said Bernie.

No answer. I heard distant sirens. And then I smelled the smell, absolutely beyond doubt. So how come the tattooed dude's eyes opened again? No idea.

He turned his head sideways a bit, maybe to see Bernie better. A red drop appeared at the corner of his lips. "We take care of business ourselves," he said.

"How's that working out?" said Bernie.

The tattooed dude started to give Bernie a real nasty look, but before he had the nastiness dialed all the way up, he got interrupted by another cough, not much of a cough, even gentler than the first. But out of his mouth rushed whole big blobs of blood, one after another. I barked once, but real sharp and loud; couldn't help it.

The tattooed dude's eyes, blurry now, moved back to me. He licked his lips and in a very soft voice, just a breath of air, said, "Ramon."

"Who's Ramon?" Bernie said.

The tattooed dude's eyes got blurrier and blurrier, and then, in an instant, lost their shine, their glow, or whatever it is that living eyes have. The siren sound grew louder.

Bernie glanced at the window, turned to me, and said, "Not much time."

For what? I didn't know. Bernie started

searching the room. He checked the closet — empty except for one shirt on a hanger and one pair of shoes on the floor — took down a mirror and tapped on the wall behind it; and then there was nowhere to check but the bed.

Bernie pulled back the sheet. There was blood, but I'd seen more, plenty of times. What there was of it had leaked out of a little slit in the front of his wifebeater, the kind of slit a knife makes. The tattooed dude was also wearing jeans and still had on his sneakers. Bernie felt in his pockets, first the front, and then, tipping him sideways a bit, the back. That was where he found a wallet. He flipped it open, took out a driver's license.

"Manuel D. Chavez," he said. "No money." He turned to the dead man. "Where's all that money, Manuel? Or at least the bundle you stuck in your pocket?"

Talking to the dead man? That bothered me, even though it was Bernie. I barked, kind of sharply again. Bernie glanced at me. "What?" he said. Then he had a thought — I could almost see it moving behind his eyes — and said, "You're a good boy." At that moment, my tail started up behind me and I knew everything was back to being cool between me and Bernie. He put a hand on

Manuel D. Chavez's middle to steady him, raised the mattress, then did the same thing on the other side: nothing under that mattress but crushed dust balls. Now the sirens were right outside.

We were kind of crowded in the little room: me, Bernie, Rick, a couple cops — Floyd and Oona — plus the body, which was what we were all looking at. Except for me, at least part of the time, on account of some cruller crumbs — no question about it — caught in Rick's mustache.

"Seen him around," said Oona.

"You're thinkin' of that other guy," said Floyd. Floyd was the redheaded type, always interesting, with pale skin and eyes of almost no color at all.

Oona, real small, hat maybe a bit big for her, dreads hanging to her shoulders, gave him an annoyed glance. "Seen this one around," she said. "Gangbanger."

Floyd shook his head. "Other guy. With the scar."

Oona looked about to say something back, but before she could, Rick handed the license to Floyd and said, "Run this on the computer."

Floyd nodded, one of those nods that says yes and means no — you see that a lot in the cop world — and left the room. Human nodding: too big a subject for going into now.

"This is Chet?" Oona said. "I've heard so much about him."

Hey! A tiny thing, no more than a kid, but she was going places.

"He's so beautiful." Like right to the top, for example. "Can I pat him, uh, Bobby?"

"Bernie," said Bernie, a bit irritated for some reason.

Oona gave me a pat. A nice one, although nothing like the kind of patting Tulip and Autumn, two friends of ours who worked for Livia Moon at her house of ill repute in Pottsdale, were capable of.

"Oona?" Rick said. "Maybe you can give Floyd a hand."

"Yes, boss," said Oona, out the door in a flash.

"Got my eye on her," Rick said.

"You're a married man," said Bernie.

"Professionally," Rick said, maybe becoming aware of those cruller crumbs at last and licking them off his mustache. "She's an up-and-comer."

"Calling you 'boss'? That's all it takes?"

"More than enough." Rick turned to the body. "So what's the story with Manny, here?"

"Couldn't tell you."

"Couldn't or won't?" Rick said.

"Never seen him before today," Bernie said.

"But he was alive when you got here."

"Told you that already."

"So you got something out of him," Rick said. "I know you."

"He was incoherent," Bernie said.

Rick gave Bernie a long look. "I'll believe you for the moment," he said. "What got you interested in this address in the first place?"

"Sorry, Rick. Can't talk about that without my client's permission."

Rick's face changed, darkening and even swelling a bit. Uh-oh. Maybe they weren't getting along. Not good: Rick was one of our best pals.

"Working on something besides the movie gig?" he said.

"We're busy these days," Bernie said. Nice to hear, especially if it meant getting paid. But as for other jobs, I couldn't think of any.

Rick took a deep breath — a way humans have of trying to change things inside — and his face came back to normal. "Anyone can get in over his head," he said. "Even you."

Floyd appeared in the doorway, his movements very quiet. He didn't notice me; some humans are like that when it comes to us in the nation within. Floyd's eyes, pale and watchful, were on Bernie.

"Uh, excuse me," he said. Bernie and Rick turned to him. "Deceased was in the system," Floyd said. He checked his notebook. "Did a year at Central State for a B and E in South P, also got an assault collar, plus a domestic violence, charges dropped." He looked up. "And the ME's waiting downstairs."

Rick nodded, then turned to Bernie like he was going to say one more thing, but he didn't. We passed the ME on her way up. She gave me a quick pat as she went by. You meet a lot of nice people in this business, even some of the perps and gangbangers.

When we got home, a big silver car stood in the driveway.

"Wonder who —" Bernie began, and then the front doors opened and out stepped Leda — and Charlie! Hadn't seen him in way too long. We pulled in beside the silver car and I hopped out, possibly while we were still rolling. Had Bernie said something about that, maybe more than once? I had a faint memory. It grew fainter and then

146

vanished completely. By that time, I was giving Charlie a great big greeting.

"For God's sake, Charlie," Leda said. "Think of the germs."

"He's just kissing me, Mom."

Leda hurried over and wiped Charlie's face with a tissue.

"Ch — et?" Bernie said in this special voice he has, just for me. I calmed right down, trotted around in a little circle, raised my leg against a tree we've got just for that purpose, Bernie says, and then sat beside Charlie. He gave me a grin. There's no grin like Charlie's and not just because of his smooth round face and jumble of teeth, some big, some little. It's all about the whole of him grinning, hard to explain.

Bernie turned to Leda. "Uh, hi," he said.

"Hello, Bernie," said Leda. She has light-colored eyes that sometimes reminded me of ice, but not now. Kind of surprisingly, she was looking at Bernie in a warm sort of way. "Hope you don't mind us dropping in."

"Um," said Bernie. "No, no, of course not. Any, ah, time." He glanced at the silver car. "New wheels?"

"Birthday present from Malcolm," Leda said. Malcolm was the boyfriend, was doing very well in apps, whatever that meant, and

147

had long skinny toes.

"Oh, right," Bernie said. "Happy birthday."

Leda laughed, made a little sweeping-away gesture with her hand, her bracelet sparkling in the light. What were those things she liked? Diamonds? They had led to an unfortunate incident in pre-divorce days, although we'd gotten the necklace back just as Amy had promised — she's the vet, a big woman with a nice voice and careful hands, but I always shook the moment I entered her waiting room. Forget all that. The point was . . . gone.

". . . new car, too?" Leda was saying. "Are those martini glasses on the side?"

"Nixon's idea," said Bernie.

"Unusual," Leda said.

"Can we go for a ride?" said Charlie.

Bernie turned to Leda.

"Why not?" she said. "In fact, if it's all right with your father, maybe you could stay here for dinner while I do some quick shopping."

"Uh, sure," said Bernie, looking a bit confused. I was confused, too. Was this an every-second weekend or Christmas? I didn't think so. But bottom line: great news!

Leda gave Charlie a quick kiss, didn't wipe it off with tissues, and got in her car. Backing out, she slid down her window and said, "Guess what Charlie's class is doing this term."

I waited for one of Bernie's quick comebacks, but all he said was, "No idea." He was a different man around Leda.

"Making a movie," said Leda.

"He's in second grade," Bernie said.

"A six-minute movie," said Leda, "all about the history of the school. We were thinking it might be a big help if he could visit a real movie set. No interference with your job, of course. I'd be happy to bring him."

Bernie's mouth opened. He might have said "oh" or "um."

Leda backed down the driveway. "On a day when they're shooting a scene with Thad Perry, if possible," she called through the window.

ELEVEN

"That was quick thinking," Bernie said. We were back in the movie bar — now deserted except for me, Bernie, and Arn, the writer dude — waiting for Thad Perry to finish napping and emerge from his trailer.

"Not following you," Arn said, taking out a pack of cigarettes. His hands trembled a bit; you see that in humans, but usually ones much older than Arn. He lit up.

"When you came up with that revised dialogue on the spot," Bernie said, eyes on the plume of tobacco smoke. Bernie had quit smoking again, not too long ago. Quitting smoking was something Bernie did a lot. He was great at it.

Arn shook his head. He had dark circles under his eyes and needed a shave, a haircut, new clothes, a shoe shine. "It's out," he said.

"That line about 'looking for someone, friend?' " Bernie said.

"Some *thing*," Arn said. "Not some *one.*

Lars saw last night's rushes, didn't think it worked. And now the whole goddamn scene's up in the air."

"The bar fight scene?" Bernie said. "How's the story going to work without that?"

Arn gave Bernie a surprised look. "You've read the script?"

"Pretty much."

"You're, uh . . ."

"Bernie. And this is Chet."

Arn took a deep drag on his cigarette, peering at me over the glowing tip. "I'm allergic to dogs," he said.

I'd heard that one before, more than once, still didn't get it. Maybe Bernie didn't, either, because he said nothing, just gazed at Arn in a way that could have meant anything. I loved that look! Bernie's a pretty tough guy — don't forget that. I've seen bad things happen to those who did.

"You're with Thad in some capacity?" Arn said.

Bernie shook his head. "Mayor's office, more or less." He gave Arn a look he has that means go on, press me on this one, but Arn did not. Instead Arn sighed and said, "You're in select company — I'm not sure even Lars has read the whole thing." He shot Bernie a sideways look. "What did you think of it?"

"I'm not qualified to judge," Bernie said.

"Go on," said Arn. "I won't bite."

"I know that," Bernie said.

The lines in Arn's forehead deepened, like he didn't care for that remark, but why? Of course he wouldn't bite! His teeth were small, and so was his mouth, now that I considered it: no chomping power there at all. We'd run across one or two human biters in our work; they'd come back down to earth when I showed them what real biting was all about.

"But," Bernie was saying, "I've got one or two misgivings about the historical record."

"Misgivings?" Arn said. He sucked on what remained of his cigarette, just the stub. "Historical record?" I was with him, not following Bernie at all.

"For one thing," Bernie said, "you've got the waterways dry like they are today. Fact is, water ran in all of them back then, at least seasonally."

"Yeah?" said Arn, not sounding interested in the least.

"And if," Bernie said, his voice sharpening, "Thad's really supposed to become a territorial ranger just before the blood brothers scene, then you'll have to change the date — the territorial rangers weren't formed until 1860."

"Hmph," said Arn. He dropped the cigarette butt on the floor. "Here's the thing, Bernie. You're not in the industry so there's no way you'd know this. Movies — going way back, right to the beginning — create their own truth. Life imitates art, as we now know only too well."

Bernie gave him a long look, then ground the cigarette butt under his heel. "What do you do with all the money?" he said.

"All what money?" said Arn. Then he did a thing humans sometimes do, blowing out through a mostly closed mouth so their lips flutter and make a *b-b-b-b-b-b* sound. Love when they do that, although the meaning isn't clear to me. "Goddamn *Hollywood Reporter*," he said. "See, Bernie, out here in the sti—" Arn stopped himself, started fresh. "In some parts of the country a certain sum of money may sound impressive, but it's not, trust me. Not in Hollywood terms. Did the *Hollywood Reporter* include the facts that I'm paying a double shot of alimony, carrying three houses — four if you include the ski place at Jackson Hole, and —"

"You ski Jackson Hole?" Bernie said.

"Who said anything about skiing?" Arn said. "We're discussing real estate."

Bernie looked like he was going to say something, maybe not totally friendly, but at that moment the swinging doors banged open and Thad entered with . . . with Brando on his shoulder. Brando looked at me immediately, not at me in general, rather at my nose in particular — I had no doubt about that whatsoever.

"Hi, Thad," Arn said, legs shifting like he was getting ready to rise off his chair. "Everything okay?"

Thad ignored him. "Bernie?" he said. "That your Porsche out there?"

"Yeah."

"It's old, huh?"

"Yup."

"But super cool."

"Thanks."

"I'd like a spin."

"Sure," said Bernie. "Whenever you get some time."

"How's right now?" said Thad.

Thad wanted to go for a spin in the Porsche, and right now? There was good in everybody.

What I hadn't realized was that Thad wanted to do the driving. Neither had Bernie: his eyebrows went way up when Thad slid into the driver's seat — Brando still on his shoulder — held out his hand, and said, "Keys?"

There was a pause. Then Bernie said, "It's a stick."

Thad laughed. "Hell, Bernie, think my Lamborghini's an automatic? Or the Ferrari? Come on, man."

Bernie tossed him the keys and turned to me. "In the back, Chet."

Me? In that tiny back space? Bernie in the shotgun seat? And worst of all, Brando on Thad's shoulder, meaning he was actually in the driver's seat? Nothing like this had ever happened to me in my life, but what could I do? I got in the back, moving in this really slow way I hardly ever use, butt practically dragging. Bernie buckled his seat belt, something he hardly ever bothered with.

"All set?" said Thad. A tiny breeze swept by, bringing the smell of Thad's breath my way: toothpaste and mouthwash on the top layer, licorice below that — the red kind — and down at the bottom, uh-oh, what was this? Cocaine? Yes. And not only cocaine, but Oxycontin as well. How did I know? K-9 school, out of which I'd flunked on my last day, with only the leaping test left, and leaping has been my very best thing as long as I could remember. Was a cat involved?

Better believe it.

Brando gazed at me in a bored sort of way, then faced front. Thad turned the key. We jolted forward, kind of how we did the one time Bernie tried giving Leda a lesson, but we didn't quite stall as Leda had done, and, of course, Thad didn't round on Bernie and scream, "Why can't you drive a normal car like every other man I know?"

We drove past the trailers — Jiggs watching us from the open doorway of the last one — left the movie set, and bumped up onto the highway, in this case a one-lane blacktop that led in one direction back to the freeway and the Valley and in the other to I didn't know what, which is where Thad headed. He stomped on the gas — Thad was one of those humans with really big feet, something I'd noticed already and forgotten and now noted again — and then *va-vroom!* We shot off down the road, actually more across it, back and forth, fishtailing wildly —

"Off the gas, for Christ sake!" Bernie yelled, exact same thing he'd yelled at Leda later in that lesson I was mentioning.

"Nope," said Thad. "In the Lamborghini I just steer right into these suckers and —"

Whatever he did in the Lamborghini got left unsaid because the next moment we were no longer on two-lane blacktop, but were instead spinning around and around in circles across the desert floor. Funny how at a time like that you notice little things, such as Brando's claws digging deep into the fabric of Thad's shirt, and Brando's mouth opening slightly and burping out a tiny yellowish blob of puke, and that blob getting caught by the wind and deposited right smack on Bernie's shoulder.

Bernie can move real quick when he has to. In a flash he'd seized the wheel with one hand and with the other grabbed Thad's leg and yanked his foot right off the pedal. We came out of all that spinning, eased back down through a bit more fishtailing, straightened out, and came to a stop. Bernie reached for the keys and shut off the motor.

It got quiet, that strange quiet that comes right after lots of noise; not a relaxing kind of quiet, more the kind that makes you want to do something to bust it up, maybe taking a nip out of Brando, for example. Would I have done that? Almost certainly not, but before I even finished getting tempted, Bernie surprised me by suddenly sniffing the air and then glancing down at his shoulder and spotting that yellowish smear of puke. He'd picked up the scent of puke with that nose of his, a nose that while not as small as many human noses, or even most, had still been pretty much useless the whole time we'd been together? That was Bernie: just when you were sure he was all done amazing you, he amazed you again.

He looked up, met Thad's gaze. Thad raised his chin, tried to stare Bernie down. Good luck with that, was my thought.

"Uh," said Thad, "the Lamborghini has a different feel."

"Yeah?" said Bernie. "And the Ferrari?"

"Also different. And, come to think of it, different from the Lamborghini, too."

"Must be a challenge," Bernie said. "What other cars have you got?"

Thad started counting on his fingers, one of those human things which always makes me like them a bit more. He paused. "Just at home in LA, or should I include the ones in storage?"

Bernie said nothing.

Thad cleared his throat. "Here's some hand sanitizer," he said. "Clean up that little mess in no time."

We drove deeper into the desert, Bernie at the wheel, Thad riding shotgun with Brando on his lap, me still in back. After not too long, Bernie turned off the blacktop and followed a dirt track up toward some big red rocks, a track that petered out before we got there. Bernie stopped the car.

"What's going on?" Thad said.

"Want to see something interesting?" Bernie said.

"Like what?" Thad checked his watch.

"Let's make it a surprise."

"I hate surprises."

Bernie smiled, one of those smiles of his that's just for himself — and me, of course, goes without saying — and we all piled out of the car, me hitting the ground first. We walked up toward the red rocks, me in the lead, then Bernie, Thad, and Brando, actually moving under his own power. Once — this was back on our trip to San Diego — Bernie said that the fog came in on little cat feet, a remark that I'd never been able to forget no matter how hard I'd tried, and that was how Brando moved along, like he was made of cloud, weighing nothing, although in fact he looked pudgy to me.

We reached the big red rocks, stepped between two of them and entered a narrow shaded space with rocky walls on both sides. At the end stood a flat rock as high as Bernie's chest. He pulled himself up with a little grunt and Thad followed with a bigger one, leaving me and Brando standing down below. Brando looked at me. I looked at Brando. Then, without any apparent effort, he glided — that was what it looked like — glided up on top of the rock.

"Chet?" Bernie called down. "You coming?"

Oh, what an awful moment: me, dead last. I sprang, one of my very best leaps, clearing the lip of the rock by plenty, and sticking my landing without the slightest bobble, but no one saw. They were all at the other end of the rock, standing before a drawing in the cliff face. We'd done some prowling around in the desert looking for drawings like this, me and Bernie, always lots of fun although the point of it I'll leave to you. Had I seen this one before? I didn't think so.

"That round thing with the rays is the sun?" Thad said. "And the guy's dancing under it?"

"It's the sun, all right," said Bernie. "But when the figures are upside-down, D-shaped like that, they're dead."

"So it's a dead guy under the sun?"

"Uh-huh."

"Wonder why anyone . . ." Thad began. He gazed at the drawing for a long time, then slowly reached out and touched the rock, but off to the side, not on the drawing.

"It's warm," he said.

"Uh-huh," said Bernie.

There was a silence. Then Thad, eyes bigger and bluer than ever — kind of like he'd taken the sky inside him, what a thought! — and still on the drawing, said, "Thanks, man." Bernie nodded. Thad took a deep breath. "Everything's so fucked up," he said.

"Like what?" said Bernie.

"You name it," Thad said.

"Jiggs?" said Bernie.

Thad whipped around toward Bernie, real quick. "What's that supposed to mean?"

"Just throwing out a name," Bernie said. "Your suggestion."

"Why that one?"

"No real reason," Bernie said. "He doesn't seem like the typical bodyguard type, that's all."

"What are you talking about?" Thad said. "Seen the size of him?"

"A big boy," Bernie said. "On the outside. Kind of complicated on the inside."

"Complicated? Complicated how?"

"Just an impression. How long have you known him?"

Thad backed away a bit. Brando, who'd been curled up on the rocks, rose and climbed up on Thad, settling on his shoulder. "Long enough," Thad said. "What are you getting at?"

"Nothing," Bernie said. "He's from LA?"

"So?"

"I hear you're from out this way originally."

Thad backed up another step. "Where'd you hear that?"

"Someone mentioned it."

"Who?"

"Don't remember offhand," Bernie said. "Is it true?"

"It's a total goddamn lie," Thad said, his voice rising suddenly in that huge, ringing way it had. The sound echoed in the rocks, boomed back over us, maybe taking Thad by surprise because he jerked slightly, like he'd stuck his tongue in a wall socket; no time to go into that now. Surprised or even — yes, I smelled it — scared. He spoke more quietly. "Not a lie, exactly. I just meant it's not true. I'm from LA."

"Cool," Bernie said.

TWELVE

Bernie stood in front of the whiteboard, the zigzag groove that sometimes appeared on his forehead now easy to see, meaning he was doing some serious thinking. We were in the office, down the hall from Charlie's old bedroom. A basket of kid's blocks lay by the window — the room was meant for a little sister or brother that never came along. Sometimes I played with the blocks myself, but at the moment I was watching old man Heydrich out on his deck with the leaf blower. We hated the leaf blower, me and Bernie. Old man Heydrich didn't use it just for leaves, of which there were hardly ever any on the ground in our neighborhood, but also for blowing the dust off his deck, probably what he was up to now, except he couldn't get the thing to start. He jerked and yanked on the cord, his bony face reddening, and finally gave the thing a real nasty kick — surprisingly powerful for such a scrawny old dude — and stalked off into his house. Nothing much new: I'd seen humans kick their machines before, also punch and slap them, throw them out windows and into swimming pools, and stomp on them till the insides came springing out — and then they sometimes stomped on the insides, too! Machines could really get humans angry, that was clear, but . . . but could humans get machines angry? Hey! What a crazy thought! I hoped nothing like it ever entered my head again.

"What's so interesting?" Bernie said, coming over to the window. He gazed out. "Nothing going on, big guy." He moved back toward the whiteboard. I lay down on the rug — a nice nubbly rug with a pattern of circus elephants — and watched Bernie. I can watch him all day, never get tired of that.

When we're working on a case, he likes to spend time at the whiteboard, drawing boxes and arrows. He was doing it now. Did it mean we were on a case? This Thad Perry gig was a case? How? Then I thought of Manuel whatever-his-name-was and that slit in his chest. Next I hoped for another thought that would come zinging in and clear everything up, nice and tidy, but it didn't.

"Over here," Bernie said, making a box inside a box — whoa, this was going to be amazing — "we have Jiggs and —"

The phone rang. Bernie went to the desk and hit Speaker. He was wearing boxers so I could see the wound on his leg, a patch of rough red skin surrounding more skin that was flat and bluish, the whole thing kind of pushed in a bit. I wanted to lick it — even started moving that way — but Bernie doesn't like when I do that, something I remembered in the nick of time, an expression that Bernie and I have, on account of Quick Nick Castenedes, a very fast perp who practically ran across a whole parking lot before I caught him. Was he getting out of Northern State anytime soon? I couldn't wait to catch him again.

"Bernie? Cal Luxton."

"Hi."

"How's it goin'?"

"No complaints."

"I hear you're doing a great job."

"Who says?"

Luxton laughed. "How come you're such a hard-ass?" Bernie didn't answer. "Nan Klein's my source," Luxton went on. "The assistant."

"Do you know her?" Bernie said.

"Know her?"

"Like from before."

"Met her the other day — you were there," Luxton said. "Not sure I understand your question."

"What about Jiggs?"

"What about him?"

"You just met him, too?"

"No."

"So you knew him from before."

"He flew in to check accommodations last month," Luxton said. "I showed him around."

Bernie didn't say anything, just made a squiggle in the box in the box.

"What are you getting at, Bernie?"

"Nothing," Bernie said.

"Is there something I should know?"

Bernie was silent again.

"Need to remind you who you're working for?" Luxton said. "You're my eyes and ears on this project."

"A spy?" Bernie said.

"Wouldn't put it that way," said Luxton.

"And I wasn't aware we were working for you personally, Cal. Thought it was the mayor's office."

"That's how I meant to put it."

Bernie made an arrow pointing from one

box to another.

"You've got a question about Jiggs?" Luxton said.

"No," said Bernie. "Do you?"

"What does that mean?"

"How about the mayor's office — does it have a question?"

Luxton laughed, normally one of the best human sounds going, but not this time, hard to explain why. "Nothing like a sense of humor," he said, "although it can open the door to misinterpretation."

I checked the door. It stayed closed. No one came in. I heard no footsteps in the house, no cars in the street. Miss Interpretation? I knew a Miss Singh, daughter of Mr. Singh, our pawn shop buddy who sometimes kept Bernie's grandfather's watch — our most valuable possession — for us, but what would she be doing here? Didn't they already have the watch?

When I turned back to Bernie, he was no longer on the phone. He just stood there, his gaze on some faraway place beyond our walls. Now and then I can feel Bernie's thoughts — normally like soft breezes flitting by — but now they were dark and cold.

He turned my way. "What are you barking at?"

Me? I hadn't even been thinking of barking.

Bernie gave me a little smile. "Wish I could lie down like that." Huh? Like what? I was just lying with my chin flat on the rug, nicely stretched out but nothing unusual. Come on, Bernie! Try it right now! I know you can do it. But he didn't. Instead he turned to the whiteboard and shook his head. "The whole thing's starting to stink, big guy," he said. What a stunner! First, although Bernie was always the smartest human in the room, he hardly ever smelled anything. Second, nothing stank: our place on Mesquite Road never did, except when Bernie forgot to take out the trash and another whole week went by. "One good thing," he said. "It's a legitimate reason to call Suzie."

Losing me there, a little bit. Why would Bernie need a reason to call Suzie? Wasn't she family? Not only that, but I missed her. Luckily for me at that moment I happened to notice a tiny tuft of rug sticking up out of the fabric. Tiny, but could I get a tooth sort of wedged up and under like so, and then try pulling with a hard, quick — yes, I could.

Bernie picked up the phone.

"Hello?" said Suzie. In the background I

168

heard ice clinking in a glass and a man laughing; also maybe a cork popping, farther off. Bernie's face changed in a way I didn't like seeing.

"Uh," he said, "it's me. Bernie."

Suzie laughed. What a great laugh she had! I missed that, too. "You dope. Think I wouldn't recognize your voice? I was just about to call you."

"Yeah?" said Bernie. "Sounds like you're kinda busy."

"Not at the moment," Suzie said. "Just a sec — I'll turn this off." Then came a click and all that partying went silent.

"Oh," said Bernie.

"Oh what?" Suzie said.

"Nothing," Bernie said. He opened his mouth, closed it, looked around, possibly as though for help. "Chet's here," he said.

"Give him a pat for me," Suzie said. "I miss him."

Bernie took a step toward me. No need for that. I was already there.

"I think he understood you," Bernie said, giving me a nice pat, although not like Suzie's; a nice patter, Suzie, but she never did that lovely scratching thing at the end that winds up so perfectly.

"He understands everything," Suzie said.

"Seems like it sometimes," Bernie said.

169

"No seeming about it," said Suzie.

"You think?"

Bernie looked right into my eyes, a sharp, close look like he was trying to see inside me. I opened my mouth wide, unfurled my tongue as far as I could then reeled it back in. What fun! I thought about doing it again. And then I did do it again. Just as much fun!

". . . strange place," Suzie was saying. "It's the center of real power and yet feels totally unreal to me."

"And what about back here?" Bernie said.

Suzie's voice thickened a bit. "That feels very real."

Bernie shuffled from one foot to another.

"Shuffling from one foot to another?" Suzie said.

Bernie laughed. So did Suzie. The conversation had to be going great.

"How's Thad Perry?" Suzie said.

"Nixon says he's a lousy actor, but I disagree."

"Yeah?"

"He has something strange inside him."

"Like what?"

"It lets him absorb things from other people and reproduce them or reform them so that while he's still sort of himself, he's also . . ." Bernie made a little throwing up his hands gesture. Humans on the phone did lots of gesturing, as though they were face-to-face; I liked that about them. "Hard to explain," he went on. "I think there's a word for it, maybe starts with P."

"Protean?"

"Yeah," said Bernie. His face softened and he looked about to say more, but did not.

"I don't want his autograph, by the way," Suzie said.

Bernie laughed again. Suzie was good at making him laugh, one of the best things about her. "You're the only one," Bernie said. He went still. I sensed stillness on the other end of the line, too, like they were both concentrating on what Bernie had just said. What was it again? When humans forgot things — Bernie's mother being a great example — they liked to say that if it was important it would come back to them. Bernie's mother, a piece of work: she called him Kiddo! But no time for that now. I was too busy waiting for whatever Bernie had just said to come back to me.

In the meantime, Bernie was now saying something like, ". . . remember you mentioning Thad Perry was from the Valley originally?"

"Or spent time there," Suzie said. "Not sure which."

"What was your source?"

"No source, really. It came up in conversation."

"With who?"

"I'd have to think," Suzie said. "Is it important?"

"Probably not," Bernie said.

"Am I missing a story, Bernie?"

"There's an irony."

"Yeah," said Suzie, all of a sudden much quieter. Something beeped on her end. "Have to take this," she said.

After that, Bernie called somebody, maybe Rick, but I couldn't be sure, on account of these dark clouds that came rolling into my mind — something that often happened when I lay chin-down on a soft rug — dark clouds that had this power of being able to make my eyes close.

It was night when we drove back into Vista City, the sky the normal dark-pink Valley night sky, the air smelling of grease; couldn't have asked for more. We turned onto North Coursin Street, stopped in front of the house at the end of the block. It was dark, as were all the houses around, and none of the streetlights were working. Bernie shone the flashlight on the door, now crisscrossed with crime scene tape, and then back and forth across the yard, passing over the kid's bike lying on its side and returning to it.

"Nobody claimed Manny's body," Bernie said. "And then there's that bike." He went quiet. "I don't know, Chet. Forcing relationships — always the danger when there's not much to go on."

Danger? Did we back away from danger, me and Bernie? Not how things got done at the Little Detective Agency, amigo. So: no surprise when the next moment we were out of the car and crossing the yard. Bernie knelt down, took a close look at the bike, a rusty bike, I now saw, with a lopsided seat and twisted training wheels. I knew training wheels from back when Bernie and I taught Charlie how to ride. The fun we'd had with that! And old man Heydrich's flower bed was now totally back to normal, just as Bernie had promised, that whole episode with the pitchfork being way over the top.

Bernie picked up the bike, carried it back to the car. He was just wedging it into the space behind the seats when a face appeared in an upstairs window of the house across the street, a lighter pink oval in the dark pink night. I barked this low rumbly bark I have for just between me and Bernie. He glanced up, not in time to see the face, but he caught the twitch of the curtain.

"Good boy," he said.

All of a sudden, the night got breezy. We'd crossed the street and were just about at the front door of this other house when I realized my tail had started up behind me. Bernie says my tail has a mind of its own. What's wrong with that? Two minds had to be better than one unless I was missing something.

Bernie knocked on the door. No answer. He knocked again. No movement inside the house, probably because someone was already right there, on the other side of the door. Was Bernie aware of that? Maybe, because he took a bill from his wallet and stuck it in the letter slot.

"More where that came from," he said, speaking in an easy, normal voice, like he was kicking back with some pals. That was just one of his techniques. I've got some myself. We've cleared a lot of cases, me and Bernie.

The door opened, real slow. A tiny woman with long, shiny black hair stood there, the money clutched in her hand and a little kid sort of behind her, clinging to her dress. They shrank back at the sight of us, or more likely at the sight of Bernie. He's a pretty big dude.

"Tengo miedo de los perros," the woman said.

"Huh?" said Bernie. "Uh, can we come in? I'd like to talk to you about —"

"No habla ingles," said the woman.

"Ah," said Bernie. "El cyclo? The bike? Es el cyclo de Manny Chavez, or . . ."

The woman frowned at Bernie, not getting him at all. Bernie took out another bill, held it up.

"El cyclo?" he said.

The kid — a girl, I saw, about Charlie's age and not unlike this great little kid we'd come across once, down in Mexico — stepped forward. "Bicicleta," she said. "Not cyclo. And it belongs to Nino."

Bernie crouched down to her level. "Who's Nino?" he said.

"Manny's kid," said the girl. "He lives with his mother."

"Where?" Bernie said.

"I don't know," said the girl. She snatched the money right out of Bernie's hand and slammed the door shut. A bolt banged into place.

THIRTEEN

We got in the car and drove off, turning at the end of the block, then turning again, and — was it possible? Yes! We were circling the block, one of our very best tricks. Tricks and techniques were pretty much the same thing: I'd figured that out early on in my career. You learned stuff in this business all the time, way too many to remember, so it was important to keep in mind . . . something Bernie often said, and might come to me later.

We parked in the dark shadows of a droopy-branched tree on the darkest part of North Coursin Street, on the other side from where the little girl and her mother lived and partway down the block. Then we just sat there, which was why this was called sitting on a place. We were sitting on that house, waiting for something to happen, doing our job. Once — this was at a speech he gave at the Great Western Private Eye convention, and just because all the pages kept getting away from him and fluttering down to the stage didn't mean it wasn't the best speech I'd ever heard — Bernie said, "There's no point in poking a hornet's nest if you don't stick around to see what comes out." I'd been sitting close to the Mirabelli brothers at the time — they run a shop in the South Valley — and they'd shared a look I hadn't liked, maybe having to do with the possibility of getting stung — which actually had been my thought, too, but I'd abandoned it immediately. Who was better at this gig, Bernie or the Mirabelli brothers, with their big gold watches and sparkling pinkie rings? I don't need to tell you. And in case you're wondering, I've had more than one nasty encounter with hornets — lots more — maybe a story for another time.

Sitting with Bernie on a hot dark night, lots of desert dust in the air, and that Vista City backed-up sewage smell drifting by: I couldn't have been happier. Bernie reached over and untangled the tag from my collar. I hadn't even realized that it was twisted up: we're a team, me and Bernie. He kept an eye on the house, actually both eyes. I kept an eye on the house and an eye on Bernie. We in the nation within have certain advantages, no offense.

Sometimes, like one night sitting on a bunkhouse from a ridge high above, we'd catch a few tunes while we waited, Elmore James, maybe, or Jamey Johnson — "Can't Cash My Checks"; Bernie loves that one! — but not on this kind of inside-the-city job. There was still plenty to hear — a trash barrel getting knocked over a couple of blocks away, a plane somewhere high above the dark pinkness, and in the background the constant hum of the Valley, which could also get broken down into all the parts of the hum, and I was just starting in on that when I heard a car coming from the opposite direction.

Was Bernie looking that way? No. But then the car appeared around the corner up ahead — those little low fog lights showing but no headlights — and he turned toward it real quick. The car — not big, not small, dark color, nothing much to make it stay in my mind, so it didn't — stopped in front of the house. The fog lights went out. Then nothing. The driver and the passenger — I could just make them out, dark forms behind the top curve of the dashboard — sat there. We did the same thing. No way they could see us in these shadows — Bernie didn't make mistakes like that — but a weird feeling came over me anyway, the kind of weird feeling that makes me want to bark. The next thing I knew, Bernie's hand was on my back, heavy and gentle at the same time, sort of resting but maybe not. The urge to bark faded and vanished, no idea why.

The door of the not big or small car opened and the driver and the passenger got out. Impossible to see clearly: all I picked up was their dark forms, gliding toward the house. Then the door opened and they slipped inside. Was there something familiar about those dudes? I came real close to recognizing both of them. The door closed.

I took a swing at figuring out what was familiar about them, and then another swing, and no more, my mind suddenly jumping tracks to a memory of a ball game Bernie bet a grand on that had ended with a swing and a miss on a ball that was a mile out of the strike zone, according to him, so it must have been. We'd paid a visit to Mr. Singh soon after.

We sat. Bernie spoke quietly, more like just a breath with a soft voice hidden in it. "Don't see a plate on the front of that car."

Neither did I, but I couldn't be sure. Bernie opened the glove box, took out the flashlight, aimed it over our windshield at the other car, but didn't turn it on. Instead he hesitated, not something you saw from Bernie very often. He even had a saying — Bernie's great at making up sayings — he who hesitates is something or other. But a good thing this time, because right about then the door of the house opened and the two dudes came out. No lights inside the house or by the door: their faces remained invisible. They walked to the car, the driver fishing in his pocket for keys; I heard them jingle. And then came another sound, a strange buzzing from somewhere above. A moment after that, just as they were getting into his car, the streetlight down at the end of the block flickered on, the light dim and sort of brownish. But enough to make out the face of the passenger, a thin face framed by long sideburns: Cal Luxton. He put on his cowboy hat and then I was sure.

And the driver? One of those redheaded types you didn't see often, but that I was seeing again, and pretty soon: Oona's partner, the uniform cop named Floyd, now in street clothes.

Bernie's heart speeded up in his chest. I could hear it. And when I did, my own heart speeded up, too, funny thing. Floyd whipped the car around in a quick U-turn and went back the way they'd come. What about us?

Weren't we going to tail them? Tailing perps was one of our best things. Bernie!

We did nothing. Bernie sat motionless, the zigzag groove deep in his forehead. I started to get the picture. Tailing perps: what a crazy thought that had been. Cal Luxton was handing out the checks, making him one of the good guys. So therefore? I didn't take it past that. Bernie took care of the so-therefores, me bringing other things to the table, in case I haven't mentioned that already.

He fired up the engine. We made a U-turn of our own, slower than Floyd's, and drove home. Bernie didn't open his mouth the whole way.

Sometimes the night feels early and sometimes it feels late: your eyelids always tell you; at least, that's how it works in the nation within. This particular night felt late as we pulled into the driveway at our place on Mesquite Road, so it was a bit of a surprise that lights were on in the house next door. Not old man Heydrich's place, where lights sometimes shone all night: mean dudes sleep less, according to Bernie, and I often heard Heydrich in the middle of the night, busy down in his workshop. "Wonder what he's making," Bernie would say. But forget about old man Heydrich. I meant the house on the other side, Iggy's crib, which he shares with Mr. and Mrs. Parsons, a nice old couple who bought an electric fence but maybe made some sort of mistake, because now Iggy — my best pal, we'd played together since I couldn't remember when — was never outside. Mr. and Mrs. Parsons went to bed early, sometimes even before full darkness — you always knew because there was no more toilet flushing until morning — but not tonight. Bernie was still getting out of the car — a little slow, maybe on account of his wound, which could act up when he was tired — when the Parsons' door opened and Mr. Parsons stepped out.

And what was this? From somewhere in their house, *yip yip yip*? Yes! Iggy! He came barreling down the hall, stubby tail — the stubbiest in creation, Bernie said — up and stiff, and crazily long tongue flapping high and low. At the last instant, Mr. Parsons felt him coming and yanked the door closed. After that there was just a muffled *yip yip yip,* followed by a single yip, amazingly high pitched; and then nothing.

Mr. Parsons came stumping toward us behind his walker. We met him at the border of our properties, a row of low cactuses that Mr. Parsons and Bernie had decided were better than the flowers that had grown there before, although I didn't see how. Marking borders was one of my jobs, of course, but maybe not at exactly this moment.

"Hi, Bernie."

"Hi, Dan. Everything all right?"

"Mrs. Parsons could be doing a little better."

"Sorry to hear that."

"But she's cheerful," said Mr. Parsons. "No complaints. And she was real pleased, the way you replaced her soap collection. Much obliged."

"Don't mention it," Bernie said.

Soap collection? Itty-bitty brightly colored things in a toilet, the water rising and rising and rising? My one visit to Iggy's house, sometime back? The plumber racing up in his truck? I came close to remembering some of that. But, as humans said, no cigar, and no cigar was just peachy with me — I'd toyed with a stub or two and cigars didn't do it, although I have no problem with the smell. And funnily enough, peaches weren't really peachy with me, either, so why did . . . ? Somewhere in there I lost the thread.

". . . puppy I was telling you about?" Mr. Parsons was saying.

"The one you saw in the canyon?" Bernie said.

"Exactly," said Mr. Parsons. "Spotted the little fella again this afternoon. Even managed to snap a picture of him on my cell phone — first time I got the damn thing to work."

"Soon you'll be uploading to the cloud," Bernie said.

Mr. Parsons gave Bernie a quick look, then nodded. "That's true," he said. "And except for how I'll miss Mrs. Parsons, I'm ready. I've had a good life."

"No, no, no," Bernie said. "I meant —" And then came a long explanation of what he'd meant, which lost me right out of the gate, and maybe Mr. Parsons, too, to judge from the look on his face.

"It's all right, Bernie," he said, "I'm not offended. But do you want to see the picture?"

"Yes."

Mr. Parsons took out his cell phone and started pressing buttons. "Cursed stupid hellish —"

"Mind if I try?" Bernie said.

Mr. Parsons handed Bernie the phone. "This one?" Bernie said.

They gazed at the glowing thing, then both turned and transferred that gaze onto me. I wagged my tail, my fall-back response in all kinds of situations.

"Guilty as charged?" said Mr. Parsons.

"But I just don't see how . . ." Bernie began.

"Doesn't he get into the canyon?"

"Only with me."

"What about when you're not home and he's out on the patio?" said Mr. Parsons.

"The gate's always locked."

"Isn't he a great leaper?"

"Not that great," Bernie said. "That gate's seven feet high — I had it built special."

Seven feet high? Lost me on that one. When it comes to numbers, I stop at two, which is plenty, in my opinion. Feet were another story: all kinds of feet in the world — I'd seen elephant feet in action! What a career I was having! — but in the end I wouldn't change mine for any others. As for the gate, my impression was that I always cleared it by plenty. I reminded myself to take a look next time.

"So what do you think happened?" said Mr. Parsons.

"Maybe a litter mate of Chet's is out there somewhere," Bernie said.

Mr. Parsons had thick, snowy-white eyebrows. I'd seen snow, by the way, once on a case, the details vague at the moment. But sometimes details can sharpen later, when you least expect it. Does that ever happen

to you? Back to snow: Bernie made a snow-
ball! We played fetch, sort of, which is when
I started finding out what snow was all
about. Back to . . . to Mr. Parsons's eyebrows. He raised one of them in this way
humans have when they want to send a
message to other humans, not friendly or
unfriendly, hard to pin down, exactly.

"Is that how you operate in your work?"
Mr. Parsons said. "Chasing after the low-
percentage possibility first?"

Bernie laughed. "Sure as hell hope not,"
he said. "Maybe the next step is to give this
big guy a test."

"Now you're thinking," said Mr. Parsons.

About what? They had me on that one.
Next thing I knew we were all of us inside
our place and walking through the kitchen
— Bernie grabbing a box of chew strips on
the way — and out onto the patio.

"Nice house, Bernie," Mr. Parsons said.
"Just imagine when your family owned the
whole parcel."

"I try not to," Bernie said.

"And a swan fountain," said Mr. Parsons
as he stumped out onto the patio, *bump
bump bump.* "Pretty funny."

Then Bernie said something about who
the joke ended up being on that I missed,
mostly on account of those chew strips, beef

flavored, from Rover and Company, the very best. Our buddy Simon Berg runs the company, and I once spent a lovely time in their test kitchen. Whoa! And Bernie had just mentioned a test. We were headed back to Rover and Company? Seemed strange at this hour, but something was up, something that included chew strips.

Bernie moved toward the gate at the back of the patio. Hey! They'd just been discussing this gate and now here we were. On the other side lay the canyon. I could hear something moving around out there, not too far away, possibly a javelina, although I couldn't be sure because of the breeze flowing in the wrong direction.

Bernie pointed toward the top of the gate. "Okay, Chet. Up and over."

Up and over? He wanted me to jump the gate? Not a good idea, the reasons why being so complicated that I didn't even try to untangle them. Instead I just sat down.

Bernie shook the box of treats. "Come on, big guy. Don't you want one of these?"

I did, big-time. But I stayed where I was.

Bernie turned to Mr. Parsons. "Maybe the low-percentage play isn't so low after all."

"Maybe," said Mr. Parsons, giving me a close look. When humans are having fun, their eyes brighten; Mr. Parsons' eyes were

doing it now. "Think it would make any difference if you took one out of the box,
showed it to him?"

"Nah," said Bernie. "He knows what's in
there, believe me. The gate's too high,
simple as that."

"Try it anyway," Mr. Parsons said.

Bernie opened the box, took out a chew
strip, gave it a little shake. "Up and over,
big guy," he said. One thing about the chew
strips from Rover and Company: they had
the best smell in the world. And another
thing about them: if they got shaken like
that, the smell got even stronger, especially
if the breeze suddenly shifted a bit, now
blowing — no, not hard — but right in your
face. How to describe it? Like a wonderfully
beefy breeze, hickory smoked? Something
of the kind, and maybe given time I could
have described it better, but it was too late.
I was already in midair, soaring over the
gate — clearing it by plenty, by the way; I
checked — and headed for a nice soft landing in the canyon.

The naked bulb over the gate went on.
The gate swung open. Bernie and Mr.
Parsons gazed out at me, caught in the
circle of light. I gazed back at them.

"Right after I took that picture," Mr.
Parsons said, "I heard a woman calling for

him and the little critter took off."

"Catch the name?" said Bernie.

"Shooter," Mr. Parsons said.

"Oh, boy," Bernie said.

Mr. Parsons leaned into the walker, letting it take more of his weight. His eyes weren't quite so bright. "I kind of like it," he said.

Where were we going with this? I had no idea. Bottom line: I'd jumped the gate and that chew strip was now mine. So what was taking so long?

FOURTEEN

Next day we swung by Leda's place. She and Malcolm, the boyfriend — but they were getting married as soon as Leda decided on where to go for the honeymoon ("never really had one the first time," I'd once heard her say on the phone) — had a big house in High Chaparral Estates, the nicest development in the whole Valley, a fact she mentioned now and then. Malcolm was a brilliant software developer, whatever that was, making money hand over fist; she'd mentioned that, too. Did humans put hand over fist to keep the money from falling out? I'd never seen it, but what else could it mean?

Leda and Malcolm had a big green lawn — the kind Bernie called an aquifer drainer — lined with flowering bushes. I lifted my leg against the bushiest of them, remembering at that moment that I'd missed out on marking our border with Mr. Parsons, so I made sure to do an extra-thorough job, and still hadn't finished when the door opened and Leda looked out and saw me. Uh-oh. Trouble on the way, and making it worse was the fact I couldn't stop just like that, not with my kind of flow, amigo. I'd tried more than once, believe me.

Then came a big surprise. She turned to Bernie and said, "You're a doll."

"Uh," said Bernie.

"Be just a minute," she said, waving her hands in a strange kind of way. "Song Yi's almost done."

"Huh?"

"She comes to do my nails."

"Huh?"

Leda backed inside and closed the door.

Bernie looked at me. I looked at Bernie. "Don't look at me like that," he said. "I know what you're thinking."

Wow! He knew I was thinking of crossing the lawn and marking the bushes on the other side? But that was Bernie: just when you thought he was done amazing you, he did it again. As for whatever he'd asked me not to do, it was like one of those feathery little clouds you see sometimes, high high up, and the next time you look: nothing but clear blue skies.

"In fact," he went on, "I was thinking the

same thing."

An absolute stunner. Bernie and I were going to cross Leda's lawn and mark those bushes together? Had anything like that ever happened? I actually did remember something of the kind, maybe in an alley behind a biker bar in Rio Vacio, but it was all too vague, and before it got clearer, the door opened and out came Leda and Charlie, followed by a dark-haired woman carrying a pink sort of tool kit. Not to worry: those bushes weren't going anywhere. And then . . . and then I had the most amazing thought of my life: given time, we could fill up the aquifer, me and Bernie, side by side. And didn't we have all the time in the world?

"So nice to meet you," Leda said, taking Thad Perry's hand and not letting go. "I'm a big big fan, your biggest. Huge."

"Thanks," said Thad, looking at something over her shoulder. " 'ppreciate it."

"And this is my son, Charlie. Say hello to Mr. Perry, Charlie."

Bernie's eyes have a way of — how to put it? Narrowing? Hooding? I give up. But the point is, I think it happens when he's starting not to like what's going down, and at that moment Charlie's eyes were doing it. He looked like a little Bernie. What a kid.

"Uh," said Charlie.

"Hey," said Thad Perry, glancing down at Charlie. Across the set — we were back on the movie set, this time not a bar in the Old West but a campfire under an enormous saguaro that some landscape dudes couldn't get to stand straight — Lars Karlsbaad was glancing at Charlie, too. Then Nan, glasses perched up on top of her head, listening to something in her earphone — I could hear it, actually, a man saying "get him on his goddamn mark" — was whispering in Thad's ear, and he tugged his hand free and moved away.

Not long after that, we were sitting under an awning not far from the saguaro, me, Bernie, Charlie, Leda. "What's the scene about, Bernie?" she said. "I'm so excited!"

Bernie leafed through the script. "Is this where the shaman —"

"Kina Molenta? She's gorgeous!"

"— starts changing the history of the west or some bull —"

"Shh," Leda said.

Thad Perry came in, cowboy hat pushed back on his head. He sat down in front of the fire. Hey! His knees cracked, just like Bernie's mom's. Then a woman entered and sat near him. I didn't get a good look at her, on account of a big distraction from the get-go, namely — was it possible? — this wolf head she had perched on her own head. From Leda came one of those quick little in-breaths humans sometimes do. Her eyes were wide; Bernie and Charlie were both in that narrow and hooded mode.

A huge camera came rolling up on a kind of train track, Lars Karlsbaad and the camera dude sitting behind it. Lars walked up to the campfire.

"Kina, looking like a dream," he said. "How were the Maldives?"

The woman shrugged.

"Excellent," said Lars, puffing on his cigar, hands balled into fists behind his back. "Comfortable with this scene?"

"Except for this fucking wolf head," said Kina. "It itches like a bastard."

Lars turned to the woman with the clipboard, standing off to the side. "I thought you took care of that," he said.

"This is the replacement, Lars," said the woman. "She tried it out and said it was —"

Lars made a chopping gesture, kind of quick and nasty. The woman went silent. He turned to Kina. "Sorry, love, we'll get it fixed by tomorrow — I give my word — but do you think you can soldier through today? It's a very short scene."

"Soldier through?" said Kina.

"Possibly a Europeanism," said Lars. "Sorry. Merely a way of saying —"

"Tough it out," Thad said.

Kina turned to Thad. They exchanged a look, not just unfriendly, more like they hated each other.

"All set then?" Lars said. "In this scene, Lolotea first sees — but subtle, subtle — that Croomer may be unlike the other white men, not a monster. At first, you both stare into the fire, possibly remembering the horror of the day. Then you, Kina, slowly turn and gaze at his profile. Questions?"

"His left profile?" said Kina.

"Why, yes, with the way you're sitting," Lars said.

Kina shrugged again. She was a great shrugger, sending messages I never wanted coming in my direction.

"Something wrong with my left profile?" Thad said.

"No, no," said Lars. "What a thought — agreed, Kina?"

She was silent. Behind his back, the knuckles of Lars's fists were white as bone and getting whiter. A crazy idea popped into my mind; I won't describe it. Lars turned to the woman with the clipboard. "For this shot we will clear the set."

"Right away, Lars." The woman with the clipboard faced us. "All nonessential personnel please clear the set."

Nonessential meant what, again? Right around then I gave up on understanding the movie business. The best thing about it was the buffet table set up near the trailers. I had some experience with buffet tables, and this one was aces. No time to go into aces now — and this card sharp name of Doc Sloman, now breaking rocks in the hot sun — on account, for example, of the steak tips, which Charlie was slipping me under the table.

"Set to go?" said Bernie.

"Oh, no," Leda said. "I'm having a blast. So's Charlie." She turned to him. "Right?"

Charlie said something, impossible for me to understand with his mouth full like that.

"That was so interesting," Leda said.

"Yeah?" said Bernie.

"Like how they had to show the horror of the day on their faces. What do you think the horror was?"

"This stupid massacre in the script," Bernie said.

"Why stupid?" said Leda, sipping her white wine. What was this? They were kind of getting along, having a human conversation with no bad feelings around the edges?

"The weaponry's all wrong, for one thing. And the Apaches would never —"

Leda laid a hand on Bernie's arm to shush him. Bernie didn't like that, gave her an annoyed look. We were back to normal. Meanwhile, Lars was coming toward the buffet table, actually right in our direction, sweat dampening his shirt in the armpits. I always watched for that.

Lars stopped in front of us. "Hello . . . Bennie, is it?"

"Bernie," said Bernie.

"Nice to see you back on the set," Lars said. "Always welcome. And this is?"

"My, uh, ex-wife," Bernie said. "Leda."

"What a coincidence!" Lars said. "I had a wife named Leda, too."

"Really?" said Leda.

What was going on? Something about two Ledas? My mind shrank away from the thought. Always a surprisingly nice feeling when my mind did that: I had one of those minds that was on my side, if you know what I mean, which I actually don't.

"And this is your son?" said Lars, turning to Charlie.

"Yes," said Bernie and Leda at the exact same time.

"Hello, Charlie," Lars said.

197

Charlie, working on a brownie, nodded his head a bit.

"Charlie?" Leda said. "Can you —"

"Like movies, Charlie?" Lars said.

Charlie stopped chewing for a moment. "Some," he said.

Lars laughed, a surprisingly squeaky laugh that caught me by surprise and which I was in no hurry to hear again. "For example?" he said.

"*Fight Club,*" Charlie said.

"What?" said Leda.

"Just the first few minutes," Bernie said. "Inadvertently. The moment I —"

"Do you think you might like being in a movie?" Lars said.

He was looking right at Charlie, but for some reason Leda answered. "Me?" she said, her face starting to pinken.

"You?" Lars said, and pink went red on Leda's face. "I was referring to Charlie. We have one nonspeaking youngster role still uncast. Your son looks the part."

"No way," Bernie said.

Leda turned to him, her complexion recovering real fast. Leda was strong inside, no doubt about that. "Bernie?" she said. "A moment?"

She pulled him aside, her fingernails, now a deep and shining red, digging into his arm. They spoke in low voices — most of the talking done by Leda, something about being provincial, completely lost on me — and in the meantime Lars grabbed a whole slice of pie off the buffet table and gobbled it down.

Bernie and Leda returned. "We've decided," Leda said, "that it's up to Charlie."

"Very sensible," said Lars, crumbs falling from his lips. I licked them up, not so much because of liking pie, more because that's what you do when a crumb opportunity arises.

"Charlie, sweetheart," said Leda, "would you like to be in a real movie?"

"Do I get paid?" Charlie said.

There was a moment of silence. Then they all started laughing, except for Charlie, who didn't seem to get the joke. Neither did I. What was so funny? Being in a movie was a kind of work, right? It was important to get paid for work, an area where we'd slipped up in the past at the Little Detective Agency, part of the reason — along with the Hawaiian pants, now filling our self-storage in South Pedroia, and the tin futures play, gone bad on account of an earthquake in Bolivia — that our finances were such a mess.

Leda was the first to stop laughing.

Then Lars. "Scale," he said.
Then Bernie.

That night we packed the twisted-up bike back in the Porsche and drove over to Vista City. The streetlights on North Coursin Street were out again, and the crime scene house was dark, but lights shone in the house across the street, where Bernie had questioned the mother and her little girl. What had come of that? I looked forward to doing it again.

We parked and walked across the hard-packed dirt yard. The front door opened and out came a man carrying a vacuum cleaner. He stopped and said, "No dogs." Or something like that: he had a huge wad of gum in his mouth.

"We don't need to come in," Bernie said. "I just want to find out where to return Nino's bike."

"Huh?" said the man. "You're not the one who wanted to see the place?"

"Not following you," Bernie said, which made two of us, but I didn't worry. We'd catch up: we always did.

"It's for rent," the man said. "Very reasonable."

"You're the landlord?"

"Yup."

"Where are the people who lived here?" Bernie said. "The woman and her daughter."

"Cleared out," said the landlord.

"Where to?"

"Back to Mexico, most likely. They're all doin' it these days — didn't turn out to be the paradise they had in mind."

Bernie nodded, a short little nod. Some of his nods meant nothing; this one meant he was starting not to like the landlord dude.

"How long have you owned the building?" he said.

"Awhile," said the landlord.

"Know much about the place across the street?"

"Nope."

"A man was killed there."

"Heard somethin' about it."

"He had a son named Nino, lives with his mother. We've got Nino's bike in the car. Any idea where we could find him?"

"Nope."

"Ever run into anyone named Ramon around here?"

"Nope."

"He might have a dog called Outlaw."

The landlord stopped chewing his gum for a moment.

"Ring a bell?" Bernie said.

"Nope." His jaws started up again.

"Would a C-note refresh your memory?"

"Nope. Anything else I can he'p you with?"

Suzie called when we were almost home.

"I remembered where I heard about Thad Perry and the Valley," she said. "Carla told me."

"Yeah?" said Bernie.

Carla? I knew Carla, a friend of Suzie's at the *Tribune,* and one of those humans who was fond of me and my kind, even made sure to always carry a little something in her purse. I waited for Bernie to whip us around in a quick U-turn.

". . . called her," Suzie was saying. "She's on assignment, back in the morning."

"Thanks."

"Bernie? You sound tired."

"I'm not," he said.

But once we were inside, he fell asleep with his clothes on. I lay down on the floor at the foot of the bed and listened to him breathe.

FIFTEEN

"Lookin' good," Carla said. "So glossy."

"Thanks," said Bernie. Bernie always looked good, of course — and even better today on account of the deep sleep he'd had, breathing slow and even, the darkness under his eyes all gone and the zigzag in his forehead hardly showing at all — but glossy? I didn't see it.

"And that tail," Carla went on, "you could power the whole city off it."

"He likes getting patted," Bernie said.

They were talking about me?

"Sure you do, you beautiful boy," said Carla.

Yes, me. How nice.

Carla gave me one more pat. She was glossy, too, at least her hair, and also had smooth skin the color of coffee the way Rick drank it — with lots of cream — skin that today was smelling of grapefruit soap. We'd met Carla downtown, in the little park across from city hall. The morning sun shone brightly on the white columns of the building, making all the details, like the chipped paint and the bird droppings, so clear. What a day this was going to be!

"Working on a story?" Bernie said.

"Zoning reform," Carla said.

"Gonna happen?"

"Soon, no. In our lifetime, yes." She checked her watch. "Starts in ten minutes, Bernie. What's up?"

Bernie got going on one of those stories with lots of twists and turns, something about Suzie and Thad Perry and the Valley, not easy to follow. I preferred a very short story with no twists and turns — only my opinion — and besides, right under the next bench, on which a drooling old guy with a paper bag drink between his knees was zonked out . . . could it really be? Yes! A half-eaten hot dog with ketchup and relish, still in the bun. Humans: how often they threw food away! I just didn't understand, and neither did those shiny black ants, some of them getting their tiny legs stuck in the ketchup. I made short work of the hot dog — don't get me started on that strange name — ants and all. Ketchup and relish: a nice combination, and pretty unusual. Didn't relish usually go with mustard? My head practically spun with fascinating thoughts about hot dogs and all the things you could put on them. I drifted back over to Bernie and Carla.

". . . but I can't remember whose uncle," Carla was saying. "Probably one of my friends at the time — I'll make a call or two after the hearing and get back to you."

"Thanks, Carla."

"Don't mention it," Carla said. She got up from the bench. "Heard from Suzie?"

"Yup."

"The *Trib*'s not the same without her."

Bernie looked down at his shoes. He was wearing his best sneakers, not the pair with the paint spatters but the ones with mismatched laces, one black, one white, on account of the other white lace breaking and . . . a thought, possibly very important, fluttered through a shadowy part of my mind and disappeared. Wait! Something about black and white? It came oh so close to where I could grab it. But no.

"I'm not, um . . ." Bernie began, and then came to a halt.

Carla, kind of hesitant, reached out and touched Bernie's shoulder. He looked up. "Not my place to say anything," she said.

"No fair to stop now," Bernie told her.

"Maybe I shouldn't admit it," Carla said,

"but sometimes I've found wisdom in sappy song lyrics."

Bernie smiled. "Like?" he said.

" 'Once you have found her, never let her go,' " said Carla. "Just an example." Did her eyes well up? I didn't get a good look because she walked away immediately, headed toward the street. "Almost forgot." She turned and reached into her purse, her eyes now definitely dry. "Can Chet have a treat?"

"Don't see why not," Bernie said. And what was this? Now his eyes were a bit misty? Was everyone getting all emotional about my treat? That was nice, but totally unnecessary. "Did you have breakfast, big guy?" Bernie said. I couldn't remember. "And even if he did, he hasn't had a bite since then." I found myself licking my muzzle, not sure why. The next thing I knew I was taking an extra-large size biscuit — my favorite of all the possible sizes — from Carla's hand, gently but firmly.

She walked across the street. At that moment I happened to see the stone stairs leading up to city hall, and there was Cal Luxton in a dark suit, watching us from the topmost step. I looked at Bernie. He was checking his cell phone. I got a bit uneasy and barked a short, sharp bark. Bernie glanced down at me. "What's up, Chet?" Then he turned to city hall. Carla was just going through the door and there was no sign of Luxton. I barked again. "You've had your biscuit," Bernie said. "Don't be greedy."

Greedy? A new one on me. I was wondering whether to try puzzling it out when the old dude on the bench woke up and started going on about a hot dog, or something like that, hard to tell on account of most of his teeth being missing. Bernie made this quick little clicking sound in his mouth that means time to split. We split.

A taxi was idling in front of our place on Mesquite Road. The rear door opened as we parked in the driveway and a young blond woman in a very small dress jumped out and ran up to us.

"Felicity?" Bernie said. "Something wrong?"

Felicity: Thad's girlfriend. The connection came to me with amazing speed, not always the case. There's a lot to keep track of in our line of work. Try it sometime.

Felicity nodded, a real quick and nervous nod. Nervous humans had a special smell, sort of thin and sour, and Felicity was giving off plenty of it. Bernie lost control of his gaze for a moment — oh, Bernie — and it slipped down to the top of her very small dress. But he snapped that gaze right back up to her eyes in a flash — so quick for Bernie, really on his game today — big, golden brown eyes, with tears maybe on the way at any moment.

"What is it?" Bernie said.

"Thad," she said. "I think he's gone on one of his rambles."

"Rambles?" said Bernie. "A kind of hike?"

She shook her head, again with that same nervous speed. One Christmas when Charlie was younger — and completely by accident — I'd taken apart this little wind-up bear that banged on a drum when the key got turned — well, who wouldn't have? — and all these springs had come springing out. I thought of that now, not sure why; funny how the mind worked.

"Rambles is Thad's word for it," Felicity said. "It's kind of a . . ." Her eyes shifted. She was searching for a word. Humans had so many, no surprise when one or two got lost. They did lots of struggling in life — humans, I mean — but no time to go into that now.

"Euphemism?" Bernie said, losing me completely.

But not Felicity. She nodded, a calmer

208

movement this time. "You're smart," she said. "That's what Thad says — you're smart in the old-fashioned way."

The old-fashioned way? And every other possible way, amigo.

"Euphemism for what?" Bernie said.

The taxi driver stuck his head out the window; he needed a shave and a haircut. "Hey, lady, wan' me to wait or what? Meter's tickin'."

Bernie made a little flick flick motion with the back of his hand — had I ever seen him do that before? I loved it! — and the window slid back up.

"Thad . . . goes off by himself sometimes," Felicity said.

"With Jiggs?" Bernie said.

"No."

"Isn't that hard for someone in his position?" Bernie said. "So recognizable?"

"He's, um, not thinking straight when these things happen," Felicity said.

"Drugs?" Bernie said.

"You can never say anything," Felicity said. "Promise?"

"I can promise I won't say anything in order to profit from the knowledge or simply hurt Thad," Bernie said. "Making it a promise with limits."

Felicity gazed at Bernie, then blinked and

turned away. "Why is everything always like this?" she said. Hey! For a moment she looked like a little kid, not much older than Charlie.

Bernie didn't speak. He just stood there. I sat beside him. We could keep that up for a long time, me and Bernie. It was one of our techniques at the Little Detective Agency. We've got lots.

She faced Bernie, met his gaze. I was starting to like her. "All right," she said. "Thad has — I wouldn't say a problem, more like the occasional issue with drugs."

"What drugs?"

"I'm not really sure — it can be just about anything."

"Have you ever seen him inject himself?"

"Oh, no, never never," Felicity said. "And I don't want you to think it's this humongous deal, not compared with . . . well, how things go down in the industry."

"Then let's forget all about it," Bernie said.

There was hardness in Bernie — although never when it came to the two of us, goes without mentioning. His hardness, when it showed up, had an effect that you could see in people's faces. I saw it now in Felicity's.

"You're not going to help me?" she said.

"Help you do what?" said Bernie.

"Find him," Felicity said. "His next call's for eight tomorrow morning."

"He's the star. They'll wait for him."

"Maybe if there hadn't been . . . an incident or two in the past. Now there's a nonperformance clause in his contract."

"Saying what?"

"I haven't actually read it." Felicity laughed, one of those quiet little laughs meaning . . . what? Something was only a little bit funny? I didn't know. "Neither has Thad. But I heard Nan talking about it with the agent. It's all about big fines and how they can fire him whenever they want."

"And he signed?"

"Thad signs tons of stuff. He doesn't even look. He's just a child sometimes — which is where his art comes from, I'm sure of it — and all these vultures —" Felicity's voice got real thick, meaning the tears were on the way at last. Instead, a bit of a surprise: she fought them off, wiping the back of her hand over her eyes and stiffening her whole body. The expression in Bernie's eyes changed.

"Any idea where he went?" Bernie said.

"I woke up in the middle of the night and he was gone. He took Jiggs's car."

"With permission?"

She shook her head. "Jiggs is pretty

211

pissed." And then came some more about Jiggs, maybe how he was out looking for Thad but had a poor record of finding him in the past, Thad always coming back on his own when good and ready, but I couldn't concentrate on account of my mind suddenly snapping back to vultures. I was pretty sure Felicity had mentioned them, and if vultures were in the case, we had problems. Birds in general bothered me. Why those angry little eyes? Would I be angry if I could soar around the big blue sky all day? And vultures were the worst. I've been circled by them. I know.

"Does Thad have any friends or acquaintances in the Valley?" Bernie was saying.

"Nobody," said Felicity. "Not that he's ever mentioned to me."

"Has he ever talked about living in the Valley at one time? Or growing up here?"

Felicity frowned. Hey! All of a sudden I noticed that she was kind of beautiful. "I don't understand. Thad was born and raised in Southern California. What are you getting at?"

"Nothing," Bernie said. "How long has Jiggs been the bodyguard?"

"From way back, I think," said Felicity. "They were friends when Thad was still waiting tables and surfing. That's how he

212

got discovered."

"Waiting tables?"

"Surfing. He was surfing Little Dume when some producer saw him. You didn't know that? It's kind of a famous story. They re-created it for *60 Minutes.*"

What was all that about? You tell me. And maybe Bernie didn't get it, either, because now he was staring in the distance, his mouth slightly open like some question was on the way. None came. No problem. When he's standing so still that way, all caught up in his mind, I could watch him forever.

"Brando's missing, too," Felicity said.

Bernie brought his gaze slowly down to her.

"I'll pay you," Felicity said. "Just say how much."

"That won't be necessary," he said.

Meaning what? We were turning her down? We weren't turning her down, just turning down the money? Oh, no: I hoped it wouldn't be that.

Sixteen

But it was that. Working for no money, and not for the first time. Have I mentioned Bernie's grandfather's watch, our most valuable possession, now in hock at Mr. Singh's? I was worried, and when I'm worried I like to gnaw things. For example: the rounded edge of the leather trim on the shotgun seat.

"Chet! How many times do I have to tell you?"

Uh-oh. Bernie sounded . . . not mad — he'd never get mad at me — more like not in his very best frame of mind. I sat up straight and tall, still and quiet, a total pro, on the job and eager for work. Keeping Bernie in the very best frame of mind was part of what I did.

"How about a chew strip instead?" Bernie said, opening the glove box.

Bernie: what can I tell you? The best.

We drove, and while we drove, listened to

some of our favorites: "Going Back to Greenville," "Lonesome 77–203," "If You Were Mine."

"Like that trumpet?" Bernie said. "Roy Eldridge, at the top of his game."

Like it? I loved it. The trumpet did things to me. We listened to "If You Were Mine" again. And again. And one more time. And were still listening to it when we climbed into the mountains beyond the Valley, passed a huge red rock — which was when I started to pay attention to where we were, so easy to get lost in music — and stopped at Boo Ferris's gate. He came out of the gatehouse, polishing off a burger. I started in on some real crazy barking.

"Chet! Knock it off!"

I knocked it off, just in time to hear my barks echoing in the hills. Hey! Not bad, not bad at all. They even scared me a little.

"I don't think Chet likes me," Boo Ferris said.

"It's not you," said Bernie. "He's in a strange mood today."

"Have you fed him?" said Boo Ferris, suddenly showing signs of being a smart guy.

"Food is not the problem," Bernie said.

Oh? What made him so sure? True, there'd been that hot dog, but not close to a whole hot dog, and hadn't it been a long time

215

since then? All at once I was ravenous.

"I noticed last time," Bernie was saying, "that you didn't ask what I was doing up here."

"You were on the list," said Boo Ferris. "That's all I need to know."

Bernie smiled. "Just like the army."

"Except we're not taking fire," said Boo Ferris.

"You were in the service?" Bernie said.

"Briefly."

Bernie nodded, like that made sense. "Fact is," he said, "we're on a job."

"Figured that."

"And I'm wondering when you came on duty."

"Midnight," said Boo Ferris.

"Long shift."

"I'm covering for one of the guys."

"Nice of you."

"Don't need much sleep," Boo Ferris said. "And I can use the money."

"Know Thad Perry?"

"Seen him come and go."

"Did he go last night?"

Boo Ferris didn't back off, exactly, but the way he was standing changed, so somehow he seemed farther away; farther away and not so friendly. "They're big on discretion up here," he said.

"Me, too, down where I am," said Bernie. "So my preference would be to take all that Boo and Bo confusion to my grave."

Boo Ferris stared at Bernie. "Why is it always me?" he said.

"Interesting question," said Bernie. "But we're in a bit of a hurry."

"Christ," said Boo Ferris. "You didn't hear it from me."

"Goes without saying."

Boo Ferris glanced around. We were all alone. The sun shone, nice and warm but not too hot up here on the mountain. Boo Ferris took a deep breath. "He drove through. Four a.m. on the nose. Honked like a bastard until I came to the gate. I said, 'There some problem?' Just letting him know, hey, I'm a human being. 'Goddamn right there is,' he said, but not like he was pissed at me. So I kind of took a close look at him, and I coulda sworn he'd been crying."

"Yeah?" Bernie said.

"Allergies, you're thinking?" said Boo Ferris. "Possible, I guess. But he stank of booze, and he had a fat old spliff burning away in the ash tray. So I told him, like, maybe this might not be the right time for a ride. But he went anyway."

"He didn't say anything else?"

"Not really," said Boo Ferris. "Just some weird shit about the time being right if everything was upside down."

"Upside down?"

"He wasn't making much sense. But what could I do? Arrest him?"

"Imagine," Bernie said as we drove down the mountain, "if we had citizens arresting each other all the time, willy-nilly?"

Not sure what that was all about, but I liked the sound of willy-nilly. I was feeling tip-top. And so was Bernie — I could feel it. Perps, bad guys, gangbangers: heads up.

"Of course, I might be wrong," Bernie said.

About what? Was it even worth a thought, what with Bernie never being wrong, plus don't forget that thinking can be hard, compared to leaping high walls, for example, or finding your way home when you were all alone and deep in the desert, or . . . I kind of lost the thread.

Meanwhile, Bernie was saying something about upside-down. ". . . no more than a thin thread, and it's not even clear that he was even listening."

Whoa. Thread? Lost, or just too thin? Was he talking about me? I always listened to Bernie. Now, sitting tall in the shotgun seat, ears up, stiff, and open to the max, I listened my hardest. I heard a plane, the faintest hum, from somewhere high high above. Gazing up, I saw one of those white trails planes leave in the sky — they turn gold at the end of the day, a puzzler but very beautiful — with the tiny silver plane at the front, although the sound wasn't coming from there, instead from farther back on the white trail. What was that all about? The white trail made the sound? That was as far as I could take it.

Meanwhile, Bernie was saying something about having nothing better to go on, so why not? "Let's roll the dice."

Uh-oh. Please, not the dice. The last time — in a late-night dive in the diviest part of South Pedroia after the Police Athletic League fundraiser — we'd had to take Bernie's grandfather's watch to Mr. Singh, and at the moment Mr. Singh already had it, if I haven't already pointed that out. So what would be our move if a financial emergency turned up, the kind of financial emergency that always enters our life when dice get rolled or cards get dealt? If only Bernie would just stick to arm wrestling: we've made some serious green from arm wrestling. Serious green: my mind got stuck on that idea and stayed there.

■ ■ ■ ■

We climbed a mountain pass, up and over, and then we were out in the desert. Bernie's hands relaxed on the wheel. I gazed at his hands, so beautiful, and even that one slightly twisted finger: beautiful, too. Soon we left the freeway and had a nice stretch of two-lane blacktop all to ourselves, pink hills rising on both sides, the kind of pink hills that shrink farther away the closer you get to them. Who could get tired of that?

"Coronado came right through here," Bernie said.

Coronado? A perp of some kind, and not the first time Bernie had mentioned him — he always pointed out places where Coronado had been, but Coronado had moved on every time, one of those slippery customers who stayed a step or two in front of us. Message to Mr. Coronado: your day will come.

We rounded a long curve — things heating up now, the heat actually visible, wavering like rising curtains in the air — slowed down and bumped off the pavement and onto a dirt track. It led us up a slope, not very steep, toward some big rocks. Hey! I'd been here before. We often revisit places at the Little Detective Agency, just one of our techniques.

The track started looking more and more like the desert, and then you couldn't tell the difference anymore. Bernie stopped the car by a lone creosote bush, its branches all yellow with flowers. I loved the smell of creosote bushes, a sharp smell that cleared my mind like nothing else. And today my mind was clear to begin with! I took a deep sniff or two, making my mind clearer than clear, the clearest ever. Chet the Jet!

We started up toward the rocks, side by side, Bernie sweating almost right away in the heat — a lovely smell — and soon we were in the slot canyon or whatever it was, this narrow space with sheer rock rising on both sides. Bernie pulled himself onto the top of the flat rock at the end of the canyon — I was already up there, waiting for him, and glanced around. Nothing to see that hadn't been there before, namely the drawing on the cliff face with — what had Bernie said? — the sun and a guy dancing under it?

Bernie pointed at the guy in the drawing. "Upside down like that means they're dead." That was Bernie! Right there, thinking along with me. That made me feel great, so great I just about forgot that I had no clue what we were doing here, or where we were with the case, if it was a case.

Bernie was gazing up at the walls of the slot canyon, steep on the two sides, a little less steep at the end with the drawing. He walked here and there. I walked here and there with him.

"I expected —" he began, and at that moment I went still. "Something up, big guy?"

Beyond a doubt. Here, in the corner where one of the side walls met the end wall: cat. A smell I don't miss — take it to the bank. Not our bank, where we've been having problems with the manager, Ms. Oxley, but forget all that. The point is that a cat had been right here, not too long ago and not just any cat.

Before I'd even realized that this corner actually formed a sort of — not a trail, really, more like simply a doable scramble to the top — I was halfway up.

"Chet! What are you doing?"

And maybe some more like that, but I wasn't really listening, my attention focused on my back legs. When it comes to steep scrambles, all the push is from the back legs — maybe something you know already — with the front legs just marking the next set point and helping out with a bit of pull. It's all in the timing, of course — Bernie often talks about timing — and here's how I handle the timing: I don't even think about it. Pound, pound, pound, and the next thing I knew I was cresting the top of the wall, a whole avalanche of rocks and pebbles clattering down behind me. I looked back, and there was Bernie, hands over his head and running for cover.

Uh-oh. I started panting, not sure why. Certainly not from this quick little climb, over in a flash. Down below the cascading came to an end and Bernie moved back toward the base of the wall, unhurt. The panting stopped.

"Chet? You all right?"

All right? More than all right — I was feeling my very best. And at the same time, here I was at the tip-top of this ledge or cliff or whatever it was. I came very close to having an interesting thought.

"What's up there?"

I turned and started on a little recon or recoy or whatever it was, something that we at the Little Detective Agency always did in new places. Yes, I was standing on top of a cliff, but on the back side it sloped down gradually, open ground on one side and some enormous boulders on the other. I trotted along that line of boulders, a no-brainer — my favorite way of doing things

and one of the best human expressions going — on account of that was where the
scent took me.

You see these big boulders — much taller
than a man — out in our desert; Bernie has
a whole explanation about how they got
here, which I'll try to remember the next
time he brings it up. Once in a while a
boulder or two will have a small sort of shelf
cut into it, where you might find some
creature resting in the shade, a lizard, say,
or possibly a rattler or a diamondback — a
lesson I've learned in the past and hoped
never to learn again. So I wasn't surprised
to find a shelf in the face of one of those
boulders, and a creature lying in the shadows. But not a lizard, rattler, or diamondback: it was Brando.

Brando gazed down at me. I gazed up at
him. He yawned, a real big yawn. His teeth?
Huge for someone his size, and cat teeth
were amazingly sharp, another one of those
lessons I've learned and relearned. After a
bit, he closed his mouth and turned his
head away from me. That was infuriating. I
barked, my short, sharp, annoyed kind of
bark. No reaction from Brando. I barked
again, shorter, sharper, more annoyed. His
eyes closed.

His eyes closed? He was planning on taking a nap while I was down here barking my head off? Could I jump up to that shelf? No way. Somehow climb the rock? Too steep, straight up and down. No other ideas occurred to me. I sat down and shut up.

Brando's eyes opened. He slowly rose, kind of unfolding himself into a long stretch — he turned out to be a not-bad stretcher, I had to give him that — and came to the edge of the shelf and stared at me. I stared back at him. Then, still with his eyes on me, Brando began to — how to put it? — walk down that sheer wall. And not in any hurry! About halfway down, he uncoiled and came gliding to earth — somehow at his own speed and not at the earth's, if you get what I mean, and I actually don't. He landed without making the slightest sound or sending the tiniest vibration through the ground. Now if he yawned again, I was going to —

Brando didn't yawn. Instead he walked right past me, within easy pawing distance and no longer looking my way, and headed for a boulder farther down the slope. I — don't want to say followed, more like I walked behind him, just as though I happened to be going in the same direction. And the next moment, that was what I believed, pure and simple: Brando and I were on similar courses, total accident.

Our similar courses led us around the farther-down-the-slope boulder. On the other side stood one of those gnarly palo verde trees, the yellow kind, and sitting with his back to the trunk was Thad Perry. He looked real bad: shirt torn, feet bare and bloody, eyes red and glassy, lots of powder caught in the sweat on his upper lip, like a white mustache. He had a gun in his hand, and was using it to make markings in the dirt.

Thad looked up, saw Brando.

"Go 'way, Brando," he said, or something like that, his voice all messed up.

Brando lay down, curled up in a ball. Thad raised his gaze a bit, saw me. He blinked a few times, and then his gaze seemed to find me again.

"What the hell?" he said. He raised the gun, slowly and shakily, and pointed it at me.

Then, from farther down, came running footsteps, heavy and not very fast. I looked that way and saw Bernie pounding hard up the slope, all sweaty and dusty.

"Thad," he shouted. "No!"

Thad turned to him. The gun swung in Bernie's direction. Bernie kept coming. The gun wobbled a bit in Thad's hand and then he did something I'd never seen before or even imagined. He shifted that gun around and aimed it right at the side of his own head.

We didn't scare easily, me and Bernie, but we were scared now. I could see it on Bernie's face, and as for me, I was terrified, terrified for the very first time in my life, my heart beating so hard in my chest I almost couldn't stand it.

"Don't," Bernie said, closer now. "Nothing's that bad."

Thad, his eyes still on Bernie, said, "Fuck you. Fuck them all."

I was already moving, had possibly been moving from the moment Thad had drawn down on Bernie. I zoomed over a low cactus, got my legs under me, and launched myself. Thad saw me at the last instant, and then came a dust cloud, the crack of gunfire, and a shot ricocheting off a nearby rock. *KA-ZING!* I got a good hold on Thad's wrist, tasted his blood. He yelled something I missed and the gun fell to the ground. Bernie ran up and grabbed it.

"Let him go, big guy."

SEVENTEEN

And I was going to let Thad go, no question about it, if not now then real soon, but before I could, I felt a sharp jab in my side, too sharp to ignore. I spun around and there in the dust, back way up and teeth bared, stood Brando, his golden eyes full of hate. He hissed at me — that horrible hiss cats have in their repertoire — in case I was missing the point about how he felt about me. Guess what. I felt the same for him, or maybe even more so. Hot rage boiled up in me — kind of a great feeling, I admit it — and I lunged at Brando, snarling my fiercest snarl, the one where spit sprays out of my mouth. And then —

Ow. That hurt. And so quick! Brando had swiped one of his claws right across my muzzle? That was what must have happened — too fast to see, but I figured it out from the way he was poised in front of me, one paw raised, still hissing. I licked my muzzle, tasted blood, my own, and decided to think things over. Sometimes I thought better if I had more space. That was the only reason I backed up a bit.

Meanwhile, Bernie was kneeling on the ground, turning Thad over on his back. Thad's eyes were closed. Bernie stuck the gun in his belt and placed a finger on Thad's neck.

"Thad? You all right?"

Thad's eyes fluttered open, big, blue, empty.

"Thad? Say something."

His eyes stopped being empty, got unfriendly instead. "Fuck off," he said.

Bernie let him go. Thad wobbled, started to tip over, then stuck out his arm and caught himself.

"What are you staring at?" Thad said.

Bernie rose. "You've got coke all over your face," he said.

Thad wiped his face on the back of his sleeve, leaving a white smear on the material. He gazed at it, the look in his eyes changing from unfriendly to more like he'd just felt a pain inside.

"What's going on with you?" Bernie said. "What's the story?"

"Nothing," said Thad, eyes downcast. "Nada, zip, zilch."

Bernie pointed to the markings Thad had made in the dirt. "What about that — 'April Sorry'?"

Thad's gaze slowly shifted to the markings. Then, in a clumsy kind of way but not slow, he lunged forward, almost a fall, and rubbed out the markings with his hand, rubbing and rubbing wildly. After that, he turned to Bernie as though he'd just beaten him at something. Thad's eyes were amazing: they told so much all by themselves.

"You think I won't be able to remember 'April Sorry'?" Bernie said. Thad didn't reply. "Did something happen in April?"

Thad smiled, now lying facedown on the stony dirt. There was something horrible about that smile, hard to explain. "Yeah," he said, "something happened in April."

"What?" said Bernie.

"Spring came," Thad said. "All the blossoms, shit like that."

Bernie looked down at him. "I can help you."

"That's what everybody says," Thad said. "Everybody wants to do me favors."

"I didn't say anything about favors," Bernie said.

"Makes you unique." Thad pushed himself up, back into a sitting position.

"Think you can get up?" Bernie extended

his hand.

Thad ignored it. "When I want. When and if." At that moment, Brando glided forward and curled up in Thad's lap. Thad's hand moved, kind of on its own, if that makes any sense, and settled on Brando's furry back. Brando's eyes closed.

"You came up to see the rock carving?" Bernie said.

"Any law against that?"

"And what else did you have in mind?"

"Nothing. Nada, zip, zilch."

"Where'd you get the gun?"

"Sources."

"Jiggs, by any chance?"

"Don't pick on ol' Jiggsy — he's just doing his job."

"Giving you a gun's doing his job?" Bernie said. "I thought he was supposed to protect you."

"Think what you want," said Thad. He looked up at Bernie and maybe didn't like the expression on Bernie's face — although I sure did — because he said, "I've got this urge to paste you in the mouth."

"How did that work out the last time?" Bernie said.

Thad tilted up his chin. "I'm not afraid of you."

"Didn't say you were."

231

"Not afraid of anybody."

"That's hard to believe," Bernie said. "What about Manny Chavez, for example? Were you afraid of him?"

Thad's hand, which had been stroking Brando's back, went still. Brando opened his eyes. "Name means nothing to me," Thad said.

"How about Ramon? That ring a bell?"

Thad started stroking Brando again. "Sure," he said. "Ramon Novarro, silent star of the silver screen, although not my role model."

"Are you gay, Thad? Is that what this is all about?"

"Guess again."

Bernie shook his head and walked away. I walked with him.

"On your way to sell me out?" Thad called after him.

Bernie turned. "Sell you out?"

"Peddle me to the gossip rags," Thad said.

"Why would I do that?"

"For the money, for Christ sake. Are you stupid?"

"Must be it," Bernie said.

Huh? I was totally lost, Bernie always being the smartest human in the room. But for some reason, I wasn't angry at Thad, actually felt bad on account of all these things going on inside him, not including the fact that he was about to puke anytime now; I could smell it coming.

Meanwhile, Bernie was saying something about Thad's car. Thad pointed down the slope, off to one side.

"Who do you want to come get you?" Bernie said.

"Flights of angels," said Thad.

And then he leaned sideways — holding Brando as far away as possible — and got the puking out of the way.

"The choices," said Bernie, "are Felicity, Nan, or Jiggs."

Thad sat up straight, panting a bit. For a moment there was no color on his face at all. Brando rose, walked over to the tree, and lay in the shade, his eyes on me.

"That's a tough one," Thad said, color returning to his face in an uneven, blotchy kind of way. "How about I drive myself back?"

"No," Bernie said.

"No one says no to me," Thad said. "Not like that, just no, period. There's always a whole song and dance."

"I don't do that," Bernie said.

Huh? Maybe true about dancing — although one time Suzie had gotten him out on the dance floor at the Dry Gulch Steakhouse and Saloon, an event that had proven too exciting for me, so I'd had to wait outside in the car — but Bernie was a great singer, sometimes accompanying himself on the ukulele. "Mr. Pitiful," for example, was one of his very best.

"Felicity won't like my aura right now," Thad said. "And Nan might quit on me."

"Why would she do that?" Bernie said.

"She has standards."

Bernie nodded. "That leaves Jiggs."

"He'll be pissed at me."

"Pissed enough to quit?"

"Nope," said Thad. "Not Jiggsy."

"How come he's so loyal?" Bernie said.

"Ask him."

Bernie called Jiggs. Not long after that, Thad got to his feet. We walked down the hill and came to Thad's ride, a big SUV parked on a track at the far side of a dry wash. Thad climbed into the backseat and fell asleep. Brando sat in the front, licking his fur in a leisurely way that turned out to be bothersome, so I tried my hardest not to watch. Then less hard, and soon not at all. Nothing worked.

A little later, a Jeep appeared on the track and stopped a short distance from us. Jiggs got out and spoke to the driver. The Jeep turned around and drove away. Jiggs came walking up, one of those real big guys who swung a bit from side to side as he moved, like the ground was rocking under him. He glanced inside the SUV and said, "Sleeping like a baby."

"A wasted, strung-out baby," Bernie said.

Jiggs turned to him. "That's when he gets his best sleeps." He opened the front door, paused. "How'd you know where to find him?"

"A lucky guess," Bernie said. "Here's another guess — Thad didn't like it when he found out where they were shooting this movie."

"He's an artist," Jiggs said. "They're temperamental."

"There's more to it than that."

"Like what?"

"You tell me," Bernie said. "Start with whose side you're on."

"Thought you were supposed to be smart," said Jiggs. He lowered his voice, spoke in a new way, more like he and Bernie were friends, which I was pretty sure they weren't, kind of confusing. "We're family, for Christ sake."

"Family?"

"First cousins."

When Bernie gets surprised — which you

don't often see — one of his eyebrows goes up in a pointed arch. That happened now.

"Not widely known," Jiggs said, "and I'd appreciate you keeping it that way."

Bernie took the gun from his belt, held it out for Jiggs. "You came close to losing him today, cuz," he said.

Jiggs's throat bulged, like he was having trouble swallowing something big. Then his eyes filled with tears. Always strange when that happens with a real big guy. Jiggs took the gun, got in the SUV, and drove away. I caught a glimpse of Brando, arching his back in the side window.

I barked an angry kind of bark. I wasn't really angry at the way Brando arched his back, or even at Brando in general; it was more than that, hard to explain.

"Go on and bark, Chet," Bernie said. "I feel like barking myself."

Whoa! Was that really going to happen? We'd howled at the moon together, me and Bernie, but never barked. I kept up my barking for a long time, hoping he'd join in, but he did not.

We were out of the desert, stuck in traffic on the freeway, Bernie talking about some dude named Malthus turning out to be right — so maybe not a perp, since perps were always wrong in the end — and me scanning surrounding cars for any other members of the nation within, when Carla called. Her voice came through the speakers.

"Bernie? Do you know the old Flower Mart in Vista City?"

"Isn't it closed?"

"Yeah, but has it been mentioned at all in this Thad Perry thing you're looking into?"

"No."

"Okay. Just checking. Most likely a dead end."

"Carla? I really don't want you spending a lot of time on this."

"No problem, Bernie. I'm having fun."

Click.

We drove for a while, maybe headed nowhere in particular, something we got in the mood for now and then.

"Flowers are important, big guy," Bernie said after a while. "Women like flowers. Also chocolate. And what's the third thing?" He thought. So pleasant when Bernie was thinking. It couldn't go on too long for me. "Jewelry!" he said at last. "That's the third thing. But it's tricky. Big mistake to give the wrong one at the wrong time, for example. Remember when I gave Leda those chocolate caramels for her birthday?"

Yes, but I didn't want to.

"What the hell," he said. "Why not swing by the old Flower Mart?"

No reason I could think of.

"Goddamn rubberneckers," Bernie said.

I didn't know what rubberneckers were, just knew Bernie hated them. A long time seemed to pass before we left the freeway and crossed the bridge over the Vista City arroyo. I looked down — and so did Bernie; we often did the same thing at the same time, taking a pee, for example, no surprise, being partners and all — and saw two ragged guys arguing over a ripped trash bag with empty cans spilling out. Bernie reached over, gave me a pat. I squeezed across in his direction, just a bit, on account of there being some reason for not squeezing over too far when we were on the road.

"Chet!"

We swerved across the yellow line. Right, that was it. You learned something every day, humans said. And it was still light outside — plenty of time left for me to learn something else. Bring it on!

We took the ramp at the end of the bridge, went by the rail yard and a couple of bars with dusty windows, and came to a boarded-up brick warehouse. Bernie pulled into the parking lot. We had it to ourselves. The wind was rising now, a hot wind off the desert. It blew a brown, dried-out bouquet of flowers tied with a faded ribbon across the pavement.

"What if I sent Suzie some flowers?" Bernie said. "Or would chocolate be better? Jewelry?"

I waited to hear.

"And how come women like all those things more than men?" he said after a bit. "What's up with that?"

I forgot what I'd been waiting to hear before, began waiting for this new thing.

"Although," Bernie went on, "there's no denying that some guys like flowers big time. Take Monet."

Tricky Mickey Monnay? A scammer with a fake laundry business, as I recalled, something to do with selling used clothing to China, very hard to understand, and now sporting an orange jumpsuit, probably used by some other perp, kind of an interesting . . . something or other, but flowers? I didn't remember that part.

We got out of the car, walked into the shadow of the warehouse; this was recon, just one of our techniques at the Little Detective Agency. A faded wooden sign decorated with painted flowers lay on the ground. Bernie wiped away some of the grime on the sign with the sole of his shoe, exposing writing. " 'Vista City Flower Mart,' " he said.

We headed toward the end of the warehouse — Bernie kicking at the dead bouquet, me snatching it up to start a game of keep-away — and around to the other side. Nothing there but cracked pavement with weeds growing through, rusted old railway tracks, a few broken pallets, and a small blue Dumpster.

I dropped the bouquet.

"Chet?"

And hurried over to the Dumpster.

"Chet?"

Bernie came running up. "Please not," he said, raising the lid.

I got my paw on the rim, peered down. It was Carla. There was a thin red slit in her chest and her hair wasn't glossy anymore. I turned away. So did Bernie. We looked at each other, not at Carla, not at the big dark pool of blood starting to dry on the Dumpster floor.

EIGHTEEN

Metro PD came, sirens wailing, the wails colliding and recolliding, very hard on my ears. Talk went back and forth, all about different kinds of knives. I didn't feel like hearing that kind of talk — or any, really — so I walked around the warehouse to the car out front and hopped in, actually almost not getting high enough, having to scramble the rest of the way with my back legs. Kind of weird, like I wasn't myself. Bernie joined me a little later. We sat.

"Not sure who to trust, big guy," Bernie said.

Me! He could trust me, of course, take it to the bank, bet the ranch, in spades. That was the way I trusted him. We were partners, something I'm sure I've mentioned before, but it's worth mentioning again. Bernie glanced over at me and smiled a quick little smile, there and gone. I didn't know why, but it was nice to see.

Rick Torres drove up in an unmarked car and parked cop style, driver's-side door to driver's-side door, the way we did at Donut Heaven, only this was different — hard to say why, but it wasn't just about the complete lack of doughnuts, Danishes, or bear claws, to name a few of my favorites.

"The victim was a friend of yours?" Rick said.

Bernie nodded. "Carla worked with Suzie at the *Tribune.*"

"Does Suzie know yet?"

"I'm gearing up to make the call."

Rick had dark eyes. When he was looking at you, they seemed friendly. From the side, the way I was seeing them now, they seemed watchful.

"Sorry for your loss," he said.

"Thanks," said Bernie.

"Bad time to talk, I know," Rick said.

"Go on."

"Maybe you can help me out a bit, Bernie. Get in front of things."

"What things?"

"The fact that this is the second stabbing homicide you've reported in just about as many days, for starters."

"Can't help that," Bernie said.

"Maybe not," said Rick. "But questions are going to be asked."

242

"Like what?"

"The obtuse thing won't work on me, Bernie."

The obtuse thing? A complete mystery, but it had come up before, Leda often telling Bernie it didn't work on her, either. Bernie got a hard look on his face, the same as though Leda had just said it. Was there something alike about Rick and Leda? A brand-new thought, but it showed no signs of taking me anywhere.

"First off," Rick was saying, "the downtown boys will want to know if the two killings are connected."

"Not that I know of," Bernie said.

"Yet," said Rick. "You left off the yet."

Bernie didn't answer.

"Was Carla working on the Manny Chavez murder?" Rick said.

"She never said."

"What were you meeting about?"

"She hadn't told me."

"Why here?"

"I don't know."

"Did you have any reason to believe she was in danger?"

"No."

"Then what prompted you to check the Dumpster?"

Bernie glanced at me.

Rick nodded. "Of course." He gave me a smile. "Good work, Chet, as usual. Too bad you're not in charge."

I wasn't in charge? Something to think about, maybe later. Right now the ambulance and the cruisers came driving out from behind the warehouse, lights turning and flashing but sirens off. Sirens off meant they weren't really in a hurry.

Rick started his car. "Hope you know what you're doing, Bernie," he said. "But . . ." He shook his head and drove off.

Bernie watched him go. In the very quiet voice he uses for talking to himself, he said, "I'm trying to protect you, you son of a bitch."

Son of a bitch? Did that mean me? He was trying to protect me? I'd thought it was Rick. Couldn't have been me — what did I need protecting from? Weren't we the ones who dished it out, me and Bernie?

He picked up the phone, punched a button, took a deep, deep breath. "Suzie?" he said. "I've got bad news."

"Bicicleta," Bernie said.

Back home, in the garage. The garage was where we kept the van we used for times when Bernie said the Porsche would be a bad idea, plus all kinds of other stuff,

244

including Bernie's beer can collection from the army, and Charlie's bike, hanging on the wall, nice and shiny, with lovely streamers dangling from one of the grips; the other grip had had streamers, too, until recently. What had happened to them? I had hardly the slightest idea.

Bernie picked up the bent and rusty kid's bike that we'd found in Manny Chavez's yard and leaned it against the wall.

"Belongs to Nino, Manny's kid, but no one claimed the body," Bernie said, dusting off the seat, a little puff of dust rising like a wave and turning silver in the light from the window. "And the bike being in such bad shape, abandoned even in a neighborhood like that, makes me think Nino and Manny hadn't been together in some time." He found a rag and an oil can, started cleaning up the bike. Soon the tools came out and the bike was all in pieces. It got very quiet in the garage. I curled up on a tarp. Bernie worked on Nino's bike until it was time to go to the airport and pick up Suzie.

The terminal doors slid open, and out came Suzie, towing a little red suitcase. Oh, poor Suzie! Her face had no color at all, and her dark eyes, which usually sparkled like the countertops in our kitchen, looked huge and unseeing at the same time. Bernie jumped out of the car and held her. A state trooper moved toward them, ticket book in hand, saw how Suzie's shoulders were shaking and backed away.

"It's my fault," she cried, tears spilling down her face. "If I hadn't —"

Bernie's hands, big and strong, squeezed Suzie's arms so hard it had to hurt. She went silent.

"That's crazy talk," he said, looking her in the eyes. "And even worse, it gives whoever did this some moral wiggle room. That's sickening."

Suzie's tears didn't stop, but she got the sobbing part under control, nodded, and climbed in the car. After that, she seemed to pull herself together pretty quick, which was our MO at the Little Detective Agency — kind of a strange thought, since Suzie wasn't part of the Little Detective Agency, which was just me and Bernie and always would be. So I forgot all that, whatever it was, and tried to make myself comfortable on the tiny shelf behind the two front seats, not easy for a hundred-plus-pounder. Did some gnawing at the back of Suzie's seat go on? Hardly any at all, not worth mentioning.

"I could stay at a hotel," Suzie was saying.

Bernie turned to her. "Is there something about Washington that makes everybody stupid?" he said. "You're staying with me."

That night, we all went into the office and Bernie got busy at the whiteboard. The whiteboard always starts off completely blank, not a mark on it, which is how I like it best. First, Bernie drew two houses. I had no problem with that. "Two houses across from each other on North Coursin Street," he said.

"Bad neighborhood," said Suzie.

Exactly. I couldn't have been following this any better.

"Manny Chavez gets killed in this one," Bernie said. "And over here is the mother and the girl who ID'd the bike, both of them now supposedly back in Mexico." *Squeak squeak:* he made more marks with the felt pen. Those squeaks, plus the smell of the pen, both pretty interesting. I felt the thread slip-slipping away.

"After Luxton's visit?" Suzie was saying, or something like that.

Bernie nodded.

"I don't understand this at all," Suzie said.

Bernie drew some arrows. "Floyd, the redhaired cop, is some kind of source for Luxton."

"I get that. But why does it have anything to do with Carla? What if there's no connection?"

Bernie added some boxes, a few inside other boxes. The whiteboard got blacker and blacker. Soon Bernie might have a pen mark on his face.

"Jiggs gave that wad of money to Manny Chavez," Bernie said at last. "That's the connection."

I tried to remember that — and sort of did! From there, it was a real short step to getting the feeling that we were on a roll. What a nice feeling, exciting and relaxing at the same time! I gave it all my attention. Sometime later I grew aware of pen marks on Bernie's face.

We went to the funeral. I'd been to a funeral before, namely the funeral for the one kid we'd found too late. That broom closet: I wanted never to think about it, but how often it came sneaking into my mind, setting up camp in a back corner before I even knew what was happening! Forget all that, even if I can't. The point is, I'd been to a funeral and knew the drill.

For example, sitting quiet and still was important. I sat still and quiet between Bernie and Suzie in a middle row, the grass soft and thick like a putting green. In front, a woman in a sort of robe was giving a talk. I'd been to a talk before, the time Bernie spoke at the Great Western Private Eye convention, but this seemed different, although one thing they had in common was that no one laughed. In fact, everybody was sad. A whole bunch of humans all being sad at once is something that presses down on you, like the air has gotten real heavy. I stuck close to Bernie. Another thing the two funerals had in common was that Bernie wore a tie to both, the only times I'd ever seen him in a tie. It was his only one, plain black. Bernie was sad, too, but also angry. I could see it in this little muscle that bulged over his jaw once or twice.

I watched the woman in the robe for a while and then shifted my gaze to the hole in the ground — a hole with very neat, squared-off edges, not the kind I'd dig. Beside the hole a long gold-trimmed white box, pretty much the same size as the hole, rested on a stand. It wasn't one of our real bright Valley days; the sky kind of hazy, the way it can get when dust storms are on the way, but a ray of sunshine appeared and caught the gold trim. Carla was in that box, something I knew for a fact. All of this so far was like the other funeral, the one for the kid, except the box was bigger. Also, Bernie hadn't been angry that time. We'd gotten rid of our anger the night before, when we'd caught the perp and done what we'd done. I lay down and curled up — aware of the voice of the woman in the robe, plus also some soft crying now and then — and kept my eyes on Bernie. Was he restless? Maybe; he did a lot of looking around.

After, there was lots of talking in low voices, some hugging, a few handshakes. We met Carla's mother and father, both big and strong, although they clung to each other like they were about to fall down.

"You're the gentleman who found our daughter?" said Carla's father. He had one of those very deep, rumbly voices that did nice things far inside my ears.

"I am," Bernie said. "May I ask how you knew that?"

"The officer told us." He turned to his wife. "What was the name of that nice officer?"

"Stine," said Carla's mother. "Lieutenant Stine." She looked at Bernie in the way humans do when they want someone to say something, but Bernie did not.

"You're a private detective, sir?" said Carla's father.

"I am," Bernie said. "And also a friend of

Suzie's."

"Which was how you knew our . . . our daughter?" Carla's father said.

"Yes."

He squeezed his wife's arm. "I just don't understand," he said. "How could anyone harm a hair on the head of a person like . . . like her? It's impossible." I could feel his voice through the ground under my paws. One other thing: there were worms in that hole. The smell is hard to miss.

Out in the parking lot, Bernie was watching two women standing by a car, both of them wiping away tears.

"Know them?" he said.

Suzie didn't answer. Her eyes had an inward look, way down there and not happy.

Bernie touched her shoulder, and said, real gently, "Know those women, Suzie?"

Suzie's eyes cleared, like she was slowly waking up. She glanced at the women, shook her head. "Maybe friends of Carla's, but the only ones we had in common were in the business."

Bernie was giving Suzie a careful look. He reached into the Porsche, handed her a bottle of water. "Wait here," he said. "You, too, Chet. Sit."

I sat, no problem. Suzie leaned against

the car, opened the water bottle, and tilted it up to her mouth. She took a sip, then all of a sudden was drinking and drinking, sucking the water from the bottle until it started crumpling in on itself.

"How did he know I was so thirsty?" she said.

Or something like that. I appeared to be no longer quite beside her, no longer sitting, to tell the truth, but on my way to Bernie; actually pretty much there, by his side, which is where it just so happens I feel my best.

". . . and was just wondering," he was saying to the two women, "if you were friends of hers."

The women nodded. They glanced at me at the exact same moment I was opening my mouth to the max, then quickly back to Bernie.

"Had she mentioned me to either of you?" Bernie said. "Possibly about setting up a meeting?"

One of the women shook her head. The other said, "Not me. You're a detective?"

"Private," said Bernie, "formerly of Metro PD. Did she get in touch for any reason recently?"

The women looked at each other. "Last time I spoke to her was at your baby shower," one said.

"Same," said the other. She turned to Bernie. "That was back in May. What's this all about? Are you trying to find out who killed her?"

"Yes," Bernie said. "I think some old friend of Carla's, maybe going back to high school or even before, might have information."

"That's not us," said one of the women. "We both came here from Atlanta after college."

"But remember that ball game?" said the baby-shower woman.

"Where Carla got those good seats?"

"Right. What was the name of that girl —"

"— who drank too much beer?"

"Yeah, blonde with the ponytail. Wasn't she an old friend of Carla's?"

Bernie glanced around the parking lot. "Did you see her today?"

"No," the women said.

"Do you remember her name?"

"Donna, maybe?"

"Dinah?"

"Dina. It was Dina, I'm sure of it."

"Last name?" Bernie said.

"Sorry," said the women. "But," added the baby-shower woman, "didn't she work in a bar?"

"That's right. She handed out those two-for-one coupons."

"Did she mention the name of the bar?" Bernie said.

"Not that I recall," said the baby-shower woman.

"But," said the other, "I bet I still have that coupon."

"Yeah?" said Bernie. "When was the ball game?"

"Summer before last. But I'm a hoarder."

The baby-shower woman laughed, a tiny laugh, hardly a sound at all, but nice to hear. Her friend unlocked the nearest car, opened the glove box. Lots of stuff came spilling out. She sorted through it. "Here we go," she said, and handed Bernie a slip of paper.

NINETEEN

"Let's eat," Bernie said. We were back in the car, Suzie riding shotgun, me on the shelf, not good, but I wasn't thinking about that. Or anything, really. All I knew was that the farther we got from that hole in the ground, the better I felt.

Suzie glanced at Bernie, eyebrows rising, like he'd surprised her. "You feel hungry?" she said.

"Not at all," said Bernie. "But one thing I've been learning in this job" — Did his head make a quick little motion in my direction? — "is you've got to keep doing the normal routine."

Suzie thought that over, nodded her head. But what was there to think over? Eating had to be the most normal move out there, maybe even better than normal. As for Bernie not being hungry, that was the only part I didn't get. I myself was famished. What had I eaten so far today? I couldn't remember a single morsel, except possibly a bit of kibble, and maybe a biscuit on top of that. A Rover and Company biscuit, yes, best biscuits in the Valley — and wasn't it about time for a revisit to their test kitchen? — but this biscuit, even if there'd been one, had been on the smallish side. Biscuits came in different sizes. What was the point of that?

"How does Burger Heaven sound?" Bernie said. "Chet — easy!"

Here's a valuable piece of information, something I never forget: there's more than one Burger Heaven in the Valley. In fact, there are lots. What a business plan! Suppose, for example, that the Little Detective Agency . . . something or other, a great thought turning into a dust pile just before I could get there. Sometimes at night when I fall asleep there are several of those dust piles in my mind; then, when I wake up, presto! — as Bernie once said when he thought he had the garage door opener all fixed, and the chain did work perfectly after that, so maybe the door falling off wasn't important — all dust piles gone, and back to feeling tip-top.

In no time at all, we'd pulled into a Burger Heaven. This was a particularly nice one, with a smooth, recently paved parking lot and fresh-painted white lines — those smells, tar and paint, sharpening my appetite like you wouldn't believe, plus a pretty yellow plastic picnic table, which was where we sat. Bernie had a cheeseburger, Suzie a chicken salad, and me a plain burger with no bun. Trucks roared by on the freeway, which was raised up above us in this part of town. I loved picnics.

". . . didn't quite catch that," Bernie said, sipping his soda. "Can you speak up?"

Suzie raised her voice. "I said I want to help."

"When do you have to be back in DC?" Bernie said.

"Don't worry about that."

"Sounds like a plan."

That Bernie! Right every time, just about. Not worrying was the best plan there was.

". . . meaning the next step," he was saying, "is paying a visit to —" He took out the bar coupon. "— Red Devil's Bar and Grill."

Suzie shook her head. "I want to help," she said. "Not tag along."

What did that mean? Not too sure. Bernie and I tagged along with each other all the time, no problem. I polished off what was left of my burger, then did a bit of exploring under the table. And what do you know? An onion ring, perfectly round, completely undamaged, even still slightly warm.

Up above, Bernie said, "Tell you what. How about looking into that flower warehouse?"

"For what?"

"Any connection it might have to Carla."

"How about a connection to Thad Perry?" Suzie said.

"Yeah," said Bernie. "That, too."

Then came a silence. Under the table, Suzie moved her foot, resting it on top of Bernie's. I tried not to do anything about that for the longest time.

We've got bars out the yingyang in the Valley. You name it. For bikers, how about Greasy Steve's? Steve's a buddy, and yes, pretty greasy, a plus as far as I'm concerned. Greasy Steve's is at one end, sort of the watch-your-back end of Valley bars. At the other end is Amadeus, where Bernie started laughing when he saw the bill. He figured someone was playing a trick on him, and then — maybe he'd had one too many, but Bernie with one too many in him is even Bernier than ever, if you get what I mean, although I'm not sure I do, and in any case I don't want to remember what happened next, the part with the maître d' who turned out to be wearing a wig and all that, a wig that came from Paris and got added to the bill, which made Bernie laugh harder, and then came the bouncers. The point is that Red Devil's was somewhere in between those two ends, maybe a bit closer to Greasy Steve's.

We walked in, Bernie taking off his funeral tie and stuffing it in his pocket. The floor felt sticky under my paws. Yes, closer to Greasy Steve's. Red Devil's had a few rickety-looking tables and a pool table on one side — don't get me started on pool balls, so hard and slippery, plus the sticks were way too long for any kind of fun play, although they made good weapons in the hands of a certain sort of human, Jumbo Ogletree, for example, now breaking rocks in the hot sun — and on the other side a long bar with a mirror and lots of bottles.

There was no one inside except the bartender, a woman with not too many tattoos for a bartender, her blond hair, the faded kind, in a ponytail. She looked up from a magazine as we approached.

"Is that a working or therapy dog?" she said.

"Yes," Bernie told her.

"That's the only kind management allows in here."

"I understand."

"How come he's not wearing his ID vest, you know, that says therapy or working right on it?"

"Chet's undercover," Bernie said.

No problem. We'd worked undercover before, including once when Bernie pretended to be blind. I'd had some seeing-eye training — this was before my days in K-9 school — seeing-eye training that ended a bit the way K-9 school ended, now that I thought about it, but I didn't want to think about it, the point being I could work undercover, although Bernie didn't show any signs of blindness at the moment — no stick, no shades — probably a good thing since that other time he'd pretended so well he fell off the balcony at the Ritz. Bernie: to the max. You just had to love him.

"That's some kind of joke, right?" the bartender said.

"Not if you didn't laugh," Bernie said.

The bartender gave him a long look, then said, "What can I get you?"

Bernie laid the coupon on the bar.

She squinted down at it. Humans never looked their best when squinting, and she was no different. "That's no good anymore," she said. "It's from, like, years ago."

"Me, too," Bernie said.

Now the bartender did laugh, kind of a

surprise. "Nice try," she said, and ripped up the coupon, tossing the scraps behind her.

Bernie laughed, too. He took out some money. "What's on tap?"

"I'm partial to the Andersonville," said the bartender.

"Sold," said Bernie. "And one for you."

"Strictly against the rules," she said. But she filled two glasses from the tap.

"Cheers," said Bernie. I always liked when he said that: just saying it made him seem more cheerful every time — you could tell from his eyes. "I'm Bernie Little."

"Dina," said the bartender.

"Nice meeting you, Dina," Bernie said. "And this is Chet."

"Short for Chester?" said the bartender.

Whoa! Not the first time I'd heard that one. Why couldn't I be Chet, pure and simple?

"Just Chet," Bernie said.

"Nice name," said Dina.

"Agreed," Bernie said. "Can't take any credit — he had it when I got him."

News to me, and of an interesting kind. Did it mean that someone else . . . A thought rose quickly in my mind, zipping through the clear part into the fuzzy part and then up, up, and out of reach, just like every bird I'd ever chased.

Bernie took a sip of beer. Dina tilted back her glass, drained quite a lot of it. He watched her over the rim of his own glass.

"You a baseball fan?" Bernie said.

"That's a funny question," Dina told him. "Not really."

"How come?"

"You some kind of sports nut?"

Bernie thought about that. "Maybe a bit," he said. "Ever go to a game?"

"In my life? Sure. Why — you got tickets?"

"That's a bit of a problem at the moment," Bernie said. "Something happened to my source."

"Oh?" said Dina. "Like what?"

"She was a reporter," Bernie said. "They're always getting tickets."

Dina, raising her glass to drink, paused in mid-motion; a tiny wave of beer rose up and almost slopped over. Bernie saw it, too: I felt a little change in him, a change I'd felt before, hard to describe. But I knew what it meant. We were starting to cook. Not actual cooking, of course, and I wasn't even hungry, what with our picnic at Burger Heaven being so recent; although Cheetos were nearby — out of sight just on the other side of the bar, very close to my nose — and who didn't always have room for a Cheeto?

262

"A reporter for the *Trib*," Bernie went on. "Her name was Carla Wilhite."

Dina lowered her glass and set it on the bar, slow and careful. Then she raised her eyes up to Bernie's, eyes that hadn't really been friendly from the get-go and now were cold.

"A lot of her friends showed up at the funeral," Bernie said. "Not you."

"I don't know what you're talking about," Dina said.

Bernie took out our business card, laid it on the counter. This was our new business card, the one with the flower, designed by Suzie. We were living with it for now.

Dina glanced down at the card, said nothing. For a moment, I thought she was going to rip it up, just like the coupon, but she didn't.

"Carla was a friend," Bernie said. "So we'll never stop working on this, not until we nail the killer and anyone else involved, no matter how peripheral."

Dina met Bernie's gaze, her face real stony. Then she crossed her arms. Humans sometimes did that when they weren't going to say one more word.

I barked, one of those barks that just sort of come out on their own, a loud, harsh bark. Did it take everyone by surprise?

263

Certainly Dina, who jumped back a bit; and also me.

Dina didn't look so stony anymore. She put her hand over her chest. "Oh, God, this is so awful. I couldn't believe it when I found out."

"How did you find out?" Bernie said.

"On the news," Dina said. "We were friends when we were little, in the same class."

"So how come you weren't at the funeral?"

Dina opened her mouth, closed it, tried again. "I wimped out," she said. "I just can't stand funerals."

Bernie didn't say anything. Silence: one of those silences that seemed to grow, if that makes any sense, probably not, but the point is most humans can't let them go on for long.

"And also our friendship was only for a year or so," Dina said. "Carla was real smart. She got into one of those magnet schools on the west side and we lost touch. I haven't seen her in years and years."

"Except for the ball game," Bernie said. "Where you handed out the coupons."

Dina glanced down at the floor, where she'd tossed the scraps. "Right, the ball game. A total coincidence — she was doing a story on the microbrewery on Airport

Road and I was pouring. She had these box seats — from one of the radio stations, I think. I went. We had fun. And that was the last time I saw her."

"So that must have been when you told her about Thad Perry," Bernie said.

"Thad Perry?" Dina said. Although she didn't say it right away, more after a moment or two, the time it took her to lick her lips. "The movie star?"

Bernie nodded. He was a great nodder, if that hasn't come up yet, had all kinds of different nods. I'd seen this nod before — not a friendly kind — mostly when we were dealing with perps.

"I don't understand," Dina said.

"Dina," Bernie said. "Maybe you weren't listening. We're going to roll up every single person involved in Carla's death, no exceptions."

"Bullying won't make me understand," Dina said.

Bernie's voice rose. "You think this is bullying?"

Dina blinked as though tears might be on the way, but her eyes stayed dry. "You're making a mistake," she said.

Bernie spoke more quietly. "Are you saying you didn't tell Carla at the ball game — or at any other time — that Thad Perry was from the Valley?"

Dina spread her hands. "My God, no."

"Or had spent time here?"

"No," Dina said. "I don't have a clue what you're talking about."

Bernie tilted up his chin, gave her a long look from that angle. I loved when he did that, although what it was all about remained a bit of a mystery.

"How about the old Flower Mart in Vista City?" Bernie said.

"What — what about it?"

"That's where we found Carla."

"I know. It was on the news."

"And?"

"And?" said Dina.

"What do you know about it?"

"Isn't it closed down?"

"Yes. What else?"

She shrugged. "Nothing else. I've never been there in my life."

"Did Carla have any association with it?"

"I have no idea."

Bernie took a step back. "Okay, Dina," he said. "You've got my card," He made a little clicking sound in his mouth, meaning we were hitting the road. The interview was over? Kind of a surprise, but Bernie was a great interviewer, one of the best things we had going for us at the Little Detective

Agency. I brought other things to the table.

We moved to the door. Bernie stopped and turned, so I did, too. Dina was watching us.

"The name Ramon mean anything to you?" he said.

"Not especially," said Dina. "It's just a name."

We walked out of Red Devil's, took a few steps and stopped again, this time looking back through the window. Dina was grabbing a bottle off the shelf.

TWENTY

We were pulling away from Red Devil's when the phone beeped. Bernie had tried some ring tones — the Foggy Mountain Breakdown banjo thing was his favorite for a long time, the longest time, in fact — but now we were back to the beep.

"Bernie!" Leda said. "Charlie got his call!"

"Call?" Bernie said.

"To the set! Come on, Bernie — don't sound so out of it all the time."

There's a red button Bernie presses when it's time to end a call. His finger shifted toward it.

"Aren't you excited?" Leda said.

"Excited?"

"For Charlie! He's your son."

"Goddamn it, Leda, I know he's —" Bernie shut himself up, got a grip. When he does that, his jaw bulges like he's lifting something heavy; once in a while, something jumps or twitches in the side of his neck, too. Like now, both together, bulge and twitch. I never liked seeing both together. Press the red button, Bernie, press the red button! But he didn't. Instead, he lowered his voice and said, "Is Charlie excited about it?"

"He's practicing his signature for when he has to sign the contract," Leda said.

Bernie smiled. "Okay," he said. "See you there."

He pressed the red button, way too late as far as I was concerned, and turned to me. "Onetime thing — can't see the harm."

Bernie was quiet all the way home, and then, just as we turned onto Mesquite Road, he said, "We were terrible together, Leda and I, yet somehow we produced a kid like Charlie. Does that mean we weren't so terrible after all?"

What was he saying — that Charlie was a great kid? I knew that already. The rest of it made no sense to me and blew away like bits off this and that flying out the trash truck when the trash truck dudes are in a hurry. And no time to think about it anyway, because an ambulance was parked next door to our place, not on old man Heydrich's side, but the other, over in front of the Parsons' place, where my pal Iggy lived.

"Whoa," said Bernie, slowing down and pulling into our driveway.

We got out of the car and just stood there, Bernie standing and me sitting, actually, side by side. How often have we done that? Lots, and it never gets old. Bernie watched the Parsons' front door, so I did, too. We're real good at watching, and watching pays off in our line of work, big-time. Then why were our finances in such a mess? We were good! Sometimes you had to try to make your mind not do things. I tried to make my mind not think about our finances ever again. It thought about our finances right away.

"I hope —" Bernie began.

The Parsons' door opened. Out came two EMTs, rolling old Mrs. Parsons on a stretcher. She had a breathing mask over her face — I knew breathing masks from this one time Bernie and I saved a kid from drowning; what a day that was! and who cared if the perp got away? especially since we collared him that night, a perp whose name was about to come to me, I could feel it — and tubes sticking out of her here and there. Mr. Parsons came stumping after them on his walker, trying to keep up and at the same time extending one hand, maybe wanting to touch Mrs. Parsons's wispy hair. He lost his balance, started to tip sideways. One of the EMTs reached out and grabbed him, saying, "Sir, please."

"But I want to come," said Mr. Parsons. "I want to ride with my wife."

"Sorry," said the EMT. "No room, no time."

The other EMT banged open the rear doors of the ambulance. They slid Mrs. Parsons inside, one of the EMTs jumping in after her, the other running around to the front and hopping up behind the wheel. At that moment, Iggy appeared in the Parsons' doorway. He paused there, his stubby tail up straight, his crazily long tongue hanging out. Iggy, my best pal! When was the last time he'd been outside? Long, long ago, back before the divorce, maybe even all the way back to when Bernie and Leda weren't fighting all the time. This was Iggy's big chance, and I knew Iggy: when a big chance came along, he grabbed it fast and never looked back. That mailman, for example, back in the long-ago time, who'd left his sandwich on the dashboard of the truck while he'd delivered a package across the street: what a great memory, Iggy with egg salad all over his face! The truth was I'd learned a trick or two from Iggy, back in the day.

But right now, Iggy wasn't grabbing his big chance. He lingered in the doorway, sniffing the air. He might not even have seen me. Then, still sniffing, he moved onto the brick walkway, sniff-sniffing his way along. The ambulance driver revved the motor and hit the siren. Iggy raised his head, saw the ambulance, began moving faster, at the same time making a little whining noise. The ambulance pulled away from the curb and started driving away. Iggy went *yip-yip-yip,* zipped around Bernie, who was about to collar him, ran right into the street, and took off after the ambulance.

"Iggy!" called Mr. Parsons.

But way too late. Iggy pelted after that ambulance, running faster than I'd ever seen him, impossibly fast, those short legs of his just a chubby blur. It took me practically the whole block to catch him.

And then it was like old times, the two of us zooming side by side, ears flattened straight back by our own wind: we were making wind, me and Iggy! Up ahead the ambulance slowed down a bit to roll through a stop sign. We came so close to catching up, but then — oh, no — a truck? Barreling down the cross street? Right at us? I swerved, swerved my very quickest, knocking Iggy sideways and off the road. The truck honked — one of those real blaring and angry honks — and blew by.

For a moment I got mad at Iggy because . . . because I didn't know why. I barked at him. He made another one of those whining noises — not like Iggy at all; where was the old *yip-yip-yip?* — and took off again after the ambulance, now just about out of sight. But did that stop Iggy? No. He ran. I ran beside him. Block after block — the ambulance long gone except for the smell of its exhaust — we kept going, Iggy panting a lot now, and also whining, out of our neighborhood, past the public school where Charlie could have gone for free — "What's wrong with public school?" Bernie asked Leda many times. "I went to public school and so did you." — and toward the freeway entrance ramp, all blocked up with a line of cars. Iggy came to a slowish kind of stop, then just stood there whining, even whimpering, if you want the truth, his stubby tail drooping down almost to the ground, the scrubby, littered ground you get beside freeway ramps.

Iggy sat down. He eased off on the whining and whimpering, took to full-out panting instead. A kid in the bumper-to-bumper line slid down his window and said, "Mommy, look at those doggies."

A woman inside the car craned her head. "They must be lost," she said. "I'll call animal control."

Animal control? Was that the pound? I had memories of the pound, not good. That biker: I'd thought we were friends. Maybe a story for another day, or possibly one I've been over already. In any case, no time now. I barked a low rumbly bark. Iggy sat. I tried the bark again, a bark which means time to split, loud and clear. He sat. I went over and gave him a nudge. The little bugger nipped me. I nipped him back, then gave him another nudge, this one meaning business. When he stopped rolling, he rose, gave himself a good shake, and started to follow me home.

We met Bernie coming the other way. He didn't say anything, didn't seem angry, just opened the door of the Porsche and let us in. We shared the shotgun seat, me and Iggy.

Back home, Mr. Parsons was stumping his way to a taxi, idling in his driveway.

"No need for that, Dan," Bernie said. "I'll go with you."

Mr. Parsons shook his head. "You're a good man, but waiting around hospitals is a killer. Wouldn't put you through it. If you really want to help, maybe you could look after Iggy till I get back."

"Of course."

Mr. Parsons turned to Iggy. "C'mere, little fella."

Iggy, limping a bit now, went over to Mr. Parsons. He bent over, one hand on the walker, and scratched Iggy between the ears. Very briefly, but a high-quality scratching, I could tell from the look in Iggy's eyes, pretty much nobody home. I wanted some of that.

"Be a good boy for Bernie here," Mr. Parsons said.

Iggy pushed against Mr. Parsons's leg.

"I mean it," Mr. Parsons said. "Need you to be a team player now."

Iggy stopped pushing, went still, let his tongue hang out. He gazed down at the ground.

Bernie helped Mr. Parsons into the taxi, folded up the walker, stuck it on the front seat beside the driver. Then he handed the driver some money and spoke a few words I didn't catch. Bernie tapped the roof. The taxi drove off. Iggy raised his head. For a moment, I thought he was about to take off again, but he didn't. Instead he sat down and watched the taxi disappear. No whining, no panting: he just watched.

Along about then, I noticed old man Heydrich — even older than Mr. Parsons,

Bernie said, although he didn't look it, trim and straight — watching from the edge of his property.

"Think he'll put his place on the market?" old man Heydrich said.

Bernie just stared at him.

"Be interesting to see what he gets in this market," said Heydrich. He turned and went back to his house, pausing on his way to pick up a fallen leaf, crush it up, and scatter the pieces.

"Come on, Iggy," Bernie said. "We've got some nice treats." Bernie headed for our house. I followed Bernie. Iggy followed me, but not in a quick way. He didn't understand treat?

Inside our house, Iggy sniffed around for a bit, then lay down under the kitchen table. Bernie reached up to the treat shelf — the very highest shelf in our kitchen — and took down two rawhide chews, the long, thin, tubular kind, just a wonderful design, in my opinion. He crouched down by the table and offered one to Iggy, but Iggy was zonked out, eyes closed.

"All tuckered out, huh, little guy?" Bernie said. "I'll just leave this here on the floor for when you —" He glanced over at me and said, "On second thought." Then he rose and put Iggy's chew back on the shelf. "Catch," he said, and tossed me mine, which I snatched out of the air no problem, and got busy with right away, but the whole time I was thinking about that strange on-second-thought thing Bernie had mentioned: What did it mean? Why bother? Why me? Those were my thoughts. They refused to come together in any way I could understand.

Bernie went down the hall to the office. I heard the pen squeaking on the whiteboard. And then, another sound, very faint, caught my attention, a sound coming from the street. Was it a sort of . . . yes: a *tick-tick-tick*. I trotted toward the long window by the front door, taking the remains of the chew with me, and looked out.

Tick-tick-tick: a car drove slowly by, that same dark car with darkened windows. The driver's side window slid down and the driver tossed out a match, leaving a tiny cloud of cigarette smoke hanging in the still air. I got a good look at that driver: a white-haired dude, not old like Mr. Parsons and Heydrich, maybe more like Bernie's age, his white hair kind of long. What else? Black eyebrows, a shiny stud in his ear, a narrow little mouth; and dark, liquid eyes. Then up popped the head of that huge member of the nation within, leaning into view from the backseat: the real gigantic dude with angry eyes and long, long teeth. I barked, forgetting about my chew, which fell to the floor. The big dude barked back, ferocious. I grabbed my chew, ran down the hall to the office, and barked at Bernie, forgetting the chew, which fell to the floor.

He turned from the whiteboard. "No way," he said. "You haven't even finished that one."

I listened for the dark car, heard the final fading away of its engine sound, and maybe the hint of one last bark.

The phone rang. Suzie, on speaker. "Bernie, can —" she began, and then, "what's he barking about? I can hardly hear you."

"I haven't said anything," Bernie told her.

"What?"

"I said — for God's sake, Chet, knock it off!"

I amped it down as much as I could.

"He's doing his chew strip thing," Bernie said. "What's up?"

"Can you come out to the old Flower Mart?" Suzie said. "There's someone I want you to meet."

Iggy was still asleep under the kitchen table. "Iggy?" Bernie said. "Iggy?" Iggy stretched

278

his stubby legs but didn't wake up. "I guess it's okay to leave him here," Bernie said. "Don't see what trouble he can get into with the kitchen door closed."

We went outside. No sign of the dark car with the liquid-eyed dude and his fierce buddy inside. We hopped in the Porsche. My chew strip thing? Meaning what, exactly?

"You're pretty quiet all of a sudden," Bernie said, giving me a look that was more than careful, maybe even a bit worried.

Hey! Had I come close to sinking into a bad mood? Chet the Jet: what was with you? I snapped right out of it, sat straight and tall, ears up, on the job and ready. Bernie laughed, not sure why, but what a lovely laugh. I felt tip-top.

TWENTY-ONE

It was the hottest part of the day when we got back to the old Flower Mart, and this was pretty much the hottest part of the year, all that heat making Bernie's Hawaiian shirt — he wore the one with the fiery volcanoes — kind of damp. Not a cloud in the sky, but no blue, either: instead it glowed a dusty, golden brown.

"I don't like that sky," Bernie said.

Then neither did I. I hoped that another one would come sliding across soon.

No sign of Suzie in front, so we drove around to the back. No Suzie, and also the Dumpster was gone. We stopped and got out. All the lower windows of the old Flower Mart were boarded up, and the door looked boarded up, too, but it opened and Suzie looked out. She gave us that little hooked finger motion that meant come. We went inside.

"What's up?" Bernie said.

He spoke in a low whisper, the low human whisper always clear as a bell to me, even from across a street. An odd thing about bells: easy to hear, no question, but their sound was sometimes so complicated, full of all these different parts separating and coming together, like *THA-roomp, tha-ROOMP*, that you couldn't really call bell ringing clear.

"How did you get in?" Bernie went on.

"Why are you whispering?" Suzie said.

Bernie laughed. "I don't know," he said in a normal voice.

I looked around. We were in a big, shadowy space with shafts of dusty light shining down through the upper windows, the floorboards all torn up, paint peeling off the walls, wires hanging from the ceiling high above.

"I heard a toilet flush inside and tried the door," Suzie said. "Turned out the boards weren't nailed to the frame."

"Because someone's been squatting in here?" Bernie said.

"You're sharp today," said Suzie.

She led us to the far end of the room, past a big pillar, down a set of dark stairs, and into a small room lit by a single, weak lightbulb hanging from a beam above. A small room — toilet and sink on one side, counter with a hot plate on the other, bed in between — and very neat, with the bed made, no wrinkles. The man sitting on it — a little old guy in a faded uniform — looked neat, too, hair cut short, face shaved, shoes freshly shined — a smell hard to miss. Another smell I was picking up: bourbon, a smell I'm very used to, and happen to like.

"Bernie, meet Mr. Albert," Suzie said. "Former caretaker of the Flower Mart."

Bernie gave Mr. Albert a close look, his gaze taking in the faded uniform. "Former Master Sergeant Albert," he said, "Korean War veteran and winner of the Bronze Star."

"Correct, sir," said Mr. Albert. "What service were you in?"

"Army," said Bernie. "Same as you."

"Overseas?"

"Yes."

"Combat?"

Bernie nodded. Mr. Albert extended his hand, a bony, spotted hand with lots of thick veins. They shook.

"Korea came before the Flower Mart, just sose you know," said Mr. Albert. "Before Korea was high school. Important to keep all these events in order."

"Mr. Albert was the caretaker here until it closed down," Suzie said.

Mr. Albert's eyes narrowed. "How d'you

know that?"

"You told me," Suzie said.

Mr. Albert shook his head, then glanced over at a bottle standing by the sink. The bourbon with the red label: sometimes Bernie bought the same kind.

"What did you do after the Flower Mart closed down?" Bernie said.

Mr. Albert turned to him. "What time is it?" he said.

Bernie checked his watch. "Three fifty."

"Military time is better," said Mr. Albert.

"Fifteen fifty," Bernie told him.

Mr. Albert nodded. Then he pointed to the dull-colored metal star on his chest. "How much for this?" he said.

"What do you mean?" said Bernie.

"How much will you give me for it?" Mr. Albert said. "What else could I mean?"

"I think you should keep it."

"Huh? Don't want it? You're telling me you already got one of your own?"

"No," Bernie said. I wondered why: could he have forgotten that he did have a star just like that, maybe a bit shinier, in one of the drawers in his bedside table? Barking started up in the little room.

"Hey, Chet," Bernie said.

Uh-oh. It was me. I put a stop to it at once, or almost.

"I had a dog once, name of Marshall," Mr. Albert said. "Not as good-looking as this one here, missing a leg, but I liked him fine." He glanced over at the bottle. "Mind reaching me that?"

"In a bit," Bernie said.

Mr. Albert looked Bernie in the eye. "You're a hard man," he said. "Hard men die, too, easy as soft."

"I know," Bernie said.

"I seen 'em die, like flies. Ever have a B-13 go off right over your head?"

"No."

"Happened to me," Mr. Albert said. "Keeps happening, too. My head's never been the same since."

Bernie picked up the bottle, handed it over. Mr. Albert didn't unscrew the cap, just held the bottle in his lap.

"Can you remember what happened after the Flower Mart job?" Bernie said.

"A whole lot of shit," said Mr. Albert. "Think I'd live in the shelter? Think again. I improvised my way back in here, wired myself up some juice, plumbed myself up some water, and hell with them all."

"Why not?" Bernie said.

Mr. Albert gave Bernie a long look. "Maybe you're not so bad." He turned to me. "This your dog?"

Bernie nodded.

"Got the dog, got the wife, you're on track," Mr. Albert said.

"We're not married," Bernie told him.

"What's the holdup?"

Bernie smiled, glanced at Suzie. She looked down. He stopped smiling.

"Life is short, never heard that?" Mr. Albert said. "B-13 goes off over your head and forget it."

"Some people's lives are shorter than others," Bernie said.

Mr. Albert sat back a little.

"Are you aware," Bernie went on, "that a woman was shot and dropped in your Dumpster the other night?"

Mr. Albert shook his head. "No, no, no," he said. "That was a long time ago."

Suzie started to say something, but Bernie made a tiny motion with his hand. "Tell me about it," he said.

Mr. Albert's fingers moved on the bottle. I thought about this blanket Charlie had had, back when he couldn't even walk yet — and what a shocker that was, seeing how long it took a human to get up and go, kind of basic, after all — and the way his tiny fingers would stroke it. Funny how the mind works.

"Long time ago," Mr. Albert said. "Very

285

hazy, like when the dust storm rolls in."

"Was this before the Flower Mart closed?" Bernie said. "Were you still the caretaker?"

"Oh, yeah, still the caretaker. They paid me . . . what was it? Three eighty-five an hour? Might have been . . ." His voice trailed off.

"It doesn't matter," Bernie said. "The point is —"

"What the hell?" said Mr. Albert, his voice rising and getting squeakier. "Wage they give a man don't matter? Ever gone hungry?"

"No."

"Damn straight. Then you'd know a thing or two, by God."

I myself had gone hungry, lots, in fact. For example, at that very moment a little something would have gone down nicely. I wanted to figure out the thing or two I knew from that, but there just wasn't time.

"I'm sure you're right," Bernie said. "But I'm getting the picture that even though you weren't getting rich, you were better off than at other times in your life."

"Yeah," said Mr. Albert, not so loudly now. "That's the picture."

"So," Bernie said, "back when you were making some money and the Flower Mart was still a going proposition —"

"Know what it smelled like in here?" Mr. Albert said. "Heaven."

Heaven. I'd heard of it, of course — it came up a lot in human conversation — but never been.

"Why did it shut down?" Bernie said.

"Forces. There are big forces at work in this world, case you haven't noticed."

"Like that night the woman ended up in the Dumpster," Bernie said.

"Exactly what I'm talking about, brother," said Mr. Albert. His fingers did that blanket-stroking thing on the bottle again. "Though you could barely call her a woman," he went on.

"I'm sorry?" Bernie said.

"A teenager's not quite grown-up, not in my book," said Mr. Albert. "And I should know — I was all of eighteen when that B-13 come a-calling. Blew up over my god-damn head and then there was blood all over. Not mine, my buddy's, which I didn't realize right away. Made no difference in the end. Don't expect anyone to understand that."

"What I'd like to understand," Bernie said, "is this story of the woman in the Dumpster."

"Not a story," said Mr. Albert. "It really happened. You can check."

"Where?"

Mr. Albert shrugged. "The records." He glanced down at the bottle. "Anything else for now? I've got to get back to my duties."

"I'll try to be quick," Bernie said. "First, are you telling me that two women have been killed and left in the Dumpster?"

"Two?" said Mr. Albert.

"I told you — they found a body in there two days ago."

"Two days ago? I'm talking about years and years."

"Where were you two days ago?"

"Here. This is where I am."

"Did the police come in the building?"

Mr. Albert shook his head.

"What about the sirens when they arrived?" Bernie said. "Didn't you hear them?"

Mr. Albert got a faraway look in his eyes. "I thought it was a dream," he said.

"It really happened," Bernie said. "A woman — a second woman, if I'm following you right, ended up in your Dumpster. She was a reporter for the *Trib* named Carla Wilhite."

"Not a teenager?"

"No."

"The one I knew was a teenager."

"You knew her?" Bernie said.

"Sure I did," said Mr. Albert. "I knew all the workers on the floor, even the part-time kids who came in on weekends."

"The girl was one of the part-time kids?"

"That's what I'm telling you. A pretty young thing, nice smile." Mr. Albert squeezed his eyes shut. "I can see her," he said. "Pretty young thing, name of April."

"April?" Bernie said. His voice didn't rise — went the other way, if anything — but it seemed to fill the room, even push against me, like the sound was taking up space.

Mr. Albert's eyes opened. "April something or other. But the April part's easy to remember." He paused for a moment or two, licked his lips. "It's a month."

"Who killed April?" Bernie said, tamping down that scary thing in his voice some; not scary to me, goes without mentioning — there was nothing scary between me and Bernie.

"Asking me?" said Mr. Albert. "I couldn't tell you."

Bernie reached out, not quickly, more like he was doing something he did all the time, and took the bottle out of Mr. Albert's hands.

"Hey," said Mr. Albert.

"Who killed April?" Bernie said.

"Already told you — I couldn't say."

289

"Why not?"

Mr. Albert gazed at Bernie. "Oh, good Christ — you think I'm the guilty party?"

"I'm not saying that," Bernie said. "I just want the facts."

"The facts?" said Mr. Albert. "Facts are scarce on the ground."

"What are you talking about?"

"Can't have facts if they never found out who did it."

Now Bernie got real quiet. "You're saying it's an unsolved crime?"

"The right way to put it," Mr. Albert said.

"Were there any suspects?" Bernie said.

"Couldn't tell you," said Mr. Albert. "All I know's what I told the detective."

"Which was?"

"What you already know — April was a nice girl."

"Who found the body?"

"Why, I did, of course — I'm the care-taker."

"You went out to put something in the Dumpster?" Bernie said.

"You're a smart one," said Mr. Albert. "Torn strip of insulation — the pink kind." He looked at Suzie. "And you, too, ma'am. Smart." And then at me. "Even the pooch here. So if you're lookin' to find out who killed April, then maybe you will."

"Who was the detective?" Bernie said.

"The name, you mean?"

"Yes."

"My apologies on that," said Mr. Albert. "But one thing I'm sure of — he had long side whiskers, like an old-time riverboat gambler. Also wore himself a tall Stetson."

Bernie handed him back the bottle.

"But it was a long time ago," Mr. Albert called after us as we climbed the stairs out of his little room. "So maybe you won't."

I heard a faint sound of metal on glass: that would be the bottle cap getting un-screwed.

TWENTY-TWO

In the car — me on the shelf, again, being very good about it, nice and quiet, nibbling from time to time at a tiny opening I'd made in the back of the shotgun seat, now occupied by Suzie, again — Bernie was talking fast, all about Red Devil's and sideburns and Thad Perry and April and lots of other stuff that flew by faster and faster, becoming pure sound, kind of like music, until Suzie interrupted.

"Bernie?" she said. "Can you take me to the airport?"

"Whoa," said Bernie, at the same time hitting the brakes, even though we were barreling down the passing lane in light traffic. Someone honked behind us. "Uh, I thought you weren't in a rush to get back," Bernie said.

"It's not that," Suzie said. "Well, maybe it is, partly." She went silent. Meanwhile, Bernie had slipped over into the most inside lane, the very slowest, where we never rode except when we were headed for an exit.

"And partly what else?" he said.

"This is hard to say," she said. "And maybe kind of stupid."

"I doubt that," Bernie said.

Suzie turned to him, a small smile crossing her face and vanishing fast. "And then you come up with something like that," she said. "Let's forget it."

"Forget what?" said Bernie.

But why bother? I was with Suzie on this one: immediate forgetting was often the way to go.

"What I just said," Suzie replied. "The whole thing."

"I don't understand," Bernie said. "You don't want to go to the airport?"

"Christ," Suzie said.

Uh-oh. Were they fighting? Was this some kind of fight between Bernie and Suzie? How could that happen?

There was a long silence. In the distance I saw the head of the huge wooden cowboy who stands outside the Dry Gulch Steakhouse and Saloon, a smiling cowboy with his big white hat tilted back on his head. He also had a six-gun in each hand, but that part was out of sight, hidden by some buildings. Were we headed to the Dry Gulch?

Seemed like a good idea to me, kicking back, having a little something, getting along. But when the exit ramp appeared, we kept going.

"You do want to go the airport?" Bernie said after a while. "Is that what I'm supposed to figure out?"

"You're good at figuring things out," Suzie said.

I got the feeling they were still fighting. That little opening in the leather seat back in front of me? It was growing. Some interesting-looking stuff in there. I tried to concentrate on it and block out everything else, normally a real talent of mine. But not right now, for some reason.

"I'm sorry, Bernie," Suzie said. "That was uncalled for. It's my fault."

"What is? I'm not getting this at all."

"Oh, hell," Suzie said. "Let's just say the *Post* wants me back ASAP and leave it like that. And it happens to be true."

"The part you're leaving out," Bernie said. "Spill it."

Suzie thought for some time and then nodded. "Okay, Bernie, and maybe you'll think it's petty." She sat up straight. "But I don't like being silenced."

"Huh?" Bernie said.

"My father did that to my mother all the

time," Suzie said. "I hated it."

"Did what, exactly?" Bernie said.

"This," said Suzie, and she made a small sideways chopping motion with her hand. "Whenever she was about to say something he didn't want to hear, he'd cut her off, just like that. And you did the same thing to me."

"I did?"

"Back at the interview with Mr. Albert, when he was starting to talk about the first murder."

"But it was a delicate moment, Suzie, and I sensed that —"

"And I can't handle delicate moments? Or sense things?"

"Of course you —" Bernie began in a calm voice, and then suddenly he got angry. "What the hell is with you right now?"

"It was demeaning," Suzie said.

"Demeaning? I'm trying to solve the murder of your goddamn friend."

I lay down flat.

Suzie made no response. From where I sat I couldn't see her face very well, but her neck flushed from the bottom up.

"Is this just an excuse?" Bernie said, his voice not so loud now, but very hard.

"For what?" said Suzie.

"For getting rid of me," Bernie said.

"Is that what you think I'm like?"

Bernie didn't answer. Suzie sat very straight, her neck pink.

Not another word was spoken driving home for her little red suitcase, or on the way to the airport, or when Suzie got out of the car in front of the terminal. By that time all the leather on the seat back was in shreds.

Bernie stopped at a store and bought a pack of cigarettes. It had been a long time since he'd bought an actual pack, not just bummed a smoke here and there. He came back, struck a match, and lit up. Hey! His hands were shaking. I'd seen that in all sorts of different humans, but never, ever in Bernie. He took a deep drag and leaned against the car, actually more like slumping against it. For a moment he seemed to have gotten smaller. I hated that.

"I'm not smart enough to figure this out, big guy," he said. "Not nearly."

Bernie not smart enough? Not possible, although what he wanted to figure out was unclear to me.

"Is it some sort of second-fiddle thing?" he went on. "How could Suzie ever think she'd be second fiddle to anybody, let alone me?"

I went from feeling unclear to totally lost.

Second fiddle? We didn't even have a first one, Bernie's instrument being the ukulele, which he played beautifully. "Dead Flowers," "Lonely Teardrops," and "Sea of Heartbreak" were some of my favorites: there's a woo-woo thing he does at the end of "Sea of Heartbreak" where I always join in.

"Who found Mr. Albert in the first place, after all?" he said. He took another drag. "Might have been a good idea if I'd worked that in somehow. But — hey, Chet, what's that all about?"

What was what all about? Uh-oh. The woo-woo thing? I was doing it now, by myself? I put a stop to that, and pronto. We drove home. Bernie seemed like he was back to his normal size.

There's a curve on Mesquite Road, and as you drive around it, our place comes into view. I always loved that sight, but now there was something I'd never seen before: Iggy standing in the long window by our door, front paws on the glass, and . . . and what was that in his mouth? Could it be? We pulled into the driveway. Yes: the ukulele.

And once we got inside the house and Bernie had snatched the ukulele out of Iggy's mouth? "Like a goddamn bomb went off," he said. "Didn't I shut him in the kitchen?" It took Bernie a long time to clean up. Meanwhile, I played with Iggy out on the patio. At first he was very thirsty, lapping up lots of water from the base of the stone fountain, something I'd often done myself. But a little later, he came up with something that had never even occurred to me, something completely new: he lifted one stubby rear leg over the lip of the basin, just clearing it, and peed inside. In all that time we'd been apart, Iggy hadn't lost a thing. You could learn a lot from friends.

It was getting dark when a taxi dropped off Mr. Parsons. He stumped up to the door and Bernie let him in.

"You're not one of those messy bachelors, I see," Mr. Parsons said.

"Um," said Bernie. "Ah. How's Mrs. Parsons?"

"Stabilized," Mr. Parsons said, "and thank you for asking. Also thanks for taking care of Iggy — hope he behaved himself."

"No complaints," Bernie said. "Iggy!" he called.

A moment or two passed and then Iggy appeared in the hall. He was chewing on . . . yes, a cigarette, but he swallowed it quickly, possibly before anyone else noticed. Iggy saw Mr. Parsons. Iggy was one of those tail waggers who pretty much wag with their whole bodies.

Night fell, and the air cooled down some. Bernie took out the bourbon, started to unscrew the top, then stopped, and placed the bottle back on the shelf. He went into the office and made some calls. I lay under the desk and let the sound of his voice wash over me, very relaxing. After a while, he put down the phone and said, "How about a walk?"

I was at the door. One of the great things about our place on Mesquite Road — wouldn't live anywhere else — is how we back right up on the canyon, pretty much wide open country, all the way down to the airport and up to Vista City. Bernie was opening the back gate when it hit me that while we'd taken a zillion walks in the canyon or even more, none had ever come at night. So: what a great idea! But that was Bernie.

He switched on a flashlight as we crossed the narrow gully beyond the gate and started climbing up the slope. Day or night doesn't make much difference to me, but it's a game changer for humans. They can't seem to see at all in the dark, and what's there to fall back on? Hearing? Smell?

Please. So it's no surprise to me that night-time is when humans tend to land in trouble. Don't get me wrong. I liked just about every human I've ever met, even some of the perps and gangbangers, but in my opinion they're at their best right before lunchtime.

We reached the top of the ridge — Bernie huffing and puffing a bit already? How could that be? — and soon came to the big flat rock. I walked across it, felt the heat of the day, still there. Sometimes the earth itself seems . . . a thought starting out on those lines almost got going in my mind.

No time for that. We walked along the ridge, then took the trail that led to the lookout, highest point on our side of the canyon, and one of our favorite places, what with its nice stone bench and view of practically the whole valley. A javelina had been this way, and not long ago. I went into my trot, cut across the trail and down the slope, then back up, the scent strong at first, then fading out. That happened sometimes, and the go-to play was to circle back and —

"Chet."

Maybe later.

We climbed to the top of the lookout and then came a surprise: a man, all shadowy, was sitting on the bench. Just as I was about to bark, I smelled who it was. I trotted over.

"Hey, Chet," said Rick Torres, giving me a pat. "Didn't hear you on the trail, not a sound." He turned to Bernie. "You, on the other hand, are one goddamn noisy hiker."

Bernie sat on the bench, stretched his bad leg. "Didn't want to sneak up on you," he said.

"Glad to hear that," Rick said. He wasn't in uniform, wore jeans and a T-shirt, but had a gun on him somewhere. It hadn't been fired, but it had been lubricated — I'd watched Bernie lubricate the .38 Special plenty of times — and grease is a real easy smell to pick up. There are actually many grease smells — pizza grease and human hair grease, to name two — something I hope we can get into later, unless it's happened already.

"Am I hearing a double meaning?" Bernie said, losing me completely.

"A funny place to meet, that's all," Rick said.

Hey! Were they not getting along? At the same time Bernie wasn't getting along with Suzie, either? What was going on?

Bernie looked at Rick for a moment, then turned his gaze to the faraway lights of the downtown towers. The lights were hazy and so were the stars, and I could see dust drift-

301

ing over the face of the moon.

"Wish it would rain," Bernie said.

"So does everybody," Rick said. "But is that why you brought me here in the middle of the night, to discuss our weather patterns?"

Bernie turned back to him, then took out his cigarettes and lit up.

"A whole pack?" Rick said. "That's a bad sign."

Bernie blew out a stream of smoke, all silvery in the moonlight.

"Truth is," Rick said, "you're pissing me off. Big-time."

Pissing. A huge subject. Where to begin? It was certainly something we'd done by the side of the road, me and Bernie, and more than once, but had there ever been any of that side by side stuff with me and Rick? Maybe something to look forward to.

"I know you, Bernie," Rick went on. "You want something from me, but you're hesitating to ask. Why? Possibility one: you're implicated in some shit and you're looking for an out. Meaning I'd get implicated, too, and that's just not you."

"Don't be so sure," Bernie said.

"Fuck you," said Rick.

Then they both laughed, a surprise to me: I'd been pretty sure they were about to

302

throw down. Quiet laughter, though, and it didn't last long.

"Possibility two," Rick said. "You don't trust me. And I can't come up with a possibility three. If it exists, let's hear it."

Bernie said nothing.

"There you go," Rick said.

Where? This wasn't easy to follow. In the not-as-far-as-downtown distance I could see the airport, the runways lit up, planes circling, landing, taking off, soaring away with blurred orange trails slowly dissolving behind them. The whole city hummed and muttered in the night like a living thing. A disturbing thought. I tried to forget it, couldn't, then tried again, and succeeded with whatever it was.

Bernie took a deep breath.

"Stop with the deep breathing shit," Rick said. "You saved my goddamn life — think I'd ever forget that?"

"Happened to be there," Bernie said.

"It cost you your job, asshole," said Rick.

Bernie shrugged. "Things worked out all right."

Well, of course: just think of the Little Detective Agency, for starters. Who was better? The Mirabelli brothers? Georgie Malhouf? Ha! But whoa. Bernie got canned on account of Rick? News to me. This felt like the kind of puzzle to take on from different angles, a project for later.

They sat in silence. Fine with me. I sat in silence, too. Rick gave me a little pat. Bernie smoked his cigarette down to practically nothing, then ground the practically nothing under his heel, ground it out extra-hard.

"I need a cold case file from Central Records," he said.

"In an informal sort of way," said Rick.

Bernie nodded.

TWENTY-THREE

"He's wearing eye makeup?" Bernie said.

"Bernie, please," said Leda.

We were back at the movie set, me, Bernie, Leda, and Charlie, all by ourselves in one of the trailers. Leda wore tight jeans, a tight little top, and lots of jewelry. Bernie was dressed like Bernie. I had on my brown leather collar — the black one's for dress-up, in case that hasn't come up yet. Charlie wore a sort of cowboy outfit — cowboy hat, cowboy boots, and one of those long duster coats. Bernie had one, hanging in the closet back home, a gift from Mr. Teitelbaum, who owned clothing stores, although not as many after the Teitelbaum divorce, a case I'll never forget. Mrs. Teitelbaum driving that earthmover right through the garage where Mr. Teitelbaum kept his antique car collection? And then back the other way? That kind of thing stays in the mind. It was also on that case that I first discovered kosher chicken, proving there's good in everything; one of my core beliefs.

But back to Charlie. There was no doubt that he was wearing eye makeup, dark and kind of purple. Also his face had whitish stuff on it, making him look pale, like he wasn't feeling well. Plus he seemed so small in that long duster.

"My son," Bernie said, "is wearing eye makeup."

"God almighty, it's for the camera," Leda said. "John Wayne wore eye makeup. Humphrey Bogart wore eye makeup."

"I don't believe it," Bernie said.

Charlie glanced up from a sheet of paper he was staring at. "I'm trying to memorize this."

"Memorize what?" said Bernie.

"His line," said Leda. "Why are you not getting this?"

All of a sudden it felt like old times. I preferred new times, especially if old times meant going back to the Leda days. In some ways — this occurring to me for the very first time, funny how the mind works — she was like Mrs. Teitelbaum. But unlike Mrs. Teitelbaum, Leda couldn't drive a stick — would I ever forget the time Bernie tried to teach her? — so the earthmover episode would never have happened to us.

"What's the line, Charlie?" Bernie said.

"Don't disturb him," Leda said. "He's internalizing it."

"Huh?" said Bernie.

"The artistic process is a complete blank to you, isn't it, Bernie?" Leda said. That tone: hard to describe, sort of like Bernie was one of those butterflies our pal Professor Bokov from the college gazes at through his magnifying lens. Once we worked a case that came down to a certain kind of butterfly; that's all I remember of it, except for Bernie losing the check on the way home.

"Artistic process?" Bernie said. "He's six years old."

Charlie, who'd gone back to gazing at the sheet of paper — his lips moving silently, an interesting thing you saw sometimes in humans, no time to go into it now — looked up again, paused for a moment, and said, "How can I concentrate in this atmosphere?"

Bernie's mouth fell open. When was the last time that had happened? For a moment, he seemed about to speak, but nothing came out. He turned and stalked out of the trailer, slamming the door after him, so hard the door opened again, good thing since now I could get out, too. We walked down the movie Western street and into the movie

307

Western bar. No one around. Bernie grabbed a bottle from behind the bar, twisted off the cap and drank, then banged the bottle down on the bar.

"Tea, for Christ sake. Cold goddamn tea."

Tea? And some had splashed down onto the floor? Water's my drink, but I didn't mind tea. I licked it up.

"Atmosphere?" Bernie said. "He said atmosphere? What the hell is going on?"

No clue, on my part. I wouldn't have minded if more tea got spilled. Bang the bottle again, Bernie! Keep spilling! And maybe he would have — there's no end to what Bernie can do — but at that moment the light, all of which was flowing in from the street, dimmed. I turned and saw Jiggs at the saloon doors. The doors swung open and Jiggs walked in, bringing the light with him.

"Trying to sneak in a quick snort?" he said, coming over to the bar.

Bernie slid the bottle toward him. "Help yourself."

Jiggs shook his head. "Not a tea drinker, myself." He sat on the stool beside Bernie's, pointed his chin at the bottle. "That's so the studio can tell the Wall Street boys how careful they're being with their money. Meanwhile, Lars gets his meals flown in every day from some restaurant he likes in Barcelona."

"And how about Thad?" Bernie said.

"How about him?" said Jiggs.

"What are his special requirements?"

Jiggs looked down at Bernie. "Not sure where you're going with that."

"Don't be so cautious — I've got no connections on Wall Street."

"You're just curious about his meals?" Jiggs said.

"Sure," said Bernie.

"He's a normal guy, eats normal food, like you and me."

"I'm partial to caviar, myself," Bernie said.

Caviar? A new one on me. Oh, wait, not quite. I came very close to remembering a party at the Ritz, possibly the Romanoffs' anniversary. What a nice old couple, and we'd brought their runaway daughter back from Reno for them safe and sound, and at that party had there been an icy bowl — on a sideboard but well within my reach — full of tiny round black glistening things, that didn't look like food but turned out to be . . . ? No. I couldn't quite remember.

"You're a funny dude," Jiggs said, although he didn't laugh. "A funny dude who's good with his fists. Don't see that every day."

"So?"

"So it's a kind of surprise," Jiggs said, "and I'm wondering what other surprises you've got in store for us."

"Who's us?" said Bernie.

"Me and Thad, who else?"

"You're very loyal to him."

"We're cousins — I told you."

"How does that work?" Bernie said. "Where's the family connection?"

"My mother and Thad's father were brother and sister."

What was that? Something absolutely impossible to follow, that was all I knew.

"Where was this?" Bernie said, meaning maybe he was somehow staying in the picture. That Bernie! I just loved him.

"Back in Kansas City," Jiggs said. "The whole family's from there originally."

"Where are they now?"

"Pretty much dead and gone."

"Any family connections here in the Valley?" Bernie said.

Jiggs gave Bernie a long look. "Nope," he said.

"How about old friends?"

"Nope."

"Mere acquaintances, ships passing in the night?"

"What are you driving at?"

"You tell me," Bernie said. You tell me:

one of my favorites! We've closed a case or two with Bernie's you-tell-me move; not actually closed, because that happens when I grab the perp by the pant leg, but just about.

"Got nothing to tell, my friend," Jiggs said. "You're barking up the wrong tree."

Whoa. Had I heard that one from the mouths of humans before? You bet, and it used to floor me every time, but finally I realized they just don't know much about chasing little critters, because what would be the point of barking up the tree where the critter isn't? No member of the nation within would ever do that. Plus after the critter's in the tree, it's too late for barking. And why bark when you're in chasing mode in the first place? Here I come, critter? What sort of technique is that? One more thing: humans don't bark. Except for Mad Dog Dutwiller, of course, a perp I never want to think of again, so I won't.

"Whatever you say," Bernie said. "As long as you're aware of your legal position."

Jiggs went still, but not the relaxed kind of still. One of the legs of his stool creaked, sort of on its own, if that makes any sense. "Legal position?" he said.

"Specifically relating to the statute of limitations," Bernie said.

"Lost me there," said Jiggs. "Kind of weird — you losing me and threatening me at the same time."

They stared at each other. I got ready for just about anything. Jiggs placed his hand on Bernie's shoulder. Up until then, I'd always thought Bernie had real big shoulders.

"Now's a good time for asking you what you asked me," Jiggs said. "Whose side you're on?"

Bernie shrugged his shoulder free. "I'm working for the mayor's office. You know that already."

"Doesn't the mayor want this movie to be a success?" Jiggs said.

Bernie nodded.

"Then just do your job," Jiggs said. "No more, no less. And it'll all turn out peachy." He rose. "Oh, almost forgot. Your son."

"What about him?" Bernie said; his hands, which had been pretty relaxed, started curling into fists.

"They're getting ready to shoot that scene," Jiggs said. "Which is what I came to tell you, before we got off-topic." He tapped his hand on the bar, then turned and walked out.

What side were we on? That was an easy one: we were on each other's side, me and

Bernie. We also had each other's backs, which made it a little more complicated. As for peaches, Bernie's mom had surprised him on her last visit by baking a peach pie. "What the hell do you mean I never baked when you were a kid?" she'd said, and then downed the rest of her G and T and gotten right to work, but there'd been an oven glitch leading to the end result being tossed in the trash — although with the lid left off, meaning I knew the taste of peaches, at least in the blackened state.

We — meaning me, Bernie, and Leda, plus a bunch of movie people — stood outside a kind of log cabin, except the roof and one wall were missing. Inside, the cameraman was mounted on a seat behind his camera, and Lars Karlsbaad was talking to Thad, who sat on a chair facing a bed. On the bed, wearing his Western outfit, lay Charlie, his cowboy hat on the pillow beside him. He looked dark-eyed and ashen, like he was real sick. I sniffed the air, smelled no sickness coming from Charlie's direction. But sickness was in the room, no question, a thin, sour sort of invisible trickle that led straight to Lars. Hey! He had the same sickness as Mrs. Parsons. That surprised me, not sure why.

Lars stuck a cigar in his mouth. The clipboard woman hurried up with a lighter. "I don't like the hat," he said.

"Should I get props in here?" the clipboard woman said.

"The hat itself is fine," said Lars. The clipboard woman looked confused. "It is the placement of the hat."

"So . . . ?" said the clipboard woman.

"So? So get props, of course."

Props turned out to be a little dude with a dangling earring in one ear and a stud in the other, one of those human looks that bothered me a bit.

"Lars?" he said, running in.

"The hat," said Lars. "Place it on his chest."

"Right side up?" said Props.

"Unless we want to throw money in it," said Lars.

Silence. Lars frowned. Then, a little nervously, the clipboard woman began to laugh. The corners of Lars's lips turned up slightly. The laughter spread. Soon all the movie people were laughing their heads off.

Lars held up his hand in the stop sign. The laughter died at once.

"Back to the salt mines," Lars said.

Props took the cowboy hat off the pillow, placed it right-side up on Charlie's chest, and went away. Lars gazed down at Charlie. Charlie gazed back at him.

"Give me more," Lars called out to a guy up on a ladder. The guy did something with a light. Charlie looked sicker.

"Still more," Lars said. "Stops are for pulling out."

What was that? There and gone, way too quick, and besides, I was still somewhat stuck on salt mines. We'd been in abandoned mines more than once, me and Bernie — gold, silver, even emeralds once, although there was just the one emerald, planted by a perp, the details murky, but not the point. The point was why bother digging for salt? Salt shakers were on every restaurant table I'd ever seen. I mean, help yourself.

The guy on the ladder did more fiddling with the lights. Charlie looked sicker and sicker.

"What the hell's going on?" Bernie said in a low voice to Leda.

"Shh," said Leda. "They're creating."

"Voilà," Lars said, a total puzzler. He rubbed his hands together, chubby, small hands. "We all understand the situation? Croomer has at last persuaded the sheriff to free the shaman and allow her to treat the boy with the special desert herbs."

"Got it," said Thad.

"She is now on her way," Lars continued, "although we know she will never arrive due to . . ." He pressed a button on his belt. "Arn? Arn? Where the —"

"Lars?" Arn's voice came over a speaker, also the sound of a toilet flushing.

"What was that plot point?" Lars said.

"Where the saddlebag falls off and —"

"No, no, for Christ sake. With the shaman's ride."

"The renegades, you mean? The renegades suddenly —"

"Yes, yes, the renegades," Lars said. "So we know the outcome, but you, Croomer, and you, boy, do not. And yet. And yet." There was a silence. "We are ready?" Lars said.

"Yup," said Thad.

And Charlie, head on the pillow, nodded a tiny nod.

After that came the quiet on the set part, the cameraman rolling in, Lars stepping back, and — action!

Thad pulled the chair a bit closer to the bed. He looked down at Charlie and smiled a small smile. A moment passed and Charlie smiled an even smaller one back at him.

"Help's on the way, boy," he said. "You

hangin' in there for me?"

Charlie nodded the tiny nod.

"When you're back to feelin' good," Thad said, "we'll track down that herd, cut you out the finest l'il pinto pony on God's green earth."

Very slowly, Charlie closed his eyes.

Thad leaned closer toward him, his own eyes changing in a powerful way, hard to describe. "Still hangin' in?" he said, his voice now kind of thick and throaty.

Charlie's lips moved, but no sound came out. They moved again, and so softly, Charlie said, "Pinto pony."

"Good boy," Thad said.

The camera moved in closer on Charlie, lying still, and Lars started to raise his hand, like he was about to make that chopping motion and say cut, when all of a sudden Charlie's hands moved, wrapping themselves around the cowboy hat and holding it to his chest. Thad's eyes misted over. And then Charlie opened his own eyes. For an instant they seemed to see Thad, and then they didn't. Charlie's eyes went totally blank and lifeless — I knew that look from my job, had seen it too often — and . . . and stayed that way!

"Charlie!" Bernie shouted, and ran onto

the set. Me right with him, of course. We're
a lot alike, as I may have mentioned before.

TWENTY-FOUR

"I have never in my whole life been so utterly humiliated," Leda said.

We were in the parking area at the movie set, out behind the trailers and close to the two-lane blacktop leading back to the city, the Porsche and Leda's minivan parked nose to nose. Good thing they weren't moving, since there'd be a crack-up right away. Hey! What a strange thought! I gave myself a good scratching under the ear and returned to feeling normal.

Bernie glanced at the minivan. Charlie sat in the front passenger seat, eating trail mix from a little plastic container and gazing out at nothing in particular. I have things I could mention on the subject of trail mix, but this isn't the time or the place, as humans say. Maybe just the time part — actually not sure how place fits in.

"For Christ sake," Bernie said. "Who cares what those pretentious morons think?"

"Those pretentious morons, as you put it, are some of the most important people in the country," Leda said.

Bernie blew some air through his lips, making a sound like *peh.*

"You've always been so transparent," Leda said. "This is jealousy, pure and simple."

"Jealous?" said Bernie. "Of who?"

"Lars, of course."

Bernie laughed, not his normal laugh, which is one of the best sounds on earth, but harsher and more through his nose, if that makes any sense. "Why would I be jealous of that, that . . ."

"Can't find the perfect put-down?" Leda said. "How unusual. But as for the question, you're jealous because Lars has discovered a talent in your son that you were unaware of and wouldn't have a clue what to do with in any case."

Over in the minivan, Charlie had stopped eating and was watching his parents. Without thinking much about it — or anything, really — I sidled toward Charlie's door. He glanced down at me through the open window. No makeup on his face now: he looked just fine. My tail started up, all on its own.

"That's total crap," Bernie said.

"This is exactly why the Europeans think

of us the way they do," Leda said.

"The Europeans?"

A new one on me, too.

"You still can't grasp what happened, can you?" Leda said. "Your son is an artist, and not just in the making."

"Don't be ridiculous," Bernie said. "He's a six-year-old kid, barely out of diapers."

The minivan door opened. I climbed up into the car and sat on the floor in front of Charlie. First time in the minivan: it turned out to be nice and roomy. Also, some interesting food products lay under Charlie's seat, out of sight, which meant a lot to humans when it came to finding things but little to me. The food products — remains of a tuna sandwich, a French fry or two, some corn chips — could wait. Right now what I wanted to do was push up gently against Charlie, so I did. He put his hand on the back of my neck. Bernie's voice rose. Leda's sharpened. They seemed to blow round and round the minivan like a big dust devil. You see dust devils out in the desert from time to time. I thought about dust devils and other desert things I knew, especially some nice little yellow flowers, the name escaping me at that moment. Charlie kept his hand on the back of my neck.

■ ■ ■ ■

We drove home. Bernie was quiet just about the whole way. Then, as we turned onto Mesquite Road, he said, "Hope to hell Charlie didn't hear that diaper crack."

Oh, Bernie.

He banged the steering wheel. "They put him in a goddamn death scene without even telling me. Leda knew, oh, yeah. Why was that okay with her?"

I started panting, although I wasn't thirsty, hadn't been running. In fact, a nice bit of running sounded like just the thing at the moment.

We pulled into the driveway. Bernie stopped the car, switched off the engine but didn't get out. He sat there. I panted.

"Turns out it wasn't even in the script, that part where he opened his eyes and seemed to . . ." He went quiet. I heard the phone ringing in the house, but maybe Bernie didn't, because he kept sitting there. "How did he know to do that? Now she's going to twist his whole childhood around. To what end? Turn him into a Thad Perry?"

What was he talking about? I had no idea. I had no ideas at all. I searched back for my last idea. What had it been? Something nice, something about . . . yes! Running!

The next thing I knew, I was running. And not just running, but zooming, ears flattened straight back by my own wind. What a feeling, in the air most of the time, all paws off the ground, practically flying! There are many ways of zooming, but my favorite is the quick-cutting kind of zoom, darting this way and that, sometimes doubling right back on myself, claws digging deep in the ground, clods of earth flying high, and not just earth but grassy turf, too, which makes a sort of ripping sound, quite faint yet very satisfying in a way that's hard to explain and no time anyway, no time to even think about the fact that we didn't have a grass lawn, no way we could, not with the whole aquifer thing, and neither did the Parsons, in their case all about no longer being able to push the lawnmower, the only grass lawn being old man Heydrich's on the other side. Zoom. Zip. Rip, rip, rip: had I ever made cuts this sharp and at this speed? Chet the —

"Chet! Chet! For God's sake!"

Uh-oh. I hit the brakes and stopped on a dime — no dimes present, of course, although you couldn't be sure, what with dimes being so small, unless I was getting that wrong, so complicated, human money

— possibly taking out a flowery bush that stood on the boundary of our place and old man Heydrich's, or perhaps slightly more on his side.

There's a voice humans use for shouting and not shouting at the same time, a sort of muffled shout. Bernie used it now.

"Chet! Get over here."

I gave myself a good shake, trotted over to Bernie. His cell phone rang. He answered, said something, clicked off, and then turned to me.

"Hop in."

Back in the car? Why not? No reason, except that we hadn't chowed down in what seemed like a long time. But then, from out of the blue, I got the idea we were headed to Max's Memphis Ribs, my favorite restaurant in the whole valley. Those ribs! And when you'd eaten every speck of meat, there was still the whole bone in your future! What a business plan, as I may have mentioned before, but it's important! Had Bernie mentioned anything about Max's Memphis Ribs? Perhaps not, maybe meaning there was no reason to believe Max's was on the schedule. I believed.

I hopped in the car. We backed out of the driveway, pretty quick, and shot up Mesquite Road. In a hurry, all of a sudden? No problem. I love speed, in case that hasn't come up yet. Old man Heydrich's porch light went on. He stepped outside, a golf club in his hand, and was turning our way just as we rounded the curve and went roaring out of sight. Old man Heydrich was a golfer? You really did learn something every day, as humans often said.

We've worked a lot of cases, me and Bernie, but the Valley's a big place, going on pretty much forever in all directions, so sometimes we ended up somewhere new. Like now for example, way out in the West Valley, past the last busted development then came another and another, a few with a light or two showing where someone was still there, most pretty dark. We followed a road, paved at first and then not, into the darkest development, a bunch of cul de sacs lined with half-built houses, empty lots, scraps blowing in the wind, and abandoned stuff, including the cement-mixing drum from a cement truck. Bernie turned into the driveway of the only complete house in the whole place, which would be the model home. We had empty model homes out the yingyang, Bernie once told Suzie, so what are we modeling? "Can I quote you?" she'd said. No idea what that meant, but they'd both laughed. I was missing Suzie already.

We sat there. A quiet night with just the wind and us. The air was always less dusty in the West Valley, the stars shining clearer and the moon brighter. Some parts of the moon were brighter than others. That was the sort of thing — although what wasn't? — that Bernie knew how to explain. Maybe he was going to right now. I listened my hardest; and heard a car coming.

I shifted in my seat and saw it: car, no lights, moving slow.

"Chet?" Bernie said. "What's up?" Then he turned and saw the car, too. "It's all right, big guy."

The car parked beside us and Rick Torres got out. He handed Bernie a folder, stained and yellowed.

"I owe you," Bernie said.

"You can say that again," Rick said, but Bernie did not. "And you'll have to read on the spot," he went on. "I'm returning it tonight."

Bernie nodded. "Does anyone know?" he said.

"Don't need you to tell me how to conduct my business," Rick said.

Rick was mad at Bernie? Everybody seemed to be mad at Bernie these days. I didn't get it.

"Can Chet have a treat?" Rick said.

How could anyone be mad at Bernie, especially a great guy like Rick?

"He's probably starving," Bernie said.

Bernie: he nails it just about every time.

Rick gave me a nice big biscuit. "That was quick," he said. "Room for another?" Yes, a great guy, and funny, too. Room for another: loved it. We went for a little walk, around the model home to the swimming pool at the back. You see lots of swimming pools in these empty developments, and the pools are always empty, too. Not this one! Not full of water to the very top, no, but there was plenty enough if anyone felt like a swim. And even though swimming had been the farthest thing from my mind — and if not the very farthest, like say, going to the vet, then at least pretty far — all of a sudden I couldn't think of anything else.

"Chet?" Rick said. "Might not be clean enough for —"

KER-SPLASH!

Ah, really nothing quite like swimming. It's actually very much like running, only in water and you never get hot. I swam around the pool, my nose just above the surface. That was something I'd learned about swimming: much more relaxing if you didn't hold your head up high. I lapped up a quick taste. Possibly not the best tasting water I'd ever experienced. No need to do it again, I told myself, and only did it once or twice more.

Rick sat on the diving board and watched me. "You sure know how to have fun," he said.

Well, of course. Who didn't? Nothing easier. I pulled a Uey and headed back toward the other end. I preferred bigger pools, but no complaints. Many, many tiny moons sparkled on the water. All those moons seemed to be making rippling sounds. What a night! Soft rippling sounds, and they didn't drown out Rick's sigh.

"He's not going to like what he sees in that damn file," Rick said.

File? I tried to remember. And, kind of a surprise, I succeeded. I scrambled out of the pool and gave myself a good shake, Rick backing quickly away. Nothing beats a shake when you're soaking wet, the way all those droplets go spraying, especially from the tip of your tail. Swimming: it's still fun even after you've stopped doing it. Rick and I walked around to the front of the model home.

Bernie was sitting on the hood of the

Porsche, smoking a cigarette, the file on his lap.

"Thought you'd quit," Rick said.

"After this pack," said Bernie.

"Sounds like a plan," Rick said. "You done?"

Bernie nodded, handed over the file. "Was this all there was?" he said.

"What do you mean?" said Rick.

"You didn't read it?" Bernie said.

Rick shook his head. Head shaking, unless I'd been way off from the get-go, meant no, and head nodding meant yes. So somehow Rick had gotten it wrong.

Twenty-Five

One thing about a nice swim: it was often followed by a nice nap. I lay curled up on the shotgun seat, the motion of the car beneath me kind of . . . dreamy. Yes, dreamy. Bernie might or might not have said something like, "How come you're wet?" I didn't know, and while paying attention to Bernie was always at the top of my list, I really didn't care. How can you care when your eyelids are so heavy and getting heavier and heavier? And heavier. I dreamed about swimming!

And I was still swimming when the dreamy motion beneath me eased and then vanished. I opened my eyes. We were back in bad air, the moon and the stars now hidden by a dirty pink sky. I sat up. Vista City, or someplace like it: parked on a street lined with apartment buildings, not the tower kind they have downtown, but lower, old with stucco walls, the stucco cracked and crumbling here and there. Bernie was gazing at the most cracked and crumbling of all the buildings. I gazed at it with him.

"When you start digging in something that doesn't want to be dug . . ." he said.

Yes, yes: go on. Bernie did not. Naturally, I've dealt with close-packed dirt in the past, but when you kept working, even if all you did at first was make shallow scratches on the surface, eventually you always found yourself happily in a deepening pit, all legs in action. So: no problem, right?

"Such a goddamn long shot," Bernie said. "And is this even where to start?"

I tried to think of some other place, found I could not. This crummy apartment building filled up my whole thought area.

"But," he went on, "what choice do we have? There's nothing in the file except the victim ID and the ME's report. Goddamn file's been gutted. By who, is the question."

Bernie turned to me. Whoa. Like I'd done it, whatever it was? Bernie smiled. Whew. "Have a nice nap?" he said. "All set?"

I hopped out, hurried around to Bernie's side of the car, waited while he got out. "If we could harness that tail of yours . . ." he began.

Harness me? There'd been an attempt once, in the time before Bernie and I got together. Never again. And of course Bernie himself would never even think of such a thing, so this had to be one of his jokes. Bernie was a great joker, in case I haven't made that clear already. We walked side by side up to the front door of the apartment building.

Bernie tried the door: locked. He turned to a row of buzzers, ran his finger down the little labels beside them. "Spears, Spears, Spears, wouldn't that be nice?" he said. "But nope."

Spears? I knew spears from this period when work dried up completely — even divorce work, which we hated — and we'd watched a lot of movies about gladiators. Spears were nasty: was Bernie really hoping we were coming up against them? So be it. I was ready.

"How about we try the manager?" Bernie said. "T. Ortega." He pressed a buzzer.

We waited. There's a lot of waiting in this business, just one more reason why it's nice to have a partner. And a partner like Bernie? That was like hitting the lottery. Once we almost did! What a drive that was, from our place to the lottery office downtown in no time flat. But Bernie had read the number wrong, an easy mistake to make, I'm sure.

Bernie pressed the buzzer again, held it down for a while. As soon as he backed off, a voice came through a speaker, angry but small.

"Who's there? What do you want?"

"I'm looking for a family that used to live in this building."

"What number?"

"Five," Bernie said. "Where Mizell is now."

No sound came from the speaker, except for a staticky crackle.

"The name was Spears," Bernie said.

More crackle.

"Hello?" Bernie said.

"Go away." The speaker went silent, crackle and all.

Bernie pressed the buzzer again, kept his finger there. After a while I heard a door close somewhere in the building, and soon approaching footsteps, the soft, slightly flapping kind slippers make. Then someone — a man actually, a man who'd been eating something garlicky, and who could have used a shower, not that I cared much about that kind of thing, although it was always interesting how humans liked to get rid of their natural scents — stopped at the other side of the door.

There was a little click which Bernie

maybe didn't hear because he kept his finger on the buzzer. Then the door got thrown open real fast and an unshaven guy in a wifebeater and saggy sweatpants stood there, a gun in his hand and pointed at the floor, but also sort of at Bernie.

"What part of go away don't you fuckin' understand?" the guy said.

Here's a strange thing: some humans have trouble even noticing members of the nation within. Also the light over the door was out, and the nearest streetlight stood pretty far down the block, so maybe things were a bit murky. The truth is I didn't really think about any of that, just lunged forward, grabbed the guy's wrist, and clamped down good and tight.

"*Aieee,*" he screamed, or something like that, very unpleasant down deep in my ears. He dropped the gun at once. Not a tough guy, obvious from the get-go, but nobody waves guns at Bernie, not while I'm around.

"*Aieee, aieee.*" He was struggling now, always fun. Did his blood have a garlicky taste? Had to be my imagination. "Call it off!" the guy screamed. "Call it off!"

"He's not an it," Bernie said, picking up the gun.

"Huh? What the hell? He's killing me."

Bernie nodded. "He — that's better.

334

Chet? Big guy? That should do it. Chet? All set on our end now. Good job. No sense overdoing it. Let's not gild the lily."

Gild the lily? I'd heard that one before, had no idea what it meant. Wasn't the lily a flower? This wifebeater guy was no flower, and that garlicky tinge in his blood hadn't gone away. I let him go.

"Good boy," Bernie said. "How about sitting for a moment or two?"

Sitting? I didn't feel like it, not one little bit. What did I feel like? Action, baby, action and nothing but.

"Ch — et?" Bernie has this special way of saying Chet, not loud, that somehow gets my attention every time. Or at least most of the time. Or sometimes. In short: this time I sat.

Bernie popped the magazine out of the gun, dropped the ammo in his pocket, then racked the slide — loved gun lingo myself, learned it back when Bernie was teaching Charlie, a lesson that led to an unforgettable scene with Leda which I no longer remembered — and dropped that last round into his pocket with the others. Then he slid the empty magazine back in place and handed the gun to the wifebeater guy.

"Here you go, Mr. . . . Ortega, is it?"

"I'm bleedin' to death," said Mr. Ortega.

Bernie stooped down, examined Mr. Ortega's wrist. "Nah," he said. "Just a scratch.
And of course Chet's had his shots, so you'll
be good as new in no time. Now if you'll
kindly be more forthcoming about the
present whereabouts of the Spears family,
we won't take anymore of your time."

"You a cop?" Mr. Ortega said.

Bernie showed Mr. Ortega our license.

"Private eye?"

Bernie nodded.

"What do you want with her?"

"Who are we discussing?" Bernie said.

"Who do you think?" Mr. Ortega. "Mrs.
—" And then he put the brakes on, too late.
That putting on the brakes too late thing
was always good for us.

"Mrs. . . . ?" said Bernie.

Mr. Ortega shook his head. "You look like
trouble for her."

"I'm guessing she's a good person," Bernie said. "We don't bring trouble to good
people."

"I'm a good person," Mr. Ortega said,
looking down at his wrist; the blood wasn't
even flowing anymore.

"The gun fooled me," Bernie said.

Mr. Ortega thought about that. Some
humans are faster thinkers than others —
you can sort of tell from their faces. Mr.

Ortega wasn't one of them. "You gonna give me my ammo back?" he said at last.

"Sure," said Bernie. "Just as soon as you tell us what we want to know."

Mr. Ortega did some more thinking.

"I take it we're talking about Mrs. Spears," Bernie said.

" 'Cept she got married and changed her name to —" Whoa! He put the brakes on again? This was going to take forever. Fine with me.

"Mizell, by any chance?" Bernie said.

"How'd you know that?" said Mr. Ortega.

Bernie reached into his pocket, took out the ammo, and said, "Cup your hands." No time to go into this now, but I like when humans cup their hands; I once drank water from Bernie's cupped hands when we were in a bad way, deep in the desert.

Bernie dropped the ammo *clink clink* into Mr. Ortega's hands. "Grateful for your help," Bernie said. "And I'll be even more grateful if you don't reload till after we're out of here."

"What are you gonna do?" Mr. Ortega said.

"Pay a visit to number five," Bernie said, stepping through the doorway; I was already inside, on account of my little dustup with Mr. Ortega. "But you can head on back to your own apartment," Bernie went on. "We'll find our way."

Mr. Ortega backed through the small entrance hall, then started down a corridor. He stopped and turned. "She's had some hard times," he said.

Bernie nodded.

We went down the same corridor, but the other way. The floor was linoleum, kind of sticky under my paws. We passed a few doors, TV voices leaking out from underneath them, plus some fast-food smells — fast food being a wonderful human invention — and also pot. Bernie says that practically the whole country is stoned out of its mind at all times, which is why we are where we are, but where we are is pretty good, right? So maybe it wasn't a problem.

We stopped in front of a door. A horseshoe was nailed to the frame. You see that sometimes, a total puzzler. And what's with horses wearing shoes in the first place? So it was kind of a double puzzler, way too much for me. Bernie knocked.

Someone moved on the other side of the door, a woman, actually, and she'd been drinking.

"Yes?" she said.

"Mrs. Mizell?" said Bernie. "My name's

Bernie Little. I'm a private investigator, and I need your help."

"I haven't done anything," the woman said.

"I didn't say you had," Bernie said. "I'm looking into an old case."

Her voice got a bit wavery. "Old case?"

"Which it would be better to discuss in private," Bernie said.

She was silent.

"Maybe I'm making a mistake," Bernie said. "But if your surname used to be Spears and you had a daughter named April, then I'm not."

The door opened.

The woman peered out. She had rusty red hair and wore very big glasses. The eyes behind the lenses looked small and watery. They took in Bernie, and then me.

"This is Chet, Mrs. Mizell," Bernie said.

"April had a dog," said Mrs. Mizell. Holding her housecoat tight at the neck, she stepped to the side and let us in.

We were in a small living room, separated from an even smaller kitchen by a counter. On the counter stood an open jug of red wine and a half-filled glass. Mrs. Mizell made a gesture toward a couch facing the TV. Bernie didn't sit there. Instead he pulled a footstool closer to the couch and sat on that. Was an interview about to happen? Maybe: Bernie always got fussy with seating arrangements when it came to interviews.

Mrs. Mizell screwed the top on the wine jug and pushed the glass out of sight, behind the toaster, then turned quickly, the way humans do when they're checking to see if you saw. So complicated. And of course we saw. We're pros, me and Bernie.

Mrs. Mizell came over, smoothing her housecoat, and sat on the couch, shifted herself away from Bernie, but because of where he'd placed the stool, she couldn't go far. She sat up straight, a kind of bloated woman, but her feet were bare and they were nice, well-shaped in a way that's hard to describe, the nails red, a very bright red I had trouble taking my eyes off.

Mrs. Mizell gave Bernie a sideways look. She was real nervous; the smell, not unpleasant to me, filled the room.

"What was the name of April's dog?" Bernie said.

"Kurt," said Mrs. Mizell. "She was a big Kurt Cobain fan." She put her hands together, wrung them a bit. "He got unmanageable after she . . . after. I had to give him away."

"After what?" Bernie said.

Now she looked him right in the eye and her voice got harsh. "After April got murdered," Mrs. Mizell said. "Isn't that the old case you're talking about?"

"It is," Bernie said.

"Old and cold," said Mrs. Mizell. She gazed down at her feet. I gazed at them, too, and was hit by a strong desire to give them a lick. Was this a good time? I wondered about that.

"What happened to her, Mrs. Mizell?" Bernie said.

She shook her head. "April was a good kid, no matter what any — no matter what," she said. "And she was as pretty as a movie star."

"Have you got a picture of her?"

"I do."

Mrs. Mizell rose, her knees cracking, and went through a door into a dark room. Bernie turned to a desk by the wall, opened the top drawer, glanced inside, closed the drawer. Mrs. Mizell returned and handed Bernie a picture. He studied it.

"Yes," he said. "She was very pretty."

"Beautiful," said Mrs. Mizell.

"Is that the old Flower Mart in the background?"

Mrs. Mizell, looking over Bernie's shoulder, nodded. "She worked there part-time."

"Who's the boy with her?"

Mrs. Mizell's face hardened. "The boyfriend," he said. "Ex-boyfriend, but this was before she dumped him."

"Why did she dump him?"

Mrs. Mizell took a deep breath. "By that time I maybe wasn't keeping the close eye on her that I should. And I had problems of my own. A single mom, in case you haven't guessed. This was before Mr. Mizell. Now is after him."

"So she didn't tell you?" Bernie said.

"I wasn't really around much, is what I'm saying. April was here alone. I'd gone up to Vegas that summer, looking for work." There was a silence. "Aren't you going to ask what kind of work?"

"No," Bernie said. "I'd like to know more about this boyfriend."

"Manny? I never liked him."

"The boyfriend's name was Manny?" Bernie said. My ears went up right away. There was a change in the sound of Bernie's voice, not big, but that change, a slight sharpening, almost always meant something.

"Short for Manuel." Mrs. Mizell said Manuel in a way that was kind of — what was the word? catty? whoa! I'd never thought about that, clearly a huge subject, and no time now. And where was I? Manuel.

Yes. She stretched it out like she was making fun of the name.

Bernie leaned forward. "Do you remember his last name?"

"Chavez."

Bernie went very still. When he spoke again, his voice was back to normal. "Do you know what became of him?"

"Became of him?"

"Since then."

"I never saw him again."

"Was he a suspect?"

"In my mind he was," Mrs. Mizell said. "April was stabbed to death, and if you're a private eye, then you must know all about Mexicans and knives."

Bernie said nothing.

"And he had a motive," Mrs. Mizell went on.

"What was that?"

"Jealousy, of course. I think April had started seeing someone else."

"Is that why she dumped Manny?" Bernie said.

Mrs. Mizell got angry. "I told you I didn't know. I just think." She glanced over at the toaster.

"What makes you think she dumped Manny for this other person?"

"It was a long time ago," said Mrs. Mizell,

eyes still on the toaster.

Bernie rose, took Mrs. Mizell's chin in his hand and turned her face toward his, not hard, even kind of gently. Her eyes got big.

"But you remember," he said, and let her go.

Mrs. Mizell nodded. "I overheard her telling a friend on the phone." Her hand went to her chin, felt it, almost like she was making sure it was still there.

"Did she mention the name of the new boyfriend?" Bernie said.

"Not that I remember. I really don't, so keep your hands off me."

Bernie made a little motion, like he was brushing a fly from in front of his face, but I didn't hear or see one. "Who was the friend on the phone?" he said.

"Probably her oldest one, going all the way back to grade school," Mrs. Mizell said. "Dina was her name. Dina . . . Taggert, I think it was. "Or maybe Haggerty. But what difference does it make?" She started getting angry again. "Manny alibied out."

"How do you know?"

"The cop told me — the cop who found poor April in the first place. I put him on to Manny first thing."

"What was the alibi?"

She shrugged. "I'm not sure I even knew."

"And the cop?"

Mrs. Mizell stared at the wall. "A serious young man," she said. "It'll come to me."

We waited, Bernie watching her face, me watching her feet. We're a team, me and Bernie, which must have come up already.

At last Bernie said, "Did he have long sideburns?"

"Oh, no," said Mrs. Mizell. "That was the detective in charge. Detective Luxton."

"Detective Luxton?"

"He had long sideburns, like from the seventies," Mrs. Mizell said. "The cop wore his uniform, of course. He cared, I could tell. He promised me they'd find April's killer but they never did." We sat in silence. "You've brought it all back to me," Mrs. Mizell said. "What gives you the goddamn right?"

"There'd only be one good reason."

She raised her head. "You've found something?"

"I can't go into details," Bernie said.

Mrs. Mizell gave Bernie an angry look, then turned away from him. Her gaze happened to light on me. The anger seemed to leak out of her. "The cop was named Stine," she said.

Twenty-Six

We parked across the street from Red Devil's around closing time. You could always tell closing time from the fact that no one was going in, plus no one coming out ever walked in a straight line. The Little Detective Agency does a lot of its best work at closing time.

When we're sitting on a place at night, we like to avoid streetlights, not a problem on this block, since none of them were working. "Infrastructure of the whole damn country's falling apart, big guy," Bernie said. "Gonna end up living in caves."

Wow! And I was hearing that for the very first time? But we could live in caves, no problem, me and Bernie. We'd been in caves, and also mines, plenty of times. Bernie loved exploring abandoned mines out in the desert, so when the infrastructure, whatever that was, finished falling apart maybe we'd be even happier. Hard to imagine, so I didn't even try.

The door of Red Devil's opened and out came a few women, none walking in straight lines. The ones in high heels took them off, which made them surprisingly short but didn't help with the straight line problem. A taxi pulled over and they sort of fell in. After that a dude appeared, started heading one way, then changed his mind, and finally changed it again and went off in the original direction.

Lights started going out inside Red Devil's and soon it was dark, except for the neon sign in the window. The door opened and Dina came out, wearing jeans and a halter top, and pushing a bike. She pulled down one of those metal screens, covering the whole front of Red Devil's, and locked it in place. Then she got on the bike and pedaled away. The bike had a small flashing red light at the back, couldn't have been easier to follow. We followed.

Had we ever tailed anyone on a bike before? Sure, and also people on skateboards, forklifts, golf carts, and once a roller coaster, maybe the worst day of my life. Bernie kept our own lights off, and we loafed along well back of Dina on her bike, real slow. The street was dark, the night was dark, and Bernie was in a dark mood: I could feel it. The only illumination was red and green, red from Dina's flashing light and green from the dials on our dash. Bernie's face was hard in that green light. Something was bothering him, but what? We weren't in danger. In fact, weren't we bringing it? Which was what we did at the Little Detective Agency, lots of fun even if we weren't always paid.

We followed the flashing red light down the street, around a corner, and past some warehouses that were being fixed up for lofts, which I knew because Bernie had thought about investing in one, opting for the Hawaiian pants play instead at the last moment; actually after the last moment, leading to a nasty meeting with some developer dudes, but no harm done, Bernie said, because real estate tanked and we would have lost everything anyway. At least we still had the Hawaiian pants in our self-storage in South Pedroia. Once we went down there and Bernie tried a few on, looking very sharp, in my opinion.

The red light stopped flashing. We moved in closer, saw Dina getting off her bike and carrying it up some steps to the door of one of the loft buildings. Bernie pulled right up on the sidewalk and stopped the car. I just loved when he did things like that! Dina

348

turned and saw us, her eyes wide and dirty pink like the sky. She whipped around to the door and started fumbling for keys, losing her grip on the bike at the same time.

"Chet!" Bernie said. "Go."

Already on it, in fact halfway up the stairs. I vaulted over the bike, which was clattering down, and hit the landing right between Dina and the front door, twisting around to face her in one smooth motion. Chet the Jet! I knew "go," baby. Dina took one look at me and booked, back down the stairs. Bernie was there, ready and waiting. Team! He grabbed her, not hard, by one arm. Dina struggled, got nowhere, then suddenly lashed out with the keys, maybe trying to swipe him across the face. But Bernie's too quick for that kind of thing — we're pros, after all, worth mentioning even with the possibility it's come up before — and a moment later the keys lay in the gutter.

Dina kept trying to get free. "I'll scream," she said, although why not scream it instead of just saying it?

Funny thought, and maybe Bernie's too, because he told her, "Go ahead."

No screaming happened. Also Dina stopped struggling. A light went on in a window across the street.

"Would you prefer talking in private?"

Bernie said.

"About what?"

"Your lies and evasions," Bernie said.

Dina started to open her mouth, like maybe a scream was coming after all, but it didn't.

Dina lived on the top floor of the building. No elevator — fine with me — so we climbed the stairs, Dina first with the bike, then me, then Bernie. He offered to carry the bike. Bernie could be a real gentleman: too often that got lost in the shuffle.

Dina turned out to be one of those shufflers. "Fuck you," she said over her shoulder. She grunted her way up the stairs, bike over her shoulder.

Sometimes when people invite you into their place, they say, "Coffee? A drink, maybe?" and often, "And how about Chet? Can he have a little something?" But not this time. Dina had a small apartment with lots of plants, so many that it smelled like outdoors, kind of confusing. We found places to sit in all the greenery.

"I'm sure you know," Bernie said, "that there's no statute of limitations when it comes to murder."

"What are you talking about?" Dina said. She had dark patches under her eyes, the way humans did when they get tired. In the nation within we just go to sleep, but I'm sure there's no right or wrong way. "I never murdered anyone."

"Maybe," Bernie said. "But you've been evasive — at best — and that makes you suspect in my book. And a suspect plain and simple to the homicide squad — they tend to paint in broader strokes."

Wow. I didn't follow that at all. Bernie was cooking.

"I told you everything I knew about Carla," Dina said.

"With the omission of one key fact," Bernie said.

He paused and watched her face. So did I. She showed nothing that I could see. Women could be tough cookies, just as tough as men, although in my experience with cookies — let's save this one for another time. Dina was a tough cookie; leave it at that.

"Carla's not the only murder victim in this case," Bernie went on, "not even the only murder victim who was also a friend of yours."

One of Dina's eyelids twitched, always a promising sign for us.

"There are three victims," Bernie said. "You knew two for sure, and I've got a

351

hunch you knew the third one as well." Bernie: a great interviewer, and right now — at the top of his game — he was something to see.

Dina's eyelid twitched some more.

"How about we start with the first one — your closest childhood pal?" Bernie said.

"I already told you," Dina said. "Carla went off to the magnet school and —"

Bernie held up his hand in the stop sign. "I'm talking about April Spears," Bernie said. "Wasn't she your oldest pal?" He paused. "Her mother thinks so."

Dina's eyes shifted. That's a human thing for when they've got to come up with something real fast. Bernie says that if they've shifted their eyes, they're already too slow.

She looked at him. "Why do I always get the relentless type?"

"Maybe there's something in you that discourages the others," Bernie said.

Her face went white.

"But none of that matters right now," Bernie said. "What matters is why you didn't tell me about April."

"You didn't ask."

"Not in so many words," Bernie said. "But we were all around it. For example, you were vague about the Flower Mart, pretended it meant nothing to you. Care to revise that statement?"

Dina said nothing.

Bernie lowered his voice, just at the time when you might have thought he was going to raise it. "Your best friend was stabbed to death and tossed in the trash, Dina. Come on."

Dina squeezed her eyes shut. The tiniest drop leaked from the corner of one of them. "When I heard that . . ." She shook her head. "It tore me apart. I've never been the same."

Bernie's face, already pretty hard, got harder. "Who killed her?"

"I don't know." Dina looked at Bernie's face. "Oh, my God, you can't think it was me. She was my best friend. We had pet names for each other, from when we could barely talk."

"What were they?" Bernie said.

A smile crossed Dina's face, very small and quickly gone, but she looked a little younger in that moment. "She called me Dee Dee. I called her Prilly."

Bernie said nothing.

"Now you're going to grill me on where I was when she was killed and can I prove it," Dina said.

"Nope," said Bernie. "Although I am

interested in whether the police ever talked to you."

"They didn't."

"Tell me about Manny Chavez," Bernie said.

"I knew Manny," Dina said. "He was her boyfriend for, like, six weeks. Boyfriends came and went back then. It wasn't that serious — we were seventeen."

"Were they having sex?" Bernie said.

"Who wasn't?" said Dina. "She wasn't in love with him, or anything like that."

"Was it more serious for him?"

She shrugged. "Maybe not because of who she was, but what she was."

"Meaning?"

"Blond and Anglo. A kind of status thing, especially for those gangbanger types."

"Manny was in a gang?"

"He was more of a wannabe — had a Harley, which was what attracted April in the first place — but some of the others were the real thing."

"What others?"

"Guys Manny hung with," Dina said.

"What was the name of the gang?"

Dina shook her head. "I'm not sure it was that well organized, with a name and everything. There was one guy, a little older, maybe. I remember not liking the way he looked at me. I was crazy back then, but not foolish."

"What was his name?"

"I don't remember. Something Hispanic, maybe."

"Like Ramon?" Bernie said.

"Might have been."

"Last time we spoke, you said that name meant nothing to you."

"So? A person can't forget minor details with you?"

Bernie seemed to think about that for a moment. "Have you seen Ramon since?" he said.

"Since . . . since the summer April died? No."

"What about Manny?"

"No."

"Heard anything about him over the years?"

"No."

"How about lately?"

"No."

"So you didn't know he was stabbed to death last week?"

Dina put a hand to her chest. "I did not."

"Happened in a foreclosed house on North Coursin Street," Bernie said. "Only a dozen blocks from here."

She raised her hands, palms up.

"April's mother told me her daughter dumped Manny," Bernie said.

"How is she?"

"Not too good. But is it true?"

"Yes."

"Why did she dump him?"

"I told you," Dina said. "Back then six weeks —"

Bernie made a chopping motion. I liked seeing that, hoped it would happen again, and soon. "Her mother heard her on the phone, almost certainly with you," Bernie said, "saying she was interested in someone else. I need that name."

Dina said nothing.

"How much did you have to drink at the ball game?"

Dina looked surprised. I was, too. Ball game? Had there been talk of a ball game, kind of vague and —

"The night Carla had those box seats," Bernie added.

Dina shrugged. "I probably had a few beers."

"I'm guessing you're one of those people who get more talkative after a pop or two."

"Guess away."

"And maybe you wanted to impress her — this successful reporter — with a tidbit of information she didn't know."

Silence. It went on and on. Not a complete silence for me, on account of a rat I heard creeping across the space above the ceiling.

At last Bernie said, "You've answered the question."

"What are you talking about?"

"You should have said, What tidbit? The fact that you didn't means you told Carla that Thad Perry was from the Valley or spent time here. The question is why you're trying to hide it."

Dina glared at him. Yes, a tough cookie.

"So far," Bernie said, "it doesn't look like you're in any kind of trouble. But once a series of murders starts up, it's hard to get it stopped. So the next one will be partly on you."

"I hate your guts," Dina said.

People told Bernie that from time to time. I knew they didn't mean it.

"Comes with the job," Bernie said.

"And what's that?" said Dina. "What's your goddamn job?"

"Retribution."

Whatever that meant, it made her stop hating him at once: I could see it on her face. She looked at Bernie in a whole new way. Not liking him, it wasn't that. More . . . respecting. We have that, too, in the nation within. Dina took a big breath and let it out real slow.

"This was long before he was famous, of course," she said. "Thad Perry was a kid, just like us. He came here that summer to visit a cousin and met April at a car wash where the cousin worked. It all happened real fast, maybe two weeks from when they met till she died. He left town right away."

"Did he kill her?" Bernie said.

"I don't know," Dina said. "He was gentler than most of the boys, and more polite. And much better looking. I saw them together just the one time, at the car wash. They were so beautiful together."

"Did they argue?" Bernie said. "Fight with each other?"

"Not that I know of," Dina said.

Bernie gazed at her. "How come you didn't want to talk about this?"

Dina rose and went to the window, pushed the leaf of a big plant aside, looked out.

"What are you afraid of?" Bernie said.

"All the usual things," Dina said.

"Including the cousin?"

Dina turned to him, her mouth opening.

"Was his name Jiggs?" Bernie said.

"If you know all this, why ask?" Dina said. "Nolan Jiggs, this king-size shithead. He blew town with Thad Perry, something I didn't realize at the time. Then, years later, just before Thad's first movie came out, he came back and found me." Dina turned from the window, the plant leaf flopping back into place. "He paid me five grand to keep things to myself."

"That was the carrot," Bernie said.

"You're not as dumb as you look," Dina said. "The stick was a promise to kill me if I breathed a word to anyone." She gazed at Bernie through the leaves. "Are you and your dog going to keep that from happening?"

Bet the ranch.

TWENTY-SEVEN

Very late at night — but a time we're used to being up at in this business — the Valley gets as quiet as it gets. That near-quiet was what I was hearing now, like everyone was having restless sleeps. Bernie, at the wheel, face harder than ever in the green light from the dials, turned to me and said, "Take us at least twenty minutes to get there, big guy, even at this hour. Why don't you grab a quick catnap?"

Say what? I sat up my straightest for the whole ride, which turned out to be all the way across town to West Side Heights, one of the fanciest neighborhoods in the Valley.

"Not sleepy, huh?" Bernie said, as we wound up a hilly street lined with big houses spaced far apart. Not if cats were sleepy, I sure wasn't. Bernie pulled into a circular driveway, outside lights coming on right away, and stopped in front of a house that looked a bit like the old mission downtown. "Time to blow up this whole damn thing and start over," Bernie said, as we got out of the car and went to the front door, one of those massive dark-wood double doors with lots of metalwork. We had no dynamite on us — one of the easiest smells going — so the explosions weren't coming anytime soon. Fine with me. We'd blown up a shed once — the wrong one, it turned out — a really exciting day, at first, but Bernie had — not miscalculated, no way that could ever happen, more like he'd gotten a little too enthusiastic when it came to the number of dynamite sticks, and in the end we'd taken out a sort of bridge as well as the shed and all the tires on the Porsche, and had to walk a long way to the nearest gas station.

Bernie rang the bell. I heard it sound deep inside the house, a big house, the size of many sheds. That worried me.

Footsteps approached on the other side of the door: a man, barefoot, powerful. Bolts slid, locks clicked, the door swung open, and there was Bernie's pal Gronk, the insurance dude from downtown. Had he hooked us up with the mayor's office in the first place, or something like that? Hard to keep all this straight; good thing that wasn't my territory. Gronk's hair was all over the place and he wore a polka-dot silk robe. Polka dots do nothing for me, but silk has a very nice feel, something that had led to a problem or two in the past. Not now, of course: we were on the job.

"Bernie?" Gronk said. His sleepy eyes were waking up fast; Bernie was like that, too, when he had to be. "What's up?"

"Need to talk," Bernie said.

Gronk paused for a moment, then nodded. "Come on in."

We went in, and at that moment a woman called from upstairs.

"Stevie? Who is it?"

"Nobody," Gronk called over his shoulder. "Go back to sleep."

"But I heard you talking," the woman said.

"It's just an old friend."

"Friend?"

"Buddy."

"Oh."

"Go to bed."

"Okay, Stevie. Don't be too long. You've got that breakfast meeting."

Gronk cocked his head, listening for more. There was no more. "My wife," he said. He lowered his voice. "The new one." He led us down the hall and into a room that looked like a sports bar, except smaller, and not even that much smaller. "The old one was a much better sleeper." Gronk gestured at the rows of bottles behind the bar. "Something to drink?" He sat on a stool.

Bernie shook his head. He leaned against the bar. When he gets tired his leg bothers him. Sit down, big guy, I thought, sit down and have that drink. But he didn't.

"There's a problem?" Gronk said.

"Lots of them," Bernie said. His voice wasn't pally. Weren't they old pals? "The one that concerns you is that story about getting me hired by the mayor's office."

Gronk stared at Bernie for a bit, and then sighed. "You never change."

"What does that mean?"

"It means you've always been and will always be a stubborn son of a bitch," Gronk said. "A stubborn son of a bitch who doesn't ever know what's good for him."

"Spill it," Bernie said.

"You can't just leave this simply as me getting a chance to do you a small favor and seizing the opportunity?"

"Not if it didn't go down that way."

"But what's the goddamn difference?"

"Life and death," Bernie said.

"I don't get it," said Gronk.

Whoa! You can smell the difference right away, poor Carla in the Dumpster, for example. But Gronk wasn't in the business, so maybe I was expecting too much.

"I'll explain when this is all over," Bernie said. "Right now, there's no time."

"Christ," said Gronk. "Anybody else, I'd . . ." He went silent before I found out what he'd do; with a big strong dude like Gronk, probably plenty. "All right," he went on. "Attaching you to the mayor's office wasn't my idea."

Bernie voice got quiet. "Whose was it?"

"A friend of yours," Gronk said.

"Who?"

"A cop. He . . . he told me about your situation, all the debt, a play you made on the commodity market, which I had trouble believing, something else about the fashion business, the whole crazy thing adding up to the fact that you could use a high-paying gig in the worst way and I was in a position to make it happen."

"The name," Bernie said.

"He didn't want you to know," Gronk said. "So you wouldn't feel obligated. He was being stand-up, Bernie — why isn't that good enough?"

Bernie waited.

"I checked him out," Gronk said. "For a Metro cop, he's got a good reputation."

Bernie kept waiting.

"Stine," Gronk said at last. "Lieutenant Lou Stine."

■ ■ ■ ■

Dawn was breaking as we drove up High Line Road, at first just a milkiness in one part of the sky. Then it spread, pushing all the stars away and getting rid of the dark. After that there was a moment in the sky that reminded me of a time Charlie spilled all his paints, and then a small rounded sliver of sun poked up into view. I felt real good. Sunshine glowed beautifully on the tissue Boo Ferris was blowing his nose in.

"Goddamn dust," he said approaching the car. He looked over at me. "Didn't realize that."

"What are you talking about?" Bernie said.

"His ears don't match," said Boo Ferris.

"I think it's a plus," Bernie said.

"Oh, right, sure, of course," Boo Ferris said. "Like if they were both black or both white, then . . ."

"Exactly," Bernie said. He made a little gesture toward the gate, meaning: open it, let's roll.

Boo Ferris checked his clipboard. "Headed up to the old Comstock place?"

"Yeah."

"Don't see you on the list for today," Boo Ferris said. "Want me to call up?"

Bernie shook his head.

"Don't want no trouble," said Boo Ferris. "Who does?"

Boo Ferris smiled. He had some teeth missing toward the back. The sight made me want to bite something, no idea why. Life can be pretty crazy sometimes. "You do," he said. "All the guys inside thought that."

"Total bullshit," Bernie said.

Boo Ferris laughed and raised the gate.

We drove to the top of the mountain and up the driveway of that huge house practically hanging over the cliff. "Not everything has to match," Bernie said.

The chopper stood on the helipad, its blades sort of droopy, which made me think of Dina's plants for some reason. This case? I didn't understand it, not one little bit. As we walked toward the house, the whole sun rose into view, the bottom wobbling and then growing steady. You could count on the sun, the same way you could count on . . . Bernie.

"Hey, Chet, what's with you?"

Uh-oh. Was that me, bumping into the backs of Bernie's legs, and more than once? Maybe, but I really felt like doing it. We were in for a beautiful day.

I headed toward the front door, but Bernie made this soft *click-click* in his mouth, meaning "come," so I did. We walked all the way around the house, real quiet. All the curtains were closed and the house was humming a low AC hum. We came to the gym. No curtains there. We looked in, saw nobody. Bernie went to the glass door, examined the lock, and took out his credit card. We'd had problems with that credit card before, maybe the worst one being a lunch at Le Desert Bistro where Bernie picked up the check and the waiter came back with the card and wagged his finger in what Bernie said was a French sort of way, French sort of ways turning out to make him mad, and things went downhill, which was too bad on account of that being the let's-all-get-along lunch where we met Malcolm for the very first time. But not a problem today since the card always worked great when it came to B and E, which was what we were doing now.

One thing I've noticed about B and Es: it's different every time. For example, at the critical moment where Bernie leans forward and starts carefully sliding in the credit card, did a bird ever fly by, real low, and drop a smear of that weird white bird poop square on his shoulder? Not that I remembered, amigo. Bernie made a sound like

"Gah," and backed away from the door, twisting his head so he could get a good look at his shoulder. Meanwhile, other stuff was happening. The bird circled around and landed on a flowering bush right behind us, the flowers bright red like the markings on the bird's wings, an unimportant detail I now realize, that almost distracted me from noticing the door suddenly opening from the inside and Jiggs, stooping down, giving Brando a little push into the great outdoors, the great outdoors being one of the best human expressions going, a subject for later or possibly never. Brando had a stretch — a real nice one: how did he get his back like that? — and glanced around. If he saw me or Bernie, he gave no sign, but he spotted the bird for sure, and that stretch turned into a kind of slow glide, hard to describe and not slow at all, really, and then, despite how pudgy he was, Brando took to the air, a fat golden streak, and pounced on the bird, caught him like there was nothing to it — far from the case, as I well knew from experience.

But back in the doorway — things happening fast now, and in more than one place, the way it goes down in our business sometimes — Jiggs, wearing faded jeans and nothing else, was noticing us big-time. His gaze went quickly to Bernie, me, the credit card, and back to Bernie. His face started to redden and his whole body, huge to begin with, seemed to expand, kind of like a balloon.

"What the hell is going on?" he said, fierce — but quiet at the same time, maybe . . . maybe because people were sleeping? Hey! Had I made a sort of . . . what would you call it? I wasn't sure. Just when things were coming together: pop. Like soap bubbles. Once Charlie blew bubbles with his plastic bubble blower and I chased them around. It turned out not to be as much fun as lots of other games.

Meanwhile, Bernie was saying something about Thad Perry, like maybe we wanted to see him.

"You were breaking in the goddamn house?" Jiggs said.

"Didn't want to wake anybody," Bernie said. "Can you send Thad out here? We need to talk."

Jiggs swelled up some more, really making Bernie look small. Meanwhile, Brando was tiptoeing off with what remained of the bird. I followed, and because of that maybe missed some of what was going down between Bernie and Jiggs. Did Jiggs ask Bernie what he wanted to talk to Thad about?

Possibly. Did Bernie say something about that being none of Jiggs's business? I'm not ruling that out. But at the moment I was following Brando through the garden. He stopped in the shade of a giant flower pot, got comfortable, and then, yes, began to eat the bird, although not the feathers. I myself had always wanted to catch a bird, but had never even thought of eating one, so this was kind of fascinating. I watched Brando. He watched me. Brando was a very tidy eater, a lot tidier than me, I admit it. And I was just on the point of admitting something else when I heard some thuds, hard and smacking, from the direction of the house.

I raced back through the garden, and there, by the glass door to the gym, stood Bernie. Oh, no! His mouth was bleeding! I ran right over to him. He patted his mouth with the back of his sleeve. I stood straight up with my paws on his shoulders: that blood had to be licked away and pronto.

"I'm all right, big guy," Bernie said, giving me a quick pat on the shoulder, which might have been a bit of a push away, too, except I knew it wasn't, "but we've got to move quick." Which was when I finally noticed Jiggs lying on the ground, out cold. One of his teeth lay on the fancy red-stone walkway, sparkling in the morning sun. Those little details stay with you.

TWENTY-EIGHT

Bernie is a big strong guy and he can lift heavy stuff. Once he even lifted the back end of the Porsche clear off the ground! Not the Porsche we have now, with the martini glasses, or the one before that that got blown up, but the even earlier Porsche, the one that flew off the cliff. What a day that was! It wasn't the same day that Bernie lifted the back end — that came before the flying over the cliff part, of course, when we still had the car, on a night that Bernie bet a bunch of bikers a thousand dollars he could do it. And guess what. We didn't have a thousand dollars at the time, in fact, didn't have enough to settle the tab at the biker bar, a biker bar called Savages out at this desert crossroads where the saguaros were all full of bullet holes. Bernie came through, Bernie being Bernie, and the chiropractor had him back on his feet in no time.

But forget all that. The point is that Bernie, strong as he is, still had a bit of trouble hoisting Jiggs up onto his shoulders. How I wanted to help him! I jumped up and down: it was the best I could do. Bernie carried Jiggs in a — I don't want to call it staggering, so I won't — way that didn't look easy-peasy, whatever that may mean, and dumped him fairly gently into the Porsche. Jiggs filled the whole car and slopped over the sides. Bernie probed around for the glove box, found the cuffs, locked one of Jiggs's enormous wrists to a door handle. He rose, straightened his back with a low groan, barely audible even to me, and said, "All set, big guy?" What a question!

No need for any of our credit card B and E moves: the glass door to the gym hung slightly open. After some confusion in the doorway, we went inside, me first; I spotted a feather with bright red markings right away. We passed the boxing ring, the whirl-pool room, another room full of exercise equipment, and entered a long hall. Bernie looked one way, then the other, hesitated for a moment, and then set off in the second direction, a good thing if we were after Thad Perry, because that was where his scent led.

We came to a closed door. Bernie turned the handle very slowly, pushed the door open just enough, making hardly any noise, almost certainly none in human terms. We peeked in: a bedroom, dark, but light leaked in through a tiny silvery gap in the curtains, enough to illuminate two people sleeping in the bed. One was a woman with short dark hair — Nan Klein, Thad's assistant. The other was the skinny, messy-haired writer dude, Arn Linsky. It took me a moment to recognize them without their glasses, which lay on top of each other on the bedside table.

Bernie closed the door softly and we kept going. In a real low voice, he said, "She's smart, meaning the old joke about the starlet and the writer isn't true." That one went right by me. No problem. We'd reached the next door, and I smelled pay dirt on the other side — not actual pay dirt, of course, although I knew that smell, too. That mine with the golden seam, the cave-in, my escape with the nugget? Hard to forget things like that. All we had to do is go back there and dig through the rubble — digging being one of my best things — and then we'd be rich! If only Bernie knew.

He put his hand on the knob, opened it just as he'd opened the first one. Another bedroom, but much bigger, with a sitting area first and then the bed, a huge round one raised on a platform. No gap in the curtains this time. We stood there, waiting for our eyes to adjust to the darkness, just one of our techniques at the Little Detective Agency. This turned out like all the other times: my eyes adjusted right away and then we waited for Bernie's to catch up.

We stepped into the room, Bernie closing the door behind us. There were some comfortable-looking chairs in the sitting area, plus a big-screen TV, lots of flowers, and a large couch, extra-deep and extra-long. Felicity lay sleeping on the couch, covered by a puffy duvet — no time to go into an unfortunate accident involving a very similar duvet once belonging to Leda — her blond hair fanned out on a pillow, seeming somehow to light up her face, not happy at the moment, as though bad things were happening in her sleep. We walked by her, real quiet on the carpeted floor, and stepped up on the platform. Thad Perry slept in the round bed, one arm thrown over his face and what looked like dried tear tracks on his face. A pill bottle lay open on the blanket and a few blue pills had spilled out; also there was coke around somewhere, one of those real easy smells for a dog in my profession. Bernie picked up the bottle, squinted at the label, then stepped down off the platform and returned to the sitting area. I managed to get there ahead of him.

We crossed the floor, checked the bathroom, the biggest bathroom I'd ever seen. The shower was a sort of rocky grotto and the bathtub was like a small swimming pool.

Back at the couch, Bernie leaned over Felicity, touched her shoulder. She groaned softly. Bernie touched her shoulder again. Her mouth opened. "I can't," she said, more of a low mumble, hard to understand, so maybe she'd said something else.

"Felicity," Bernie whispered. "Wake up."

Her eyes opened in a slow, uncertain sort of way. At first they were a complete golden brown blank, like she wasn't really there, and in that blank period Bernie placed his finger across his lips in the human sign for not a peep. Felicity's eyes came to life, went through some quick changes all about surprise and fear, but she didn't make a sound.

"It's all right," Bernie said, lowering his hand. "We're here to help."

Went without mentioning: that was what we did. Although who were we helping, exactly? I hoped to find out soon, but if not I was cool with that, too.

Felicity nodded.

"Will you stay in the bathroom for a few minutes?" Bernie said quietly. "I need to talk to Thad."

"About me?" said Felicity, even quieter.

"Why would it be about you?"

"I don't know," she said. And then: "We usually sleep together."

"I'm not the togetherness police," Bernie said.

Whoa! A totally new one on me. Policing was more than Metro PD, the state troopers, FBI, ATF, Secret Service, Game and Fish? Even with someone like me who'd been in the business just about forever, there were still new wrinkles. But I was in good shape on account of wrinkles never bothered me, Leda's obsession with ironing every single piece of clothing remaining a total mystery.

Meanwhile, Felicity was nodding again, like she was having no trouble following all this. "It was just that he was having such a bad night," she said.

Bernie held out the bottle. "How many of these did he take?"

"He needs them to sleep," said Felicity.

"But how many?"

"There's nothing I can do to stop him when he gets . . . the way he gets."

"Was he drinking, too? Drugging?"

"Probably. He has demons."

"What kind of demons?"

"I don't know," Felicity said. "It's all tied up with him being an artist, but sometimes they take over."

Bernie took a long breath. "Okay," he said. "Just go in the bathroom and stay quiet."

"What are you going to do?"

"Try to beat back the demons a little," Bernie said.

"Thank you." Felicity rose. She wasn't wearing any clothing — my preference as well: once Bernie's mother had tried to get a vest on me! — and Bernie did a pretty good job of trying not to watch her, sort of, all of that a bit of a puzzler, while she took a robe off one of the chairs and threw it on. Felicity went into the bathroom and closed the door. Bernie and I returned to the big round bed. The darkness in the room had a sort of feel, like weight pressing on my back.

We gazed down at Thad, still sleeping with his arm thrown over his face, a big strong arm, although now the muscles looked soft. Bernie's face was hard. I stood very straight and still, ears way up. We know how to send a message at the Little Detective Agency. Thad made a low sound and shuddered in his sleep.

"Dreaming about April?" Bernie said in

his normal voice, no lowering or whispering.

There was a long silence. Then Thad's face — the visible part, below his arm — twitched, and very softly he said, "Oh, April, no, no."

"What's happening to April?" Bernie said.

Another silence, not as long as the first. Then, even more quietly, Thad said, "It's too horrible."

"What is?" Bernie said.

Thad groaned. "Blood," he said, "too much. Way, way too much."

"Whose blood?"

"Everywhere," Thad said, his voice rising. "Blood all over us, all over the sheets." And he suddenly threw off his covers. He had a lipstick stain on his chest: I had time to spot that just before he opened his eyes, those huge blue eyes, now all blurred and foggy. "A knife?" He twisted sharply toward his empty hand, gazed at it. Was he expecting a knife to be there? I didn't get it.

Thad turned, jumped at the sight of us, his eyes clearing fast. He sat right up. "What the hell?" he said.

"What happened to the knife?" Bernie said.

Thad licked his lips. He looked very bad, dark purple patches under both eyes, his skin kind of pasty and waxy, like he'd gotten a lot older since the last time we'd seen him. But his eyes were clear now and he was wide awake. "Knife?" he said.

"The knife you used to kill April," Bernie told him.

"No," Thad said, shaking his head. "No, no, no." He glanced around in that desperate way perps do when they've got a notion to book. "How did you get in? Where's Jiggs?"

"Waiting for us to finish our conversation," Bernie said.

"Jiggs knows you're here?"

"No question."

"But . . . but he'd never do that."

"Maybe he's decided it's time to cut his own deal."

"Deal?" Thad said. "He knows I'd give him anything."

"Not a deal with you," Bernie said. "I'm talking about the law."

"The law?" Thad reached for the covers, pulled them back up, meaning . . . meaning it would be harder for him to book. At that moment, I knew one thing for sure: Thad was no perp.

"There's no statute of limitations on murder," Bernie said. "And from information we've developed it's pretty clear that

380

Jiggs was an accessory after the fact."

"Who's 'we'?" Thad said.

"Chet and I," said Bernie. What was wrong with Thad? Wasn't that obvious?

Thad's gaze shifted to me, then back to Bernie. "Where's Brando?"

Bernie shrugged.

Thad licked his lips again. They were all dry and cracked. He glanced at the bedside table. An empty water bottle lay on its side in a little puddle on the tabletop. "I need water," he said. "Can't think straight."

"Try easing up on the drugs," Bernie said.

And all at once, I was thirsty, too: funny how the mind works. I went over and licked up that puddle.

Meanwhile, it looked like Thad was starting to get angry. "A real feather in your cap, huh, bringing down a movie star?" he said.

"I couldn't care less about that," Bernie said.

Or something close, my mind getting stuck a bit back at the feather part. That feather on the gym floor, glossy black with the red markings, would probably look great in a cap, but Bernie never wore one. And just as I was thinking about the feather and how it got to end up in the gym, from out of nowhere came Brando, sort of flowing across the room, up onto the bed, and settling down in the crook of Thad's arm. Brando settled some more. He could settle like nobody I'd ever seen. Thad gazed down at him, then back at Bernie, and now the anger was gone.

"I knew it would be someone like you," he said.

TWENTY-NINE

"What are you talking about?" Bernie said.

"Someone ruthless," Thad said. "Who came to take me in. That's what you're doing, right? Arresting me? Aren't you a cop or something?"

Bernie's laughter is one of my great pleasures in life, but there's one laugh he has that's not so nice. Still pretty nice, since it's Bernie, after all, and it's not that I didn't like hearing it. I just didn't like hearing it quite as much, and I hardly ever did. But Bernie laughed that not-quite-as-nice laugh now, laughed it in Thad's face.

"You think I'm ruthless?" he said. "Just wait."

"For what?" Thad said.

"For what's coming."

Thad's eyes shifted. "Maybe I should call my lawyer."

"Who's that?"

"I've got lots of lawyers," Thad said. "Nan

will know." He glanced toward the door. "Where is she?"

Bernie shook his head. "You're on your own right now."

Thad pulled Brando in a little closer. Brando wasn't in the mood. He rose, sort of drifted off the bed, and vanished in the shadows.

"What about Felicity?" Thad said.

"You're dealing with me," Bernie said. "Me and Chet."

Thad looked at me. For no reason at all, I chose that moment to bare my teeth; actually, it was more like my teeth chose the moment to bare themselves. Has that ever happened to you? But even if it has, so what — no offense — human teeth being what they are?

Thad turned quickly away from me and back to Bernie. "What do you want?"

"Start with the facts about April's murder," Bernie said.

Thad took a huge breath, let it out in a way that was almost a sob. "I was just a kid."

"So was she," Bernie said.

And then Thad did sob, one big teary cry that he muffled by putting his hands over his face. "I don't even know where to start," he said, or something like that, not too clear what with his hands like that.

"Start with the car wash," Bernie said.

Thad peeked at Bernie through his fingers. I'd seen Charlie do the exact same thing. Did that mean Thad was some sort of child? What a thought! It disappeared from my mind, and not a moment too soon.

"How do you know about the car wash?" Thad said.

Bernie just gazed down at him. Slowly Thad lowered his hands.

"The car wash," he said. "It was in Vista City. Jiggsy worked there. He's my cousin, although nobody knows it, so I'm asking you not to . . ." His voice trailed away.

"You came from LA to visit him?" Bernie said.

Thad nodded. "Just for a couple weeks. It was my first time away from home. I was sixteen, knew nothing about nothing, except for surfing. Then one day April drove into the car wash."

"Alone?"

"With her friend."

"Boyfriend?"

"No. Her friend Dina."

"And then?"

"I sort of became the boyfriend. It all happened so fast. And so intense. I was a virgin up until that time, believe it or not."

"And April? Was she a virgin, too?"

Thad shook his head. "She was only a year older, but way more experienced. And kind of wild. I loved that about her." He gazed toward the window, hidden by the dark curtains. "In fact, I actually just loved her, period."

"So why did you kill her?" Bernie said.

Thad sobbed again, this time more than once; his eyes teared up, but they didn't overflow. Bernie watched with a real cold look on his face. I raised my tail, high and stiff.

"I don't know," Thad said, shaking his head from side to side. "I've tried and tried and tried and . . ." He kept shaking his head like that, faster and faster. Bernie reached out and slapped him across the face.

Thad stopped shaking his head, looked real angry. He glared up at Bernie and his hands balled into fists. But then they un-balled and those big blue eyes — kind of like a movie all by themselves — went dead. "Just kill me. Kill me now."

"I'll take a rain check," Bernie said.

Uh-oh. That was a bit of a baffler since it never rains in the Valley. So did a rain check mean never? I'd been over this ground before, always with the same result, meaning zip.

"Right now," Bernie was saying, "let's get

386

back to why you killed April."

"I already told you — I don't know," Thad said. "I don't remember a thing about that night."

"What night?"

"That goddamn night. I'd never done drugs before, not even pot. I'd hardly ever been drunk."

"You did drugs that night?"

"April was kind of wild, like I said."

"What drugs?" Bernie said.

"Oh, man," said Thad, "I'm one of those people that drugs just live for, you know?"

Bernie didn't say whether he did or didn't, whatever Thad's question might have been. That was one of his interviewing techniques and this was an interview, no doubt about it, and not close to being the first one we'd done with someone or more than one someone in bed. In fact, that kind of interview often went well for us.

"Stick with that night," Bernie said.

"I told you I don't —"

Bernie cut Thad off, his voice rising. "Where were you?"

Thad kind of cringed, just at the sound of Bernie's voice. "If you're going to hit me again, don't stop. You'll be doing me a favor."

"There's no time for your dramatics," Bernie said. "Where were you?"

Thad laughed, a harsh little laugh, quickly done with.

"Something's funny?" Bernie said.

"The opposite," said Thad. "I've trained myself to shut out the critics. Now you come along." Bernie stared down at him. Thad looked away, turning again to the curtains; he seemed to be seeing something far away. "We were at Jiggs's place," he said in a voice that got quieter and also stranger as he went along, almost like he wasn't really with us, hard to explain. "Jiggs was living at his dad's and his dad was usually gone — he worked in the oil patch out in Texas. This particular night was my last one. I had to go home the next morning for summer school on account of my lousy grades. I wanted April to come with me. She wanted me to stay. We had a little fight about that."

Silence. We waited. That was another part of our interviewing technique. Bernie had explained why more than once, but it was one of those reasons that just didn't stick. I tried not to worry about that; actually, I didn't even have to try. I'm lucky that way.

One thing about this particular technique: there was no point in waiting forever. Just before we were about to hit forever, Bernie said, "What kind of fight?"

Thad glanced at Bernie, squinting as though Bernie was too bright. "Nothing physical, if that's what you're thinking," he said. "We argued a bit, that's all. Maybe she cried. But then she came up with this idea to take LSD. Go on a trip together after all, kind of thing. I wasn't that enthusiastic — we'd smoked some pot and we were drinking vodka, too. But I went along. All I remember — I still see them — were these terrible visions, in a tunnel, April and me, although we were actually in bed, and claws."

"Claws?"

"Horrible long hooked claws, clawing and clawing at us."

Big claws? I'd been up close to an angry mama bear, knew more than I wanted to about big claws. I started feeling kind of sorry for Thad, but not much, since I was getting the feeling he'd done something real bad long ago.

"And?" Bernie said.

"And nothing," Thad said. "We just clung to each other, shaking and crying. At least I was. She might not have even been there."

"April might not have been there?"

"I don't know." Thad's eyes turned deep and murky. He closed them. "I feel like — I felt like — I was all alone, clinging to

389

myself." His chest rose, fell, rose again. "April, April," he went on, very softly. "But she won't answer. Still mad? I have to go to school, babe. It's my whole —" His eyes opened. He blinked a few times and his eyes returned to normal, if eyes like Thad's could ever be called normal. Was he back in the here and now? I myself preferred the here and now at all times, maybe something we can go into later.

Thad tried to meet Bernie's gaze and actually did. "But she must have been there," he said.

"Why?" Bernie said.

"Because when I woke up she was right next to me." Thad shuddered. "Blood all over her, all over me, and the knife was still in my hand."

"What knife?" Bernie said.

"This ordinary kitchen knife."

"From Jiggs's kitchen?"

"I guess so."

"How did it come to be in the bed?"

"I must have gotten up and brought it there."

"Do you remember doing that?"

"I told you — I don't remember anything."

"Where was Jiggs this whole time?"

"Hanging with friends. He didn't come

back until morning. By that time, I was freaking out. He kind of took over."

"In what way?"

"Handling the situation."

"How did he do that?"

"Calmed me down, to begin with," Thad said. "Getting me to understand that I hadn't been in my right mind, like temporary insanity."

"Making you not responsible?"

"Legally, right?" He gave Bernie a challenging sort of look.

"Your nightmares tell a different story," Bernie said.

Thad hung his head. At that moment, I felt something soft move against me. I looked down, and there was Brando lying at my side, curling around my back legs. The feeling wasn't the worst in the world.

"Whose idea was it to dump April behind the Flower Mart?" Bernie said.

Thad winced. "Jiggs's," he said. "It was meant to be . . . misleading, I guess you'd say."

"I guess."

"After that, we . . . we cleaned up the place, and Jiggs drove me to LA. He decided to stay when we got there. His old man didn't care."

"What happened to the knife?"

Thad shivered like it was cold, even though the AC wasn't nearly as cranked up as it often is in Valley houses. "Jiggs cleaned it and put it back in the kitchen drawer."

Bernie nodded like that made sense. "You got away with murder," he said.

"I sure don't feel like it," Thad said.

"You're too sensitive," said Bernie.

Thad turned red.

"When did the blackmailing start?"

"How do you know about that?"

"Everything comes out eventually," Bernie said. "In the real world," he added.

"Christ, stop," said Thad. "Just stop tormenting me. I already confessed. And I'll tell you something — the only reason I took this pissy role was because of the location. My subconscious wanted to come back here, to — I don't know — make things right."

"By killing the blackmailer?" Bernie said.

"Huh?"

"Come on," Bernie said. "You don't know who was blackmailing you?"

"Of course I do," said Thad. "It was this old boyfriend of April's, Manny something, and a gangster pal of his. I kind of remember April mentioning she dumped him, but it turned out he was stalking her. He saw us that morning through the window."

"How do you know?"

"Because they dropped in on me unannounced not long after *Ninety-nine and Forty-four One Hundredths* came out."

"What's that?" Bernie said.

Thad looked surprised. "My first film," he said. "They wanted seventy-five grand, one time only. We paid, but of course it hasn't been one time only."

"When did you last see Manny?"

"That was it. The one time."

"And his pal?"

"The same."

"The pal's name?"

"Ramon Cardinal, a real dangerous guy. Jiggs deals with Manny."

"Heard any recent news about Manny?" Bernie said.

"Jiggs made a payment last week, if that's what you mean by news."

"And he found Manny in good health?"

"What are you saying?"

Bernie gave Thad a long look. "Nothing," he said.

There was a silence. It went on for a while. Finally, Thad said, "Now what?"

Bernie didn't answer. He was having thoughts, but maybe Thad was missing that.

"If it can be done discreetly, I'd appreciate it," Thad said. "Not for me. For the others."

Bernie snapped out of it. "What the hell are you talking about?" he said.

"Taking me in, booking me, all the procedures."

"They can wait," Bernie said.

Thad's head came up so he was sort of looking down his nose at Bernie, something Bernie was not fond of, not one bit. "Why do I always miss the obvious?" Thad said. "You're blackmailing me, too."

Bernie didn't punch Thad, exactly; it was more like he put his hand on Thad's forehead and pushed him down on the pillows.

"Let's go, big guy," Bernie said.

"You're leaving?" Thad said.

"Where can you hide?" said Bernie.

I stepped carefully over Brando. He seemed to be asleep, but also purring softly. We walked through the sitting area. The bathroom door was still closed. Felicity stood right on the other side of it. I could hear her breathing.

We went outside and got a bad surprise: no Jiggs. The whole passenger door of the Porsche — meaning my door, although I seldom used it, preferring to hop over on my way in and out — was missing, ripped right out. Bernie glanced around real quick, and leaned into the car, opening the glove box and taking out the .38 Special. I loved the .38 Special, the sight, the sound, the smell, everything; Bernie was a crack shot, in case that hasn't come up yet. Coke bottles on a fence rail? Smithereens!

I could almost hear those smithereens, in fact, got a bit distracted by their almost sound, meaning I just about missed a scared cry coming from the direction of the helipad, the cry of a voice I knew. It was Leda.

"Chet? What are you growling about?" And then Bernie heard it, too, and we took off toward the helipad. Parked on the other side of the chopper was Leda's big silver minivan. Leda and Charlie were outside the van, but not together. In between stood Jiggs, one arm still cuffed to our door, now hanging down to the ground. His other arm was sort of around Charlie's shoulder, like they were pals. Leda was trying to get to Charlie, but Jiggs blocked her with his huge body.

"What are you doing?" she screamed. "Let him go."

"Back the hell off," said Jiggs.

Bernie raised the .38. "Freeze."

They all whipped around toward us. Leda and Charlie actually did freeze, although I was pretty sure Bernie hadn't meant them. He'd meant Jiggs, and Jiggs was the one who didn't freeze. Instead, he yanked Charlie in front of him and curled his enormous arm around Charlie's little neck.

"Drop the gun," Jiggs said, but Bernie already had; it clattered on the helipad pavement.

"Hands up behind your head," Jiggs said.

Bernie put his hands behind his head. At the same time he made this quick tiny whistling sound, more like just air, *fwwt fwwt. Fwwt fwwt?* Was that something we'd been working on? I tried to remember.

Meanwhile, Leda was calling out to Bernie, "Bernie, Bernie, do something." And Jiggs was saying, "Shut your goddamn mouth." And Charlie had turned white and was starting to cry. I saw red, and just as I saw red, remembered what *fwwt fwwt* meant, or almost, something about sidling around and coming up on the perp from behind and then getting lots of treats; but too late for any of that. Jiggs was making Charlie cry? I saw red, really saw it, the whole world smeared over with bloody red, even if Bernie says I can't be trusted when it comes to colors.

Way too late for *fwwt fwwt:* I was already on the move, across the helipad on the first

396

bound and launched on the second. Jiggs saw me coming, his eyes opening wide, and started to raise Charlie right off the ground, trying to turn my Charlie into a shield. But Charlie struggled — what a kid! — and Jiggs had to grab him with his other hand, and that meant dealing with the car door, and then: *KA-BOOM!* I hit Jiggs full in the face, both paws stretched out to the max. Jiggs cried out in fear and pain, and began toppling backward, losing his grip on Charlie. That cry of Jiggs's sent a thrill right through me, from nose to tail and back. I wanted nothing more than to hear it again.

THIRTY

But I didn't hear it again, because in what seemed like no time I had Jiggs by the throat, and no human does much screaming in that situation, not in my experience. Why the throat? Hard to explain: it's just one of those things we in the nation within know how to do when it needs doing. Terror: not something you often saw in the eyes of a dude the size of Jiggs, but there it was, out in the open and unmistakable. I stopped seeing red.

"Easy, easy, big guy." Bernie was at my side, his voice low and strangely thick, like there was something wrong with his own throat.

I was already taking it easy, sort of. Had there ever even been a question of actually biting? The truth was I hadn't broken skin, or hardly at all.

"C'mon, Chet. You did great."

I felt Bernie's hand on my back — one of

the best feelings going — and eased up a bit, almost letting go of Jiggs's neck completely.

"Chet?"

Okay, okay. Completely.

Bernie stepped in between me and Jiggs. Jiggs felt his neck with his free hand. He was breathing heavily, like he'd been on a long run, but he went still when he saw the look on Bernie's face. So did I. Bernie had the gun again, although he wasn't holding it the usual way, instead gripped it by the barrel, the butt all of a sudden turning into the weapon part. He started to raise it. For a moment, I thought he was about to do something really awful, and so did Jiggs, couldn't have been clearer on his face. But Bernie paused — the muscles in his arm popping even though it couldn't have taken much strength to stop raising the gun — and didn't end up doing anything awful. Bernie was Bernie.

Jiggs started to sit up, propping himself on his elbows. "Look," he began, "I —"

"Not one goddamn word," Bernie said.

He turned to Charlie and Leda, standing over by the chopper and hugging each other. "You okay, Charlie?"

Charlie nodded, maybe keeping it up for a bit too long. Leda began moving toward us,

her voice high and unsteady. "I don't understand any of this," she said. "Why did he
—"

"Leda. Stop. I'll explain later."

"But —"

"And what the hell are you even doing
here?" Uh-oh. Bernie was starting to lose
his temper in the way he only did with Leda.

"We were invited, of course," Leda said,
starting to lose hers right back. "For breakfast. Thad's being so nice, in case you
haven't noticed. Arn has a very cool idea
for a script with a major role for an actor of
Charlie's age, and Thad's —"

"Get in the car," Bernie said, raising his
voice over hers, actually making the air
tremble. "Take Charlie home. Don't come
back here."

Whenever Bernie wanted Leda to do
something, she either just straight out didn't
do it, or put up such a huge fight that Bernie gave up, or changed it into something
else that got Bernie all confused. In short,
she never simply did it, not ever.

Until now. Leda took Charlie's hand, led
him to the minivan, got in. As they drove
off down the mountain road, Bernie calmed
down; I could feel it. "You're a brave boy,"
he said, so quietly I almost didn't hear.
Meaning me, of course, although his gaze

was on the minivan.

"What's that word?" Bernie said, turning to Jiggs. "Charade?" First I'd heard of it, so no surprise Bernie seemed uncertain; we're a lot alike in some ways, don't forget. "The charade, Jiggsy," he went on, "is over."

"Don't know what you're talking about."

"Sure you do," Bernie said. "The murder of April Spears. Thad made a full confession."

"You're lying."

"I even know you cleaned off the knife," Bernie said. "And helped Thad flee the scene of the crime, making you at least an accessory, possibly an accomplice — I'll have to read up."

Jiggs glared at Bernie and said nothing. Perps had that right, so it was cool with me. Was Jiggs a perp? Big-time, for what he'd done to Charlie. And there might have been even more to it. I waited to find out.

"What I don't know," Bernie said, "is whether you were skimming from the payments."

Jiggs kept glaring. He kind of swelled up, like an explosion was coming. Good luck with that, amigo, you down there and us up here. A big vein, thick as this huge worm I'd once dug up — a bit of a shocker, when all you're trying to do is locate an old bone — pulsed in the side of his neck, and then, like he just couldn't hold it in an instant longer, out came a loud "Huh?"

"A minor point, but I'd like to clear it up," Bernie said. "Manny was skimming, so why not you?"

"I'm not a parasite, you goddamn —" Jiggs began and then cut himself off.

"Maybe you're a killer instead," Bernie said.

"Setting me up?" Jiggs said. "Forget it. I never laid a finger on her. Wasn't there that night, and I can prove it."

"Who said anything about April?" Bernie said. "I'm talking about Manny."

Jiggs was silent for a few moments. I watched the worm in his neck. When it got to pulsing pretty fast, he said, "Why would I kill that little prick?"

"Killing the blackmailer is one of those classic go-to moves," Bernie said.

"Doesn't mean shit," said Jiggs. "I didn't do it."

"But you knew he was dead."

Jiggs made the slightest little nod.

"How come you didn't tell Thad?" Bernie said.

"Wouldn't have made any difference," Jiggs said. "All it woulda done is upset him,

402

and that's not my job."

"What is your job?" Bernie said.

"Looking out for Thad, what do you think?"

"How much does he pay you?"

"He doesn't have to pay me squat. I'd do it for nothing."

"Why?"

"I'm loyal," Jiggs said. "Probably not a concept you understand."

Had I ever heard anything crazier? The biting urge started up in my teeth, also crazy, since we had Jiggs where we wanted him, meaning the biting period had come to an end. By the time I got all that confusion back under control, or close to it, Jiggs was saying, ". . . a great artist. He'll be remembered long after you and I are dead."

"So will Heinrich Himmler," Bernie said.

"Who's he?" said Jiggs.

Bernie smiled. "You win," he said. He held out his hand, as though to help Jiggs to his feet.

Jiggs ignored Bernie's hand. His eyes narrowed. "I win? What does that mean?"

"It means I'm offering you a deal," Bernie said. "If you cooperate, I'll get you booked on something trivial for what went down today — threatening, harassment, that kind of thing. If you don't cooperate, it's the whole enchilada — kidnapping, assault with intent, possession of a deadly weapon."

"Weapon?"

Bernie pointed to our car door, still cuffed to Jiggs's wrist, but I wasn't really paying attention. The whole enchilada! How often had I heard that? Had an enchilada ever put in an appearance? Never. Forget about a whole one — how about just some measly enchilada crumbs? So I was hoping pretty hard that Jiggs would walk away from the deal and maybe I'd get my chance at last.

". . . cooperate how?" Jiggs was saying.

"Set up a meeting for me," Bernie said.

"With who?" Jiggs said. A clever look glinted in his eyes. "Thad's management?"

"In a way," said Bernie. "I'm talking about Ramon Cardinal."

Jiggs gazed up at Bernie, his eyes narrowing more. "What do you want with him?"

"Have a drink, kick back," Bernie said.

"He's not the type."

"What type is he?"

Jiggs shrugged. "I haven't seen him in years."

"But he must have contacted you, and recently," Bernie said. "There's got to be some new system for making the payments now that Manny's gone."

Jiggs said nothing. He watched Bernie real

404

carefully, the way perps did when they started getting hip to the fact that Bernie was always the smartest human in the room. And we weren't even in a room right now, meaning he was the smartest human in the great outdoors! No one was hipper to the fact than me.

"Plus you're a sharp guy, Jiggs," Bernie went on. "So when he called, you got his number. I'm betting it's on your cell phone."

"Don't have it on me," Jiggs said.

"Jiggs? I can see the outline on your pocket."

Jiggs reached into the pocket of his jeans, gave Bernie the phone.

Bernie squatted down like a catcher, getting closer to Jiggs. He winced the tiniest bit from his leg wound, but you had to be watching real close to spot it. "You're going to request a face-to-face meeting," he said, "just the two of you."

"What if he says no?"

"Tell him you want to make one final payment, a big one on condition it's also the last."

"There's never a last payment with bloodsuckers like him," Jiggs said.

"You'll have to do some make-believe," Bernie said.

"Make-believe?" said Jiggs.

"Like acting," Bernie told him. "Pretend you're too dumb to know there's never an end with bloodsuckers like him. I have faith in you."

"You're an asshole, you know that?" Jiggs said.

"The time for recrimination is over," Bernie said. He pressed a few keys on Jiggs's phone, checked the screen. "This it?" he said, turning the phone so Jiggs could see. Jiggs nodded. Bernie gave him the phone. "Say you want to meet in the park across from city hall."

Jiggs made the call, had a brief talk, clicked off.

"He'll meet," Jiggs said, "but not there."

"Where?" said Bernie.

Jiggs got a new look in his eye, like something was funny. "Behind the old Flower Mart," he said.

We headed back down the mountain road, Jiggs in the shotgun seat, still cuffed to the door, which rested on his lap, and me on the shelf in back, not at my happiest. Boo Ferris raised the gate.

"You didn't see anything," Bernie said.

"I'm saving up for Lasik," said Boo Ferris.

We drove through. Did Bernie make a

quick call? Possibly to Rick? I was too caught up in staring at Jiggs's neck — scratched up, but I'd seen way worse — to be sure. The shotgun seat was rightfully mine.

Before we got down to the valley floor, Bernie pulled off on a narrow track and parked at a lookout. Below us the city went on and on as far as I could see.

"What about Thad?" Jiggs said.

"What about him?" said Bernie.

"You're separating us," Jiggs said. "Meaning you've got something in mind."

"Have you read the script?" Bernie said.

"What the hell is that supposed to mean?" said Jiggs.

Bernie did not reply. A little later a black-and-white appeared on the track, drove up beside us, parked cop-style. Rick looked past Bernie at Jiggs with the door in his lap.

"Hope you know what you're doing," he said.

"Makes two of us," said Bernie.

Which had to be one of Bernie's jokes. Of course he knew what he was doing. I was totally sure that the case, whatever it was about, exactly, couldn't have been going better.

". . . some out-of-the-way precinct," Bernie was saying. "San Marco, maybe."

"Fighting traffic coming and going?" Rick said.

"Ocotillo Springs, then, for Christ sake. Book him on something minor —"

"Drunk and disorderly?"

"Whatever you like. Then just hold him, no calls in or out till you hear from me."

"What about his rights?"

"He's waiving them."

Jiggs stared straight ahead.

Bernie uncuffed Jiggs from the door, and Rick sat him in the back of the black-and-white, behind the cage. I hopped up into the shotgun seat, made myself comfortable. Meanwhile, Bernie and Rick had moved over to the railing at the edge of the lookout.

"Did you know Stine worked with Cal Luxton in Vista City?" Bernie said.

"That's not news," Rick said. "They hated each other."

"How come?"

Rick shrugged. "Happens with partners sometimes."

It did? What a crazy idea!

"Luxton's connected," Rick went on. "No way Stine ever would have made lieutenant if Luxton had stayed on the force. And no way he ever makes captain, not as long as Luxton's in the mayor's office."

"Does Stine know that?"

Rick nodded. "Eats him up inside."

THIRTY-ONE

"What am I sposta do with that?" said Nixon Panero, his cheek bulging with tobacco chew.

Back at Nixon's Championship Autobody. Spike came right over and gave me a nip. I gave him a nip. We nipped each other to our hearts' content, which came sooner for Spike — a warrior, but getting older now, his face whiter than ever — than it did for me. He went and lay down in the shade of a jacked-up limo.

"Huh?" Bernie said. He was trying to give Nixon the door Jiggs had ripped off the hinges, but Nixon had his hands in the pockets of his greasy overalls and showed no sign of taking them out anytime soon.

"Fix it, of course," Bernie said. "Can't have Chet riding around with no door."

"Know something, Bernie?" Nixon said. "You're hard on automobiles." He spat a thin stream of tobacco juice into an empty can that should have been out of reach but somehow wasn't. I could watch Nixon do that forever. "It's psychological," he went on. "I made a study of this."

"Of what?" Bernie said, shifting the door to a more comfortable position and maybe sounding just the tiniest bit irritated.

"Guys like you. You're basically jealous of your car. It's, like, perfection, and you're flawed. So it figures you'd want to take it down a peg or two, even things up."

Bernie was flawed? How? I couldn't come up with a single way, and knew right then that this idea of Nixon's made no sense. But funny thing: maybe Bernie himself didn't realize that. I could sort of tell from this look on his face, a still look that meant he was having deep thoughts. When Bernie went still like that, I often found myself going still, too. The stillness went on for sometime, and then Bernie did something pretty amazing: he gave himself a shake! Yes! Just like a member of the nation within. He gave himself a shake, snapping out of the deep thoughts, and said, "So based on my psychological profile, you're refusing to fix my car?"

"Exactly the opposite," said Nixon. "Based on your profile, I'm gonna do it. But not with that door." He gave the door a glance, shook his head. "Beyond my powers, Bernie. Hope you got it out of your system."

There's an old couch outside the front of Nixon's shop. That's where Bernie and I waited while the door got fixed, and while we were waiting a black car with tinted windows pulled up right in front of us. The driver's window slid down and the driver looked out at us. Cal Luxton: with his swept-back hair, long sideburns, cowboy hat.

"Well, well," he said. "This is serendipitous."

"Yeah?" said Bernie.

"Running into you like this. Best mechanic in the Valley, of course, and you're the type who's in the know." Luxton gave Bernie a long, slow look, the probing kind that made me uncomfortable. "Problem is, you're not passing on that knowledge in a timely manner."

"No?" said Bernie. Bernie giving real short answers like "yeah" and "no" was a sign of him being careful. I got ready to be careful myself, starting by gnawing on my leg. And what was this? Some kind of thistle? I went to work on it.

"We're not paying you enough?" Luxton said. "That the issue?"

Now Bernie gave him a long, slow look

right back. I just loved Bernie when he did stuff like that, and also when he didn't. As for what it was all about, you tell me.

"I'll pay it back if you want," Bernie said. "Every cent."

Whoa! That was what his long slow look was about? Paying back? With our finances being what they were, meaning a mess? Tin futures. Hawaiian pants. They swirled round and round in my mind until I began feeling pukey. I actually considered puking, went with making my mind a blank instead, which took less time.

Luxton smiled. "No one's suggesting that," he said. "What I'm looking for is better communication."

"About what?" Bernie said.

"You're supposed to be keeping an eye on things," Luxton said. "Today's on the shooting schedule and now I find out all of a sudden they're not shooting. How come I didn't hear it from you?"

"They forgot to run it past me," Bernie said.

"Any idea what's going on?"

"With what?"

"This schedule change," Luxton said, his voice sharpening. He gave Bernie another one of those eye probes. "What else would I be talking about?"

"Search me," Bernie said. "But it's hard to know why they do anything, Cal. They're artistic types, different from us."

"How about the bodyguard, Nolan Jiggs — is he the artistic type?"

"You never know," Bernie said. "Everyone in Hollywood's got a script in the drawer."

"So maybe he's off in a cabin somewhere, banging away on his laptop," Luxton said. "Because no one can find him."

"Wouldn't know anything about that," Bernie said. "My job's making sure Thad Perry keeps his nose clean, and last seen he was stone cold sober and looking forward to breakfast. Chet here had a nice time playing with Brando."

"What the hell are you talking about?"

"Thad's cat. You met him. He and Chet are pals."

Luxton made the kind of sideways gesture with his hand that humans have for whisking away flies. Where I come from we have tails for that, but I'm not saying one way's better than the other. No time to think about that, or the fact that some humans miss out on what's going on with other creatures, almost like they're not there, because problems were coming at me in waves. I was pals with Brando? When had that happened? And what was this about breakfast? I remembered no breakfast. Breakfast is not something I forget. So therefore — whoa! I came very close to doing a so-therefore. But so-therefores were in Bernie's territory. I backed off.

"What's pissing me off," Luxton was saying, "is this feeling I get that you're not taking the job seriously."

"Yeah?" said Bernie. "That's really what's pissing you off?"

Luxton's face darkened like a shadow was passing over him, but there wasn't a cloud in the sky. "What else would it be?"

Bernie looked right at him. "You tell me," he said.

Luxton looked at Bernie right back. "Hope you know what you're doing, buddy."

"People keep saying that," Bernie said.

Luxton drove off. Not long after that, Nixon had the Porsche all fixed.

"What do you think?" Nixon said.

"The new door is yellow?" said Bernie.

"Golden," said Nixon. "I'd call it golden. See how it's shiny?"

"The rest of the body is red."

"Not the martini glasses."

Bernie gazed at the car.

"I could paint the door to match, but you

415

won't have it today," Nixon said.

"Need it today."

"Now Chet has a golden door," Nixon said. "Think of it that way."

Bernie looked thoughtful.

"All depends on how you think about things," Nixon said.

"You're right, Nix," Bernie said. "So tell me how I should be thinking about the fact that Cal Luxton just swung by."

Nixon opened his mouth, closed it, shuffled his feet, the kinds of things guilty perps did. What was going on? Nixon had been a perp, of course, and we'd sent him away, for what I no longer remembered, but now weren't we friends?

"Coincidence?" said Bernie. "Or not?"

Nixon gazed down at the ground.

We pulled into the empty parking lot of the old Flower Mart late in the afternoon. The wind blew hot and hard, full of grit. The sky, so red and dusty, made me uneasy. Bernie took the .38 Special out of the glove box and tucked it in his belt. We got out of the car and walked around the boarded-up warehouse to the back. No one there. Bernie checked his watch.

"We're a little early, big guy," he said. "But early's good when it comes to meetings like this." Early: a tricky one. It had something to do with late, the exact relationship murky. But if Bernie said it was good, then that was all I needed. We paced around a bit, checked the rusty railroad tracks, the space where the Dumpster had been, and the nailed-shut back door which I knew from before wasn't really nailed shut. We paced around some more, returned to the door. Bernie tried it. Nailed shut after all? It wouldn't open.

He knocked. "Mr. Albert?" he called. "Mr. Albert?"

No answer. Sometimes I hear when someone's around, sometimes I smell it, and sometimes I just get a feeling. Right now I got the feeling that no one was inside.

We waited. Time passed, how much I couldn't tell you. Bernie checked his watch. The wind blew hotter and harder, and the sky turned redder and darker. We huddled in the doorway. Huge roiling clouds rose in the distance, much more solid-looking than regular clouds; the air got drier and drier, and dust blew into my eyes and ears. Bernie gave me a little pat. It was kind of nice, here in the back doorway of the old Flower Mart, just me and Bernie. I had no desire to be anywhere else.

"Why wouldn't he show?" Bernie said.

"Any reason why he'd want to screw Jiggs around? Probably a shitload."

Uh-oh, not that. I thought of one of our very worst cases, not the details of the case, all gone now, but just the nighttime ending when the flatbed truck we were hiding on rolled over and all the portapotties came tumbling loose. I got ready for anything.

"Would help right about now if we had a solid theory of the case," Bernie said.

A solid theory of the case: hadn't heard that in way too long. Soon after the solid theory of the case came me grabbing the perp by the pant leg, which was how our cases closed just about every time, although not the portapotty case, which I'd rather skip for now.

The wind died down in a strange way, and as it did, the huge roiling clouds grew and grew and there seemed to be less air to breathe. I panted a bit, my tongue getting coated with dust.

"Is it basically about money?" Bernie said. "Maybe, but there's a sicko element. Three killings, knife the weapon in every one. Knife because it's handy at the moment, that's one thing. Knife by choice is sicko. So therefore?"

Good news: we were back in so-therefore territory, Bernie at the controls. I waited, and waited some more, but Bernie went silent.

The sun, real low now, all of a sudden peeped through dust clouds, a deep, deep red like a light flashing on, and then quickly off. After that it got much darker and the wind started back up and in no time blew even stronger than before. All sorts of scraps began flying around, and I smelled the desert like I never had, huge and mighty.

We huddled closer together, Bernie kneeling down beside me. "Goddamn dust storm," he said, raising his voice over the wind, which now had a voice of its own, like an angry creature working itself up to a howl. "No way he'll be coming now. We'll just have to wait this out."

Fine with me. The dust storm moved in, rising and rising, towering over us. The sound rose, too, hurting my ears in the worst way, and I could barely see a thing, even though the sky wasn't as dark as night. Besides, I see pretty well at night; the problem now was this strange thickness in the air, unlike the emptiness of night air, if that made any —

Whoa. What was that? A tiny sound barely cutting through the enormity of noise, kind of like a propeller going *whap-whap-whap,* or maybe actually more of a *tick-tick-tick.*

That *tick-tick-tick* reminded me of something. I tried to think what.

"Christ," Bernie said, and began rubbing his eyes, all teary like he was crying, an impossibility, of course. Now we were dealing not just with dust, but sand, too, desert sand somehow airborne, rasping like sandpaper against my muzzle and *pock-pock-pocking* the bricks of the warehouse, and on account of the *pock-pock-pocking* mixed into the roar of the storm — this strange dry storm, way drier than normal dry, hard to explain — I lost track of the *tick-tick-tick*. In short, we weren't at our most alert, me and Bernie, and in that moment the *tick-tick-tick*ing suddenly came closer, and a dark car partly emerged from the reddish swirl of the dust storm and stopped in front of us.

Bernie, hand over his eyes to block that sand, didn't see the car and probably hadn't heard it, either, not a big surprise since I'd barely picked up on that *tick-tick-tick* myself. The driver's window slid down and the driver peered out.

Not Cal Luxton, which was my first thought. This was the white-haired dude, not old, more like Bernie's age: white hair kind of long, heavy black eyebrows, narrow little mouth; and those liquid black eyes. In the passenger seat beside him sat that gigantic member of the nation within, long teeth bared. I had the strangest thought: that was me and Bernie in a nightmare.

The liquid-eyed dude nodded to himself and said, "Thought it'd be you."

He had a liquidy voice that somehow matched his eyes and kind of made me feel sick. Bernie turned his head in the direction of the liquid-eyed dude's voice and squinted at him through puffy eyelids.

"Ramon?" he said.

"Hello and good-bye," said Ramon.

He was leaving? I had just enough time to think: good news. And then Ramon had a knife in his hand. There are all sorts of knives — for butter, for steak, for carving the turkey on Thanksgiving. This particular kind of knife — all steel, thin and flat, with a round hole at the top of the grip — was a kind I'd seen before — and seen in action — on a visit to Otis DeWayne, our weapons expert. What Ramon had in his hand was a throwing knife, which he now drew back behind his ear with the same soft easy grip Otis had used before letting it go and popping a pink balloon hanging from a branch in his yard. *Pop* went the balloon, shriveling down to nothing, and the knife sank deep and quivering into the tree. Those liquidy dark eyes locked on Bernie. Shriveling down to nothing? No!

I got my paws under me and sprang, maybe not my best spring on account of the brick pavement in back of the warehouse being so slippery with dust. But no excuses, not in this business: that's one of our rules, mine and Bernie's. The point was I straight up didn't get there in time, in fact sort of didn't even get there at all. Ramon's arm whipped forward and he flung that flat steel knife. It whistled in the air and I felt the blade cut right through the tip of one of my ears before I crashed against the side of the car. Then came a grunt of pain from Bernie. I picked myself up, wheeled around toward him.

Oh, Bernie. The knife had stuck him — not in the head or the chest, which I knew from my experience in this business were game changers — but in his leg, the bad leg with the war wound. Plenty bad enough, and worse was the fact that the knife had cut clear through and sunk into the door, pinning him to it. Bernie reached down, obscured by a sudden whirlwind of dust and sand — like it was taking Bernie away from me! — and gripped the handle of the knife, his movements slow and . . . yes, even uncertain, as though he was confused. In that horrible moment, I sensed movement inside the car, quickly turned, and saw Ramon drawing another knife from a sheath he wore behind his neck. And the .38? Somehow it had fallen from Bernie's belt, and now lay on the ground, out of his reach.

No time to think, but that's often when I do my best work. I leaped straight up and through that window, clamping my mouth around Ramon's wrist, good and hard. Our cases usually ended with me grabbing the perp by the pant leg, not the wrist, but this was a start. Or maybe not, because the next instant Ramon shouted, "Outlaw! Kill!"

And then that huge dude beside him with the long teeth and the angry eyes was all over me. So strong! So heavy! I thrashed around, tried to throw him off, couldn't budge him.

"Kill! Kill 'im, Outlaw!"

Outlaw growled the most ferocious growl I'd ever heard and got me by the neck, although not right under at the very softest part, more to the side. My heart pounded like it wanted to get free and fly away, but somehow that gave me more strength. I twisted around, got a paw free, dug it right into Outlaw's face. He barked a furious bark and then we were in the backseat, crashing around so hard the car rocked. Outlaw rolled right over me, went for my throat again. I kept rolling, slipped away, twisted around suddenly, and there I was, on top! Outlaw didn't like that. He bit my shoulder, bit it real hard. That maddened me so much that what came next was a blur of fighting and blood and pain, all of this with the dust storm howling outside, and the next thing I actually knew was that I somehow had Outlaw by the throat. That didn't make him let go of my shoulder. Those long teeth were still there, digging in deep, Outlaw growling this rough burry growl the whole time, a growl I felt in my body, through and through. More than anything else it was the growl I didn't like: it sent a message that in some way Outlaw was enjoying all this. Didn't he realize I had him by the throat, the softest part? My jaws started to squeeze and I tasted blood and a thrill went through me and I squeezed harder and —

And Outlaw stopped struggling, stilled himself, lay defenseless down on the floor in the back of the car, throat exposed. In short, he submitted. That was something we have in the nation within. My role now was to call a halt to the neck biting thing. Not an easy role at all: I barely pulled it off.

But as soon as I did, backing away from Outlaw — who didn't move at all, his eyes, now dull, gazing at nothing — I realized

424

that Ramon was no longer in the car. I vaulted into the front. The driver's door was open. I shot outside.

The air was thick with dust, like a screen between me and everything. But I could see Bernie, sort of sitting against the door, all twisted around, still trying to pull the knife out and get himself free. Ramon was walking toward him, not in a hurried sort of way. He stood over Bernie. Bernie glanced up at him, his eyes swollen almost shut from the dust. Ramon's own eyes were wide open, darker and more liquid than ever. He smiled and reached behind his neck.

Oh, no. He had another knife in that sheath? I charged. Or tried to. But my shoulder — the one Outlaw had been working on — let me down, and I crumpled to the ground.

Ramon drew the knife. He held it over Bernie's head and said, "Adios." But as he raised the knife higher so he could jam it down even harder into the top of Bernie's skull, Bernie at last yanked the other knife out of the door and out of his leg. It took all the force Bernie had, and because of that the blade came slicing up real fast, almost slipping from his grip, and that blade cut deep into the inside of Ramon's leg, high up.

Ramon staggered back. Blood jetted out of his leg in thick red pulses. He sank to the ground, pressed his hand against the wound. His hand was soaked red in a moment and then the thick pulses started up again, shooting right through his fingers.

"Lucky son of a bitch," he said. "You killed me."

THIRTY-TWO

"I'm not that lucky," Bernie said.

By now I was at Bernie's side. He ripped off his own shirt — Hawaiian, with the red palm trees, one of my favorites — tore a strip from it and tied the strip tight around Ramon's leg, above the blood-spurting part. Blood spurted once more, and then not again.

After that Bernie cuffed him. Ramon lay down in the dust, his skin white, pasty, damp, staring straight up, his eyes kind of lifeless, reminding me of Outlaw at the end of our little scrap.

Bernie turned to me, examined the tip of my ear and my shoulder. "Might need a stitch or two, big guy." Then he rolled up his pant leg. "Me, too." His poor leg: the knife had gone right through his calf where all the old scars were and out the other side. But there wasn't much blood. Bernie tore off another strip of Hawaiian shirt and fixed himself up. Meanwhile, the storm was fading, the wind falling off, the air clearing, the roar amping down and down. Reddish dust covered everything — the old Flower Mart, Ramon's car, Ramon, Bernie, me. Outlaw poked his head up out of the car window. He was all dusty, too. He gazed at Ramon. Ramon gave him a cold look. Outlaw ducked back out of sight.

Bernie shifted over, picked up the .38, tucked it back in his belt. Then he sat right beside Ramon.

"Sign that the ecology's going absolutely haywire," Bernie said.

"Huh?" said Ramon.

"Dust storm like that," Bernie said. "Once the rivers all ran free. Keep that in mind."

"What the hell are you talking about?" Ramon said.

"Doesn't matter," Bernie said. He touched the strip he'd tied around Ramon's leg. "Know much about knots?"

Ramon gazed down at his leg, didn't reply.

"This here's a slip knot," Bernie said. "Meaning all I have to do is give a light little pull on the end right here and it's all undone."

Wow! Was there anything Bernie didn't know?

"Now that we've laid the groundwork,"

Bernie went on, "let's go over the three murders you've committed."

Ramon gave Bernie a hard glare.

"Not selling you short," Bernie said. "There may be more in your whole career — I'm just focusing on the ones revolving around Thad Perry."

"You're full of shit," Ramon said.

"How about simplest one first?" Bernie said. "You killed Manny Chavez because he was skimming off the blackmail payments. The only way he could have done that without your knowledge was by telling Jiggs the amount had been raised and then pocketing the difference. So the question is, what put you onto him?"

Ramon turned his head and tried to spit, but only dry dust came out.

"All I can think of is that Jiggs called you to complain about the bump," Bernie went on. "Was that it?"

Ramon gave him another one of those hard glares.

Bernie reached out, took hold of one end of the torn-off strip, held it lightly in his fingers. Ramon looked down, his eyes losing the glare real fast. Bernie tightened his grip just the littlest bit.

Ramon, his gaze locked on that knot in the Hawaiian shirt material, nodded his head. "Manny was a goddamn loser all his life."

"But Carla was a winner," Bernie said. His hand curled into a fist, the torn-off strip end lost inside. "How did she track you down? Through her friend Dina?"

"The hell with you," Ramon said. "I got rights."

Bernie started to pull.

"Stop," Ramon called out. "Yeah, that was it, Dina. I was gonna have to —" He cut himself off.

"Kill her, too?" Bernie said. "But you ran out of time?"

Ramon said nothing.

"Which leaves us with April," Bernie said. "She dumped Manny for Thad Perry, back when they were all kids. But you weren't a kid — hard to imagine you as a kid ever. Also hard to imagine Manny feeling so humiliated he'd actually want to kill her. Unless some older buddy got him all stirred up."

"He was a goddamn pussy," Ramon said. "We — he — was just gonna throw a scare into her. But he went too far."

"You're saying Manny killed April?"

"Yeah."

Bernie shook his head. "Don't believe you."

Ramon shrugged.

Bernie didn't like that shrug; I could tell from his eyes. He yanked the end of the torn-off strip real hard. A red jet came pumping right out, the most powerful one yet. It struck Bernie in the face, ran down his chin, made him look so scary.

Ramon got scared through and through, no doubt about it. "You don't understand," he screamed. "The feel of the knife sliding in — I was just going to make a scratch. It was an accident."

Bernie gazed down at him. Another red spurt: Bernie shifted his head out of the way, just like he was slipping a punch.

"Please," Ramon begged. "Please."

Bernie retied the knot, not quickly, but he did it. Ramon was making little whimpering sounds.

"Then you framed Thad for the murder," Bernie said.

Ramon nodded.

"But Stine and Luxton started poking around," Bernie went on, "and Stine was smart. For some reason Luxton alibied you out. Possibility one — you had dirt on him. Possibility two — you paid him off."

"Everyone in Vista City knew Luxton was on the take," Ramon said.

"So that was that?" Bernie said, wiping

Ramon's blood off his face with what was left of the Hawaiian shirt.

Ramon nodded again.

"Except for the nice bonus years later when Thad hit the big time," Bernie said.

Ramon looked into some far-off distance. He'd lost all his color, making him sort of invisible, except for the dark eyes. "Couldn't believe my goddamn luck," he said.

Bernie and I each got stitches, took it easy for a day or so. Less than a day, in my case: taking it easy gets old pretty fast.

We had visitors. Lieutenant Stine, for example — although he arrived in a brand-new captain's uniform, with all the gold. He had a whole case of bourbon for Bernie.

"Don't want it," Bernie said. "Don't want anything from you."

"Aw, come on, Bernie," Stine said, softening that voice of his, normally so harsh and hoarse-sounding.

Bernie shook his head. "You used me as a cat's paw."

Whoa.

"I don't like that," Bernie said.

Well, of course not. Who would? Yes, Brando and I'd come to an arrangement, but no point pushing things too far.

■ ■ ■ ■

Then there was Thad Perry.

"Can't thank you enough," Thad said. "And I'm sure Jiggs will want to thank you, too. Right now he's on an extended vacation."

"What's this?" Bernie said.

"A check."

"No, thanks."

"Aren't you even going to look at it?" Thad said. "There are lots of zeroes."

"Nope," said Bernie. In this business you get good at spotting tricks, and didn't zero mean zip, nada, zilch? No way we were falling for that, me and Bernie.

"But I want to do something," Thad said. "You . . . you redeemed me, man. And way less important, but it counts — you kept me out of the news."

"Okay," Bernie said. "Here's what you can do — stop encouraging Leda about my son and the movie business. In fact, discourage her."

"But why?" said Thad. "Charlie's talented. Lars says that scene we did is the best thing in the film."

"Can you get him to cut it?" Bernie said.

Thad laughed, like maybe he thought this

was one of Bernie's jokes. "You can't be serious," he said, "but I'll try if you insist."

Bernie sighed. "Just do the discouraging part," he said.

The mayor's office called and the mayor himself came on our speakerphone.

"Not sure of all the details, my friend, but the movie people seem very pleased with your work."

"Uh-huh," Bernie said.

"And what with Cal Luxton taking early retirement, I was wondering if you'd be interested in the job? Head of security for the mayor's office, starting salary a hundred and —"

"Nope."

After that, Bernie poured himself a stiff drink. "Some dark night let's you and me pay Cal Luxton a visit."

I looked out the window. It was night. But not dark enough? I didn't get it.

We were back on our feet by the time Suzie flew in. I kind of remembered that things weren't right between them, but you wouldn't have known from their faces when they saw each other. We had a nice dinner out on the patio, the night cooler than any night we'd had in a long time, the sky so clear after the dust storm. We all gazed at the stars.

Suzie reached for Bernie's hand. "Crazy to screw up the time we have for no good reason," she said.

"Sounds like the beginning of a sappy song," Bernie said.

"What?" said Suzie, withdrawing her hand.

"That's a good thing," Bernie said. "Sometimes there's wisdom in sappy songs."

Suzie looked surprised. Bernie took her in his arms. And just at that moment, when their lips were touching and I was thinking of doing something about it, barking started up in the canyon, beyond our back gate. Funnily enough, it sounded something like my own bark, but higher-pitched.

"What's that?" Suzie said.

Bernie shot me a strange sort of look, no idea why. I wasn't the one barking; I was the one sitting quietly, keeping my nose clean. Just to be sure, I gave it a nice wet lick.

"I think I know the answer," Bernie said. He picked up a flashlight, limped across the patio, and opened the gate.

ACKNOWLEDGMENTS

Writing the Chet and Bernie series is the best kind of labor — that of love. And one of its greatest pleasures has been the constant feeling of enthusiasm from my wonderful publisher, Atria Books. My grateful thanks to everyone at Atria, and especially Peter Borland, Judith Curr, and Ariele Fredman.